J

I Am

By Cris Beam

LITTLE, BROWN AND COMPANY
New York   Boston

Little, Brown and Company

Hachette Book Group
237 Park Avenue, New York, NY 10017
Visit our website at www.lb-teens.com

Little, Brown and Company is a division of Hachette Book Group, Inc.
The Little, Brown name and logo are trademarks of Hachette Book Group, Inc.

First Edition: March 2011

Library of Congress Cataloging-in-Publication Data

Beam, Cris.
    I am J / by Cris Beam.—1st ed.
        p. cm.
    Summary: J, who feels like a boy mistakenly born as a girl, runs away from his best friend who has rejected him and the parents he thinks do not understand him when he finally decides that it is time to be who he really is.
    ISBN 978-0-316-05361-7
    [1. Transgender people—Fiction. 2. Identity—Fiction. 3. Emotional problems—Fiction. 4. Friendship—Fiction.] I. Title.
    PZ7.B362Iaj 2011
    [Fic]—dc22

                                                            2010008640

10 9 8 7 6 5 4 3 2 1

RRD-C

Book designed by Ben Mautner
Display type is Monotype Modern Wide
Body type is Sabon Roman

Printed in the United States of America

For Lo,
mon coeur

In fond memory of
Bella Martinez
1980–2004

J

CHAPTER ONE

J could smell the hostility, the pretense, the utter fakeness of it all before they even climbed the last set of stairs. He was going to this party for Melissa, though she knew he'd hate it, though she'd have friends to talk to and J would stand there in the corner like a plastic tree, sucking at a beer, steaming in his too-many shirts and humiliation. The stairs were already sticky with spilled drinks, and reggaeton thumped through the door.

"Come on, J, you have to go with me. Daniel's gonna be there," Melissa had whined to him earlier that day at school. They were sharing a Diet Coke in the school's emergency stairwell. The place was littered with cigarette butts and graffiti; every few days, some student dismantled the alarm, looking to sneak off and smoke. Daniel was Melissa's latest crush, a quiet guy who played chess with the old men in Washington Square Park and who always had a Strand book bag over one shoulder. J thought he was pretentious.

"I hate parties," J had said. "And I hate everyone at this school."

"You're so dramatic," Melissa had answered, tapping the brim of J's cap. She leaned her head on J's shoulder. "What happened now?"

"Got called a dyke again." It had happened a thousand times before. Dyke, aggressive, AG, butch. Whatever the names, none of them fit. He'd considered the possibility briefly, when he first realized he was in love with Melissa a few years back, but he'd never felt like a lesbian.

"Oh, sweetie," Melissa said, lifting her head from J's shoulder and trying to meet his eye. She sounded exactly like Karyn, her mom.

J shrugged off her concern even as he longed for it. He stared straight ahead, steeled his jaw.

"I know you're not one," Melissa said. "I know you just have your own style, like me. Screw this school. And..." Melissa paused. She pulled at a binder clip holding back a strand of curly hair. "Even if you were gay, it wouldn't be the biggest deal. It's not like a tragedy or anything."

J jiggled his knee. "I'm not, though."

"Okay, dude. I didn't say you were."

Melissa had recently taken to calling J "dude," which J loved. In J's mind, if not in anyone else's, he was a *he*. He couldn't go so far as to actually think of himself as male anymore; he had let that dream go at puberty. Now he tried not to think about gender at all, except when the world outside his brain barged in and forced him to. Which happened about every other minute. Still, saying *she* felt like something close to blasphemy. In J's head, he was nothing; in J's head, he was just a head, floating, trying to forget he had body parts he hated.

"J—" Melissa started. "Come to the party tonight. I want to be with you."

Melissa smelled like amber, cinnamon, and cigarettes. J inhaled, but quietly, so Melissa wouldn't notice. He leaned his head back against her wild hair and gave a tiny nod.

Melissa jiggled open the door to the party, knocking aside some sophomores who had been leaning there. Pot smoke obscured his vision, but J could tell this was a nice place. There was a dining room, separate from the kitchen, with African masks on the wall. Three girls J recognized from math class were sitting on the table, legs swinging, all vying for the attention of a senior boy, who was twirling a drumstick and tapping it alternately on each of their knees. Another couple was making out in the foyer, with the boy's oversize jacket wrapped around the girl so people couldn't tell he had his hand up her shirt. J averted his eyes as Melissa took him by the hand. "Let's get a drink," she said.

The kitchen counter was a pool of spilled soda and Cisco; next to this were giant bottles of gin labeled in a language J didn't recognize. "They're out of mixers," somebody said, walking away. "You'll have to drink it straight."

Melissa filled two red plastic cups (one already had lipstick on its rim) with warm gin and took a sip. J swallowed a long gulp and tried not to shudder as it burned his throat. He held the cup by his side and followed Melissa toward Daniel, who was smoking a joint and reading in the corner.

"Hey," Melissa said, and Daniel looked up, putting a finger in his place. His straight brown hair and pale skin made him look like a zombie. "What're you reading?"

"Proust," Daniel answered. "But I'm getting sick of all the madeleines."

"That's cool." Melissa giggled and turned her foot inward a bit.

J hated how Melissa acted around her crushes—overly sweet and dumb. *He's a fake,* J tried to psychically transmit to Melissa. *Can't you see that? A total ass.*

"If you don't like girls named Madeleine," Melissa said, giggling, "maybe you should put down your book. You know J, right?"

Daniel glanced mildly at J and said, "I don't think so." J widened his stance and grimaced. They had met several times before—sitting next to each other on the same ramshackle stage at a school awards ceremony for high math scores, and through Melissa in the hallway. Daniel turned his attention back to Melissa. "Have you read Proust?"

Dios mío, J said in his head, just the way his mother would. *God.* He put on his toughest scowl, but he felt, in his mouth, that it looked more like a pucker.

"I don't read at parties," Melissa said, smiling flirtily. "I socialize." And then, as though she owned the apartment, she added, "Can I get you a drink?"

J marveled at Melissa's social skills as Melissa and Daniel pushed their way back into the kitchen. He sat on the arm of a couch and drank some more gin. This apartment was *nice*; the old dark thoughts of pocketing a few valuables rushed through J's mind. He shook his head to get rid of the thought. *Bad*, he thought. And, *Who are you fooling? You're no gangster.* He looked at his shoelaces, which Melissa had played with just the night before.

She had toyed with them, those very laces, in her apartment, right after their squabble about the cutting. Most nights, after school, J went to Melissa's apartment. Melissa lived on the Lower East Side, in a studio apartment with her mother. It was even smaller than J's family's place, and much messier—with books and dance tights strewn about, two cats nuzzling against the worn furniture. Melissa and her mom were close; Karyn was in school herself, studying psychology in college, and she was full of ideas. She read the tarot cards of anyone who came through her door, and loved to stay up late drinking wine out of miniature jelly jars. Karyn was black and had been with a white man, Melissa's dad, who had been little more than a hit-and-run, and this too was fascinating to J. His own parents were so conventional, hanging out in the building, talking with the neighbors, making dinner, watching TV. They'd stopped talking about whose sons back in PR were growing up, getting handsome, might make a good match for J, but still. J knew that aside from college, his parents' slowly slipping dreams for him involved a white dress and a three-tiered cake.

Yesterday, like most days, they got to Melissa's place and just hung out. J went online, and Melissa changed into dance clothes to stretch. He'd looked over at Melissa, who was flexing her biceps in a sports bra in front of the mirror. Melissa was a dancer and a cutter; like J, she was obsessed with her body, but unlike J, she admitted it. She wore her drapey sleeves long to cover the pine needle–length lines on her arms, nicked out every few nights with a razor she kept in her purse. She studied these cuts closely, monitoring their progress, scanning for infection, and she examined her musculature, too, wanting her legs to be both strong and lean, so she could jump higher, her shoulders perfectly broadened for lifting. Melissa's dream was to join a company like the one Pina Bausch had founded— athletic, urban, and strange. Whenever she could, she stretched, pushing an elbow up and down her back like a cricket, bending in half and curling her forearms around her knees.

Melissa was smart, and J loved her for that. Melissa didn't mind J's long silences, the way he couldn't muster a witty comeback, didn't seem to have a political bone in his body. Melissa said she liked J's photographs—she was the only one he showed them to—though Melissa spent most of the time talking about Melissa. Melissa's curly wild hair, always tied up with pieces of yarn, or multicolored rubber bands, or even paper clips, matched her personality. Melissa's hair, Melissa's clothes, even Melissa's cutting said, "Look at me."

"Melis, those cuts look nasty. You should talk to a counselor or some shit, for real," J had said, nodding at the fresh scars on the inside of Melissa's forearm. "Why do you do that?"

"Shut up," Melissa answered, pulling on a shirt. "They're from the cats."

Melissa plopped on the floor and stretched her upper body out over one leg. "Why do you wear fourteen million shirts when it's a hundred degrees outside?"

"I don't know. It makes me feel better."

Melissa looked up at J from the floor, checking to see whether she'd stung him with the shirt comment. When she saw that J was still looking at her, she playfully untied J's sneakers. "I read a book about people who cut themselves. It was called *Cuts*. Anyway. Supposedly tons of people do it, something about bringing the pain of your insides to your outside world so you can see it. Or master it. Or something."

Melissa's cuts were close together and scabbed up in little black dots, like several short strings of beads. J wondered if he'd ever have the courage to let someone cut into his skin, if a scalpel or a knife could help get the tormenting thoughts out of him.

Melissa went on. "But people stop. So I'll stop, too. Probably when I get into a dance company, and I don't have so much stress in my life. It's not like I ever go deep—so stop worrying."

"Okay," J said, but he had already stopped worrying, if that's what he'd been doing, already stopped paying attention to the words Melissa was saying. Instead, he was watching Melissa's fingers twisting and untwisting the laces on J's sneakers, as though they were the ears of some animal. She was so gentle with the laces, so tender and attentive, it made J feel dizzy.

J remembered learning to tie his shoes when he was a kid. He was probably four. His dad had bought him a pair of Nikes that almost matched the Air Force 1 mid-tops the older kids in the neighborhood wore; J had begged for them at the store, and Manny had given in. That was back before his dad had gotten so involved with the union. J worshipped his father then; he remembered copying the way Manny walked and sat and smoked his endless packs of Marlboros. J would pick up unlit cigarettes and hide them in his fist, puffing into his curled thumb, making his dad laugh and laugh.

"These are bunny ears, Jeni. You just have to cross them," Manny had said, taking J's tiny hands in his own. "And then you just make a tunnel for one loop to go through, and you're done. Look. Like this."

"My dad taught me to tie my shoes," J said to Melissa, trying. There always was more to say.

"Mmm-hmmm," she answered. She was still playing with J's sneakers. She had undone the laces and restrung them, looping them through the holes in straight lines instead of X's. "Your shoes look better like this."

As she worked, the sides of her palms brushed J's ankles. He wished he weren't wearing socks, wished it were summer.

"My dad used to be so great," J continued.

"Your dad *is* great."

"Yeah, but…" J trailed off.

"At least you have one." Melissa narrowed her eyes at J again, tugged at the hem of his pants. She reached up under the cuff, above the socks, and felt his calf. "You're hairy."

J glared at her. Melissa knew better than this, he thought. And still, the pull of her touch—she felt like landing the perfect photograph in the viewfinder, just before you pressed the button. That mix of jittery stomach and absolute stillness—that rare sense that somehow all is right in the world. He loved it. He hated it. An image of a car crash he'd seen on *Cops* flashed through his mind.

"M, I gotta go." J stood up and bolted out the door.

*   *   *

Suddenly, at the party, someone tapped his shoulder. J looked up from his laces.

"Hey, J." It was Mischa, a kid from the group at school that called themselves the Alchemists. J sometimes tinkered around on the computers with the Alchemists after everyone else went home.

"What are you doing here?" J asked, jutting up his chin. Alchemists never went to parties.

"I dunno. Same as you, man. I got invited," Mischa answered, his accent thickened by alcohol.

J got up and walked away. He didn't care about this party, but he didn't want to be seen talking to an Alchemist, either. And was Mischa throwing a punch with the *man* comment, or was it a figure of speech? He was so sensitive, it seemed. Mischa was a social climber; he was talking to J only to be seen talking to *someone*, and J didn't want to help him out. Mischa smelled like body odor, and he looked stupid in his polo shirt. At least J smelled good. Comforting himself with these thoughts, J turned and saw Melissa and Daniel leaned up against a fireplace. The mantel was littered with red plastic cups, and the fireplace was filled with burning candles and melted wax. Melissa was laughing with her head tilted back—a fake laugh J had seen only when Melissa was talking to older boys or bragging about dance companies she was too insecure to audition for. Daniel was running his hands through his hair and looking very serious. He reached out and touched Melissa's cheek, and she hooked her forefinger into the front pocket of his jeans. J turned abruptly toward the kitchen for more alcohol.

Hadn't Melissa said she wanted to spend time at this party with *him*? J fumed as he poured himself another cup of straight gin, warm and sharp-smelling, the bottle slightly gummy from so many hands. When they'd arrived, Melissa practically flew toward Daniel and left J in this nest of vultures, all looking to one-up each other with their sex appeal and their sophistication. J felt like a bald baby bird, waiting to get gobbled up.

As if to prove the point, a Dracula-ish older girl in all black with spike-heeled boots swooped down on J and sneered. "Are you going to let go of that bottle, or do I have to fight you for it?" J was gripping the neck of the gin bottle with his fist. He looked at the girl; she was pretty. He nodded toward the cup she was holding and reached over to pour her some gin. "Thanks," she said coyly, and half-smiled. Her lips were outlined in black.

Damn, J thought. *Does she know who I am? How come I haven't seen her before?* He opened his mouth to say something, to ask her her name, maybe, but only a raspy sound came out, something between a choke and a gasp.

"Are you all right?" the girl asked, concern briefly lighting her eyes.

"I'm fine," J said, covering his embarrassment with a coughing fit. "I just have a cough."

"Okay," the girl said. She looked into her cup as though J might have contaminated it, and then clacked away in her heels. "See ya."

Loser! J thought. *You are such a loser!*

J roamed away, too, and found a den, or some kind of office, lined with books. The lights were off, and kids were dancing to someone's iPod. He thought they looked like a single blob of flesh, an undulating sea creature, tentacle-like arms flailing out here, a butt in tight jeans jiggling out there. The room was hot and short on air, and he sucked at his gin, though it just made him thirstier. He wondered what it would feel like to live at the center of the sea creature, enveloped by bodies. Would he stop noticing his stomach, his back, his stupid legs, and just feel like a whole person for once? Would he belong in some kind of primal, physical way? No. The alcohol was getting to him. He would never belong. He would never wear tight jeans and bangles on his wrists. That much was obvious. He would never be able to talk with other people the way Melissa could—he would never be funny and graceful and easy. The only place J could be himself was on his computer, and there he was Rico, which wasn't himself at all but a rich man in his twenties, which J wouldn't be, either.

J was a joke, and everybody knew it. Here he was, in oversize jeans, a baseball cap, and three shirts, looking like an eleven-year-old boy. The top shirt was a ripped sports jersey, and that's what he was, nothing but an empty shirt, something to be tossed off and thrown away. Why had he worn such a dumb shirt? Suddenly, he wanted to yank it off and just wear the thermal beneath. The room was so hot. Why was it so hot at parties? His head was spinning now; he was definitely drunk. He couldn't take the top shirt off— people would look at him. And then his breasts would be more obvious. God, he hated those things. Every single day he thought about destroying them. When he first began to develop, at thirteen, J had slept on his stomach every night, trying to stop their growth. But the breasts were determined. They pushed forth from his ribs like animals, fisting their way up from beneath. Even with two sports bras and the extra shirts, you could see their roundness, their adamant shout: *I am a girl.* J finished the last of his drink and went back to the kitchen for more. At least with a drink in his hand, he thought, he looked something like everybody else. Everyone held a red cup.

All the bottles on the counter were empty, so J splashed his face with water from the sink. He was starting to feel thickheaded, bleary—and sad, the sadness that settles with drinking too much, too fast. A small girl with a face like a mouse said, "There's beer in the fridge," and at first J thought she was talking to him, but she was motioning to her boyfriend, who was trailing behind her, red-eyed and spacey. J found a can of Schlitz next to takeout containers and jars of condiments and opened it with a fizz. He took a long swallow. That was better. Lighter than the gin, at least, and cold.

"Dude, you got a light?" a guy with a goatee was saying to J from across the counter. He had a cigarette dangling from his mouth. He seemed to be very far away and too close at once. J reached into his pockets but knew he didn't have any matches.

"Nope," he answered.

Goatee Guy walked over to the stove and lit his cigarette from the flame. J studied the way he bent at the waist, feet parted—the way he shoved his hair from his eyes so as not to catch it on fire. Every move was quick and deft, though somehow also thick, as if his bones carried more weight than J's. "You go to PS three eighty-six?" he asked. It was the New York City public magnet school for math and sciences, in midtown.

"Yeah. You?" J was surprised a stranger—a guy—was talking to him.

"Yeah. I hate it."

"Me, too." J tried to look tough, but the room was swaying.

"You know Stacey Ramirez?" the guy asked.

J thought. The name sounded familiar, but his thoughts were sticky, slow. He shook his head.

"She's only a freshman...and I'm kind of worried about her. She's in the master bedroom right now giving head to seniors—twenty bucks to anyone who wants it. She was advertising at the beginning of the party."

"Cool," J said. He was so surprised that Goatee Guy was talking to him, he almost didn't register what he had said. J tried to copy the way the other kid was leaning against the counter. He wished he had a cigarette, too. He thought about Stacey, about the line of guys, briefly wished he had twenty bucks, then erased the impossible thought.

"It's not cool, actually," Goatee Guy said, now eyeing J suspiciously. "Don't you think we should get someone to intervene? I mean, she's so young, and I don't think she knows what she's doing." Goatee Guy took a long pull on his cigarette, flicking his eyes briefly over J once more, and then stared upward at a spot in the ceiling, like he didn't care.

But Goatee Guy obviously did care, and J wondered

why. The word *intervene* sounded so weird. *Intervene.* Like *intravenous.* Like the rat J's biology class would be dissecting on Tuesday. What would it be like to be Stacey Ramirez? What would it be like to give head? Gross. It would be gross.

Goatee Guy was now staring at J as though he expected some kind of answer. J didn't know what to say. He was thinking about Melissa. Would Melissa do that with Daniel? Suddenly he was angry, very angry. Melissa had come to this party with J, and now she wanted to mess around with Daniel, who sat in corners and read books like he was better than everybody, smarter than everybody. J was Melissa's real friend; J was there when Melissa fell apart after a bad dance class, when she cut her arms, when she fought with her mother, when guys broke her heart. But where was J now? Talking with Goatee Guy about some stupid girl giving it up for money.

"Look, I don't care about some dumb-ass bitch," J said.

Goatee Guy looked shocked. "You're an asshole," he said, and walked away.

Wait, what went wrong? J thought. *Did that guy think I was a dude? I was being cool to him. Everybody here's an ass.* And he went to look for Melissa.

*   *   *

17

Melissa and Daniel were still in front of the fireplace, but they were standing closer now. J took a long swig of beer and positioned himself behind a ficus tree that somebody had strung with Christmas lights. Melissa was laughing at something Daniel was saying—what could he be saying?—and Daniel was looking serious and pompous, as usual. Melissa reached out and touched Daniel on the nose, and then touched her own nose, as though connecting them by an invisible string. Suddenly, Daniel leaned in and, very gently, kissed Melissa. J threw up in the plant.

"Nasty!" two girls standing nearby shouted. "Get this bitch to the bathroom!" J felt himself being shoved from behind, and he saw a pathway between the bodies open up before him. Another heave welled up inside him but, mercifully, a toilet bowl materialized, and J made it in time. He slumped down against a bathtub and leaned his head against the cool porcelain. He flushed the toilet, then lay down on the floor. After what seemed like a long time, Melissa's pink ballet slippers, which she had striped with black paint, appeared in front of J's face.

"Dude—what happened?" Melissa was shouting. "You just barfed all over a tree!"

J moaned and closed his eyes.

"Come on, let's get you home," Melissa said, pulling

J up from the elbows, her tone a little gentler. "You can sleep at my place."

In the taxi, J drank some water Melissa had in her bag, and Melissa gushed about Daniel. "First he was talking about chess and the way it mirrors life. The way most of us think we can move in only one direction, one step at a time. We're so restricted. But the knights—they get to jump over everybody else and make unexpected side-swipes." Melissa was glowing. "Daniel feels like he's the knight, all erratic and misunderstood. He thought maybe I was a knight, too."

"Are you?" J asked weakly, his head against the taxi window.

"I told him I was a queen, but unprotected. All my pawns have left me."

"That's dramatic," J said.

"Daniel's the type of guy who likes to hear himself talk. But he's smart, too." Melissa looked out the taxi window at Fifth Avenue streaking by. J could tell she was hurt he didn't like her crush. True to form, she fought back. "At least he doesn't throw up in strangers' trees."

J felt a hot rush of shame. "How was the kiss?" It was torture to ask, but he had to know.

"Wet. Too much tongue. He didn't know how to be delicate, you know?"

J didn't. At seventeen, he'd never kissed anybody save for the neighbor girl he'd played "bar" with in fourth grade. The girl, Laureleen, used to live in the apartment downstairs, and after school she and J would take their cups of juice and lean against Laureleen's bookcase, pretending they were in a bar. J would be the man; Laureleen, a chick he was picking up. They must have seen this on TV. They'd "practice" making out for hours, Laureleen pretending to resist and J encouraging her to take a ride in his car. They never talked about what they did, but they played the game several times. "Daniel's a fool," he said.

Melissa ignored him and paid the fare.

Melissa's mom was out for the evening. The apartment smelled like cloves and candle wax, and the cats were underfoot, meowing for dinner and attention. J had known the cats since they were kittens, rescued from some bodega's back room in another winter, years ago. Melissa had begged to keep them, and when Karyn relented, J and Melissa had tried to train them to do tricks, one kitten with a ribbon around its neck pulling the other in a plastic toy wagon. J had tired of the game quickly—the kittens were always jumping away and dragging the wagon under the bed—but Melissa was patient, rewarding them with treats and cooing in their ears. She was often patient like this with J, too, encouraging him to talk about the pictures he took, stretching her legs again and again while he struggled to find words. Once when his father and mother had argued about money, Manny left the house and didn't come home for three days. J went to Melissa's, and she let him watch all the music videos he wanted on her computer, even though she usually hated the female dancers. That time she didn't press J to talk, but when he spent the night, she took his hand and held it, kissing his thumb once before he fell asleep. Nobody understood J's moods like Melissa; nobody else let him be who he was.

Melissa started boiling some water for tea, and J crawled into Melissa's bed, his head throbbing. The comforter felt thick and warm, like being inside a loaf of bread, and when the kettle whistled, J covered his ears.

"Here, drink this," Melissa said, handing J a cup of chamomile. "You'll feel better." She took off her shoes and pulled her bra off from under her shirt and climbed in bed beside J. He wondered, briefly, if she didn't want him to say anything about the cuts. Usually she tossed off her clothes with abandon and scrutinized her body in front of the mirror, pinching imaginary fat or looking for blemishes before she pulled on some boxers to sleep. He'd seen her naked countless times. "Want to watch *Late Night*?"

"No, too noisy," J said. "My head hurts."

"Okay. So let's talk. What do you think of Daniel?"

"I think he's a pretentious prick."

Melissa mock-slapped J on the arm, sloshing tea onto the comforter. "No, he's not! He's just quiet."

"I'm quiet," J answered.

"So? What does that have to do with anything?" Melissa touched the razor lines in J's hair, above the ears. "Why'd you shave these stripes in?"

"I dunno. Better my hair than my arms."

"Ouch," Melissa said, pulling back but watching J closely. "What's the matter? You mad at me or something?"

J considered this. "No. I'm not mad. I don't know what I am. I think I'm just sick from the alcohol."

"Okay," Melissa answered, snuggling down into the bed. She curled her feet around J's. "Let's go to sleep, then."

In the dim light cast by the street lamps outside, J examined Melissa's face. He could see the shape of the large eyes beneath her lids, and he watched her eyelashes twitch slightly, as though some invisible breeze were touching them. Her lips parted, and her breath came slowly; she made a *kaaah* sound with each exhale, and a curl fell across her forehead. Was she really sleeping? Could a person fall asleep so fast? J wondered. Or was she faking it?

J and Melissa had slept this way dozens of times before. It was the only reason J could appreciate being born female: girls like Melissa—well, actually, only Melissa—let J in on their secrets, their biggest plans, their most frightened, sad places. Melissa let J see how smart she was. Other girls, of course, rejected J, saw only the most superficial aspects of him—the way he was so butch and tough-looking—and they'd run away, thinking he was a freak or a dyke or both. Something predatory, something hard and impenetrable. They'd never know, as Melissa knew, that J was a photographer, that he loved the interplay of light and dark and finding the wavering balance between them. They'd never know how gentle J was inside, and how scared, how he wanted to do the right thing but often couldn't. They'd never know how confusion and cruelty change people, make them hard—the way the deepest cuts make the toughest scabs. As long as he could remember, J had been taunted, tested, and mistreated for the way he looked.

It was, in fact, in the middle of a schoolroom taunt that J and Melissa had met. It was in middle school, and both of them had been placed in a program called Arts for Gifted Children. Sixth grade was well under way, but J had skipped most of the arts classes—until a six-week photography rotation was announced. All the other "gifted artists" knew one another when J showed up, his old 35 mm stuffed into his backpack. The teacher was reading the roll, and she came to J's name.

"Jenifer Silver."

"Um, it's J," J said quietly, looking down.

"I can't hear you; what did you say?" The teacher was bottle-blond, middle-aged. She sat next to a tall stack of magazines that she had brought from home.

"My name. It's J."

"Okay," the teacher said, smiling just a little. "You might be J in your other classes, but this is photography. In photography, we strive for accuracy, for telling the truth in pictures. That's why we're not doing digital work here—so nothing can be altered. So in this class, I think it's important for you to be as honest as the subjects you're photographing. You'll be exactly who you are—no deception, no fooling."

J had no idea what the teacher was talking about, but his head was starting to swim. The other kids had turned to stare at him. The teacher continued. "In my class, you'll be Jenifer. Roberto will be Roberto, Frances will be Frances. No changes, no alterations, no lies. It's an important part of the learning process. Understood?"

J couldn't answer. His tongue felt like a thick sweater in his mouth, and his hands started to sweat. Somebody laughed.

"I can't hear you," the teacher persisted.

Suddenly, a girl in neon tights and braids piped up.

" 'Scuse me, ma'am?" she said, completely unafraid.

The girl had a tough street accent, which J would later learn could be adopted and abandoned at will. "J is my cousin, and something real bad happened in our family. She can't be called Jenifer no more, 'cause of the memories. That's why her name is J."

"Oh!" the teacher said, her mouth a small circle, her eyebrows lifted in surprise. She weighed the situation for a moment, seemingly steeling herself for a battle. Then she dropped her armor. "Okay, then. I'm sorry. J it is. Let's go on."

After the class, J thanked Melissa. It took all his courage to stop her in the hall.

"Don't worry about it," Melissa had said. "That teacher was an idiot. I mean, since when is photography honest? There's a Picasso quote from the first teacher— the one who taught painting. I love it! It goes, 'Art is the lie that tells the truth.' That teacher was waaaay better."

J knew, right then, that he loved her.

More than five years and countless sleepovers later, J wondered: could Melissa feel J's own breath as he moved microscopically closer to her in the bed, his own lips now almost touching Melissa's? He was sure Melissa shifted toward him, too. J thought suddenly of Stacey Ramirez and wondered whether she had really wanted to do that, or whether she just craved attention.

Or money. Melissa's knees pressed harder into J's, J was sure of it, and a flame rose up in J's stomach. J's eyes were closed now, and he didn't dare open them; Melissa might see him watching and move away. He could feel Melissa's breath on his upper lip, and though the alcohol smell made him queasy, he didn't want the moment to end. And yet he wanted more. He wanted to be in the lineup of guys with Stacey Ramirez, he wanted to be in Puerto Rico, he wanted to fly a plane. He wanted Melissa.

Suddenly, they were kissing. J's mouth on Melissa's, his hand lightly hovering above her hip. J felt Melissa's lips part in response, her tongue dart out and back again.

Melissa sat straight up. "J!" she said. "What are you doing?"

Melissa got up and walked across the room. Her bare feet made a slapping sound on the wood floor, and then an overhead light shattered the darkness. J threw the comforter over his head to protect his eyes. "I was sleeping!" J shouted, his voice muffled. "Same as you!"

"No," Melissa barked. "You kissed me."

J peeked out from the blankets. Melissa's face looked strained and confused.

Melissa came back and sat on the edge of the bed. She hung her head and looked at her toes. Her black nail polish was chipped in several places, and she leaned down to pick away at some more. "People warned me about you, again and again and again," she said. "But I ignored them. I thought you were my friend."

J just looked at her. His headache was worse than ever.

"J—" Melissa started again, "I'm not a lesbian."

J sat up straight in bed. He screamed at her, inside his head, louder than anything he'd ever screamed before. *I'm not, either!*

Melissa, of course, couldn't hear him. She picked up J's bag from the floor and said, "I think you should go home."

CHAPTER TWO

"Jellybean, wake up." J's mom was standing over his bed and shaking his shoulder. Carolina was wearing her hospital nurse uniform and looking at her watch. "It's after eight o'clock. You have to go to school."

J had spent the weekend hiding from his cell phone, hoping Melissa wouldn't call or text him, yet checking the screen every hour to see if she did. So far, she'd ignored him completely. On Monday, he played sick, and Carolina went for it; he couldn't face the school hallways and their wretched stink of raspberry body wash and bleach, and the risk of Melissa's disdain.

Today in biology, they'd be continuing a rat dissection. Melissa wasn't in that class. Maybe he'd just go to biology and then come home again. He murmured from his pillow. "Okay, I'm up."

J slept in the living room on the pullout couch, and his parents let him decorate that corner of the room. He'd put up a few of his own photographs from last year, when he was taking pictures of shadows on sidewalks. One showed the outline of what looked to be an old man in a bowler hat; another was a bird that seemed caught in barbed wire, even as it was flying. He'd also taped up magazine photos of Daddy Yankee, surrounded by women in bright, skimpy dresses. There were other shots of Yankee, in Puerto Rico or somewhere warm, standing on the hood of a car, with a mic, arm outstretched, reaching for a crowd that loved him.

Dressing that day, like all days, was painful. J kept his clothes in an old trunk his dad had brought home from the lost and found of the MTA; Manny worked there and was forever trekking in treasures. The trunk was ancient cracked leather, with shiny brass hinges and locks, and J liked the way it always looked packed and ready to go somewhere better. J hated his clothes. His mother had long ago given up on taking him shopping; now she handed him money and let him fend for himself. But J couldn't stand dressing rooms with their multiple mirrors or clerks with their snarky smiles, so he just grabbed jeans off the stacks in the neighborhood shops, bought sports jerseys on the Internet, and got thermal underwear from a Target in the Bronx, where he bought his boxers, too. Every size was a guess, and then he guessed three sizes up, which made everything swim on him. It was a style, but it never looked good.

That day, like every day, J pulled out three shirts—a tank top, a thermal, and a flannel for the top. It was mid-October and already cold, and J loved the winter, when he could legitimately cloak himself in layers. J's body was scrawny and long, his hair shaved close to the scalp, with razor lines around the ears. He tried to stay skinny by not eating much; he'd heard that really skinny girls could make their periods stop, but that had never happened to him. Besides, by dinner, usually, he was starving and would throw back a large portion of whatever his mother served. Luckily, J had a high metabolism from all his years of swimming, and he still lifted free weights at night. He hoped that the muscles would develop, thick and ropy beneath a thin layer of skin, if he could continue to keep the fat, and the way it maddeningly clung to his hips and backside, at bay.

J guessed he looked like a mixture of exactly what he was: Puerto Rican and Jewish. There wasn't really a word for this; in his head, he sometimes called himself

Jewto Rican, but his dad never made much of the Jewish part. J's face was thin, with some baby fat around the cheeks that he hoped he'd grow out of, and he had a dimple in his left cheek when he laughed. His eyes were probably his best feature, round and chocolaty, framed by long lashes that his mother cooed over but that J thought were too feminine. His jawline was also too soft for J's standards, but he tried to toughen up the look by pressing his full lips into a permanent hard line. He could raise one eyebrow easily, and often did, making him look quizzical and accusatory at once.

If J let his hair grow, it would be curly and black, but he liked the buzzed look with the razor-straight hairline across his forehead. Most people didn't even see this, as J always wore a baseball cap. They couldn't see much of his body, either, as he hid his hips in the baggy jeans and his chest in two sports bras and all the shirts. On this morning, like all mornings, he pulled on his clothes as fast as he could to avoid even looking at his bare skin. Then he grabbed his camera, scratched Titi behind her ears, and ducked out the door.

"Hola, Jeni."

J spun. His stomach clenched hard, as though he'd been hit. For a blessed half hour, he'd been in the world of his head. And then, before he'd even left the building, the other world was slamming him again. The glass doors to the outside turned to water in his eyes, and he slowly turned around.

It was just the neighbor lady Mercedes, in a stained shirt, sitting in the vestibule with a basket of laundry, gathering her strength to haul it up the stairs. Mercedes had known J since he was a baby, had been to his christening. J's mother and Mercedes traded recipes and gossip from home in PR, at night or on Saturday afternoons. J couldn't muster a "hello" back, not now that Mercie had screwed up his day; he didn't care that she'd tell his mom he'd been rude. *Fat pig Mercie*, J thought. *She should know better. Nobody calls me Jeni anymore.*

The dissection was already in full swing when J slipped in the door. Today they finally had the animals, though J likely wouldn't get to touch one, since there were thirty-six kids in biology class and only three rats. Why they couldn't get more was a mystery; J's dad worked for the subway and said tens of thousands ran through New York City's tunnels every day. His teacher ordered the animals—cleaner, pinker, and bred to be carved up—from a lab in Iowa.

Berkin assigned J to group three. Dominic had

already cut a thin slice through the rat's belly, along a purple line someone had drawn with a marker. Dominic's eyes were wide, almost hungry, and the girls in the group were pulled back behind him in a knot, *ewww*-ing to each other. The insides were shades of gray and brown; they looked like swollen little sponges snuggling in for protection under the rib cage. Below this was a mass of intestinal tubing, shiny and green. Dominic lifted a ribbon of intestines with some tweezers; another kid told him to shove aside, give someone else a chance. J moved in closer. The kids all had worksheets; they were supposed to identify the heart, the diaphragm, the stomach, the spleen, and the pancreas. If the rat was female, they were to "excise the uterus"; if male, they should simply locate the testes and write it down. J rolled his eyes in disgust. Of course Berkin wouldn't make them cut off the balls.

Their rat was female. J looked at its face. The rat's head was tipped back in the tin dissection pan, and its teeth protruded like two yellow bits of corn. The whiskers were intact, the fur sticky from the formaldehyde but still white, the arms splayed open like a T.

Suddenly Dominic was dangling a long worm of intestine in front of the girls' faces, saying, "Mmm, lunch…"

The girls jumped back in horror. One said, "You nasty!" Everybody in the small group was pushing and shoving around the wiggling flesh, trying to make somebody else get closer to Dominic, who was wagging the thing and cracking up. J, who was feeling woozy anyway, was thrust face-to-face with Dominic's evil grin. The slick intestine brushed J's nose.

"Ugh!" he shouted, and tried to get away. Where was Berkin? The formaldehyde made J feel faint.

"What's wrong?" Dominic taunted, pushing the tweezers toward J's face as J swerved and ducked. "I bet you eat intestines all the time, you freak."

"Fuck you," J said, and tried to hit him. The other kids laughed.

"Awww, baby girl wants to fight with a poor little dead mouse?" Dominic purred, backing himself into his posse of boys. "Little dead mouse can't defend herself. She all cut up."

No, J thought, *you asshole. I want to fight you.*

J had been getting into serious fights since the fifth grade, when people had started harassing him more intensely for his clothes, for the way he looked. He wasn't afraid of fighting anymore; in fact, sometimes he relished it. He often felt lighter after a fight, even if he lost, like an extra burden of guilt had been lifted, or shame for a crime he knew in his heart he hadn't committed but sometimes in his head imagined that he had. He sometimes fantasized about being tough enough to carry a gun, or dreamed about clocking one of his tormentors from behind late at night when he was alone standing somewhere desolate. He picked up an X-Acto knife from the lab table.

"You wanna go there, Dominic?" J said. "You really wanna go there?"

"Fiiiiiiight!" Several kids shouted at once, joy in their voices. "Fight!"

Berkin was at their table in an instant. "What's going on here?" Dominic's and J's faces were suddenly blank, innocent. Other students, from other lab groups, gathered around. Berkin's voice was serious. "Somebody speak up!"

The bell rang, and J pushed out of the room with the rest of the class, becoming invisible in the swell of bodies in the hall. He decided he didn't really want to fight, not today. He remembered Melissa, heaved his backpack over one shoulder, and dropped deep inside himself, leaving school with one of the passes he had stolen months ago.

"¿Quieres comer algo?" J's mom called out when she heard the front door slam. J had wasted time at a comic-book store on St. Marks before coming home at a reasonable hour; Carolina was cooking plantains at the stove.

"Sí. What are we having?" J kicked off his sneakers by the door, the way his mother liked, and padded over to the computer.

"Rice, beans, plantains—no chicken. Just juice," Carolina answered. "Your dad isn't coming home for dinner—union something."

"Yeah," J said, scanning the computer screen, noting there were no messages from Melissa. He took a plate from his mother and hunched over it at the little table, its top scattered with mail. Carolina looked at her daughter shoveling food and sighed. She handed J a napkin.

"You can breathe between bites."

"Sorry," J said, not looking up, his eyes shielded by his baseball cap.

"I'd understand you eating so much if you were still swimming, but now all you do is play on the computer," Carolina said, stirring her rice and beans together. "How does that burn calories? How is that healthy for a girl?"

J stopped. He shifted his jaw left, then right, glaring hard at his plate. The g-word, and then the swimming thing again. Did she have to bring it up today? Ever since he'd quit the team in eighth grade, his mother couldn't let it go. He'd been the top of his team, made it to the state finals, and Carolina believed J would get an athletic scholarship to college one day. Until that year,

J had loved swimming. He was good at it, natural. He learned young, on a family trip to Puerto Rico, the salty water supporting his body as though he were made of rubber and air instead of bulky flesh and bone. In the pool, his arms naturally pulled the water in smooth, strong strokes, the trunk of his body thin and still as a knife. The pool was an escape; as he swam in his lane, his muscles could scream for relief, but he would hear only the thrumming quiet of the water in his ears.

J remembered the argument. "What do you mean, you quit? You can't quit!" J and his mother had been on the interstate bus, coming home from a meet in New Jersey, a towel damp and cool between them. For weeks, J had been mustering the courage to tell her.

"I already did," J said quietly, fingering the nubs on the towel. "I already told the coach."

"But why? You love this! We already paid the fees. Swimming will pay for college! You think we're made of money? Did you go crazy?"

"I just don't like it anymore," J said.

"Why the hell not?"

"I don't know," J said, but the truth was, he did: he didn't want to wear the swimsuit anymore. His breasts had grown two cup sizes since the seventh grade, and the team suits were horrible. At home J could flatten his breasts with sports bras, but in the full, bright squint of the sun, J was a piece of glazed ham. The pool employees, the boys on the team, even the coach looked at his body hungrily, and the other girls saw his body changing, too; J knew it. Every day his breasts hurt his body; he could feel the strain of their growth beneath his skin Showering after a workout was an exercise in disassociation; he'd hold his head high and turn the water on hot, hoping the steam would obscure his vision. He hadn't looked at his body naked in a mirror since fourth grade. He'd soap his arms and his legs quickly, keeping his gaze high, but he'd try not to touch anything else. He figured it all would get clean enough through the soapy-water runoff. The coach, a skinny guy named Red, never let him swim with a T-shirt and shorts over his suit, the way he could when he trained on his own. The latest insult was Red's suggestion that J shave his legs, an offhand comment he made after practice. The humiliation was endless. J looked at Carolina apologetically. Carolina picked up the wet towel, smacked it across her daughter's lap, and went to sit at the back of the bus for the rest of the trip home.

J shook his head free of the memory and dropped his plate in the sink. He sank into the couch to watch television. He turned the volume up loud. The party, Melissa, the rat fight, and now his mom. It was all too much.

"¿M'ija?"

J winced. "Yeah?"

"Can you turn it down?"

J shut off the television.

Carolina tried again. "Jay-jay, is anything wrong?"

"No," J answered, clicking on the computer screen.

"Did anything happen between you and Melissa?"

J started to scroll through his e-mails. He tried to keep his voice neutral, but it shook just a bit. "No. She's fine."

That tremble in the voice, it had been giving J away since he was little. Carolina plunged on. "Did you and Melissa have a disagreement?"

J was getting annoyed. "Mami, no. Everything's fine."

"But you didn't go there after school today, and you didn't even *go* to school yesterday."

J's palms were starting to itch, and he rubbed them on his jeans. His mother, he thought, was somewhat psychic, and she was especially watchful over his relationship with Melissa. Sometimes, though, she was off base. He remembered eavesdropping on an argument Carolina had with his father, back when J was in sixth grade.

It came on the night J had asked his parents to stop calling him Jeni. Manny had gotten angry and stormed into his bedroom and slammed the door. Carolina followed.

"It's a beautiful name—it was your sister's name—don't you care about that?" Manny had shouted. Even if J hadn't been crouching behind his parents' door, he would have heard the whole thing. It was one of the few things J knew about being Jewish; you named your kids after some relative who had passed away. Mostly, Manny didn't care about his own heritage—he did Christmas and even let Carolina baptize J, because it mattered to his wife. But Manny wanted to give his child a *J* name, as his mother's name began with *J*, and that's just the way you did things. J's aunt Jeni had died the year J was born.

From behind the door, J could hear his mother murmur something, but he couldn't make out the words.

"I don't like that you let her get away with everything!" Manny shouted back.

"She's not getting away with anything," Carolina said. "She's being herself."

"But this is too much. J is a boy's name." Manny's voice had shifted from rage to a kind of firm authority. "Jeni isn't the parent here. We are."

"Manny—" Carolina started. "You know what Jeni is, yes?"

"Don't say it." J could hear his father pacing around the room.

There was a long silence then, punctuated by what sounded like his mother's crying. That usually worked on his dad.

"Okay," Manny had said finally. He sounded resigned, sad. "What do we do?"

"We hope she changes," Carolina said. "Until then, we wait."

"She's not going to change," Manny answered, his voice almost a growl.

"We accept her," Carolina had said. "What else can we do?"

"No," Manny said, sounding angry again. "You're not listening to me. We're the parents. Jeni can't be—and we don't have to accept anything. We pay the bills in this house."

And that was the last they'd spoken of it, and of course J didn't change. He'd grown even more masculine, coming home in sports jerseys and boy's jeans, lifting free weights at night when Carolina and Manny were sleeping. Manny had dealt with the situation by staying away, getting more involved in his union, or at least that's the way J saw it. Carolina tried to be home more, though J didn't know how to cut a path through her endless questions.

Carolina looked at J, still fiddling with the computer. "Jay-jay," she started, trying to get the words just right, "I know you love Melissa, that she's your really good friend, but there's more to life than girls."

J's hands froze at the keyboard.

Carolina continued. "I mean, there's your school, and college applications, and you shouldn't focus all your attention on one person, anyway." Carolina picked up the cat. "I think you spend too much time with Melissa."

So this was it, J thought. His mother didn't like Melissa. *Now* she tells him. "Don't worry about it," he said. "I won't be seeing her that much now."

"I thought you had a fight!" Carolina sounded triumphant.

"We didn't have a fight," J said, tightening his jaw. "I don't want to talk about it."

Carolina looked at her daughter, miserable and rigid at the desk chair. "Oh, sweetheart," she said, her voice breaking. "Love is love, no matter who it is. There are other girls besides Melissa."

J jumped up from the desk and ran from the room. He thought he was going to be sick. He locked the bathroom door, grabbed onto the sink, and stared at his face in the mirror. *A lesbian!* he said to himself. *Your mother thinks you're a lesbian, too.* His eyes were dilated, and his face was pale. *I hate you,* he said to the mirror, and sat hard on the floor.

He wondered how long he could stay in there, whether he could sleep in the bathroom, how long a person could live on water from the bathroom sink. But

Carolina was already tapping at the door, asking if he was all right. J barked out an answer, said he just had eaten his dinner too fast. Why was this all happening? Had everyone around him conspired to make him gay? And why did his mom, his Catholic mom, seem so fine about it? J just wanted to sleep. To sleep and sleep and sleep. He pulled a towel from the wall, covered himself, and shut off the light.

Sometime later, J's dad got home and kicked at the bathroom door. J stumbled awake and blinked his way into the bright living room and his foldout bed. "G'night," he mumbled to Manny, trying to look sleepy to avoid a conversation. Still, once he heard his father tuck in for good, J got up to check his computer. There was a message from Melissa.

The subject line read: *Read this: Don't call me.* J clicked *Open.*

J—I've thought a lot about Saturday night, and I think right now we should take a break from our friendship. I've been thinking about this anyway. It isn't just the kiss. We're really different people, J, and we've been growing apart. I've been becoming more serious about my dance career, and I need to think really hard about who I spend my time with. I can't drain myself with people who pull me away from my art. I need to be around artists, J—real artists who commit themselves to their work. Not stupid high school kids who have no goals. I'm not saying that's what you are, but you know what I mean. I feel like I don't know you anymore.

I know what you're thinking, and this isn't about Daniel... although we have been spending more time together since Saturday. He said that if you were a guy and you did what you did, it would be almost like rape. I was SLEEPING and you TOOK ADVANTAGE of me. I don't know if I can ever forgive you for this.

Well maybe we can talk sometime. Until then, good luck with everything. m.

J stared at the screen and felt a silent panic rise within him. Daniel knew. Melissa, his best friend, had practically accused him of *raping* her. Ex–best friend. He pulled at his fingers, trying to make the knuckles crack. Faster and faster he pulled, until it felt as if he could pull them off. *How dare she?* He slammed his hand on the table and stood up, catching a glimpse of his face in the mirror. It was white. J picked up whatever was nearest—it was one of Titi's fuzzy cat toys—and hurled it at the mirror. The cheap balsa wood frame shook against the wall, but the glass didn't break. His own stupid face still stared back at him. The face that said *fool* all over it. The face that would never be what J wanted. J picked up his boot; he wanted to smash that mirror face into a thousand pieces.

"J?" His mother's muffled voice came from the bedroom. *She thinks I'm a lesbian, too!* "You okay out there?"

J put down the boot and stuffed his foot inside. "Fine," he shouted back as he laced the boot up tight. "Go back to sleep."

The cold air hit him like a punch. Under the coat he'd grabbed on his way out the door, J had only two T-shirts. He instinctively slumped his shoulders and ducked his head against the wind. Nobody on 170th was out. J jogged to the corner, toward the light of a deli.

If nobody saw J as he really was anyway, he raged inside his head, then who would notice if he changed? What did he have to lose? A non–best friend? Some loser computer geeks? A school he hated anyway? He kicked at some loose gravel at the curb, felt around in his pockets for cigarettes. An old, crumpled pack was empty.

At the beginning, when J was a really little kid, he had been surprised whenever anyone thought he was a girl; the world seemed confused and backward to him. He was clearly a boy; everybody else was just wearing the wrong glasses. He remembered the first bad experience of this, like a sour, twisting pit in his stomach— a feeling that would repeat itself throughout all his seventeen years. It was summertime and he had just learned to run, so he must have been about two and a half. Manny had taken him to a little park near their apartment, and J remembered it because Manny had brought him alone, without Carolina. After J had clambered around on the ladders and the slides, he wanted to run through a sprinkler the other kids were playing in, spouting out of a seal's head. Manny had allowed him to take off his shirt, and he'd joyfully splashed around in his shorts. Until somebody's mom spoke to Manny. "Your son's so cute!"

J felt proud and happy, but Manny's tone—gruff, embarrassed, strained—stayed with him still, fifteen years later. "That is my daughter." And Manny yanked him roughly by the arm and stuffed him back into his flowered T-shirt, marching him home, as though he was the one who had said something bad. That was his first full memory.

He started preschool when he was three, and when he ran to play with the other boys at school, nobody seemed to care much. Carolina hadn't fussed for long over the dress situation, though she had cried when J took scissors to his long hair, trying to cut it as short as his dad's, or make himself look like his school best friend, Axel. That was another stomach-twisting memory. He had pocketed some scissors from school, excited to get rid of the long curls his mother combed after baths and tied into pigtails, and thrilled with the sudden knowledge he could just cut them off, the way he cut shapes in class. The scissors had rounded tips and red handles, and J snipped the curls off by himself in the bathroom. He stood on his little stool to see the mirror, but basically he just chopped—big cuts, all around his head, again and again, singing a little song. Carolina screamed when she saw him, called it a massacre, and J cried. Carolina took J to her own hairdresser and had her style the remaining clumps of hair like a pixie.

After a while, his parents didn't talk to J about his masculine appearance. They just fussed over J's grades, praising him for the *excellent*s he got in science, the *very good*s in English and spelling. Whenever J came home upset that someone had teased him, Carolina would take J on her lap and say, "Oh, m'ija, you just have to be yourself. Because if you aren't, who else will be?" J's dad said, "Don't let the bastards get you down."

Still, J's parents didn't know a lot of things; J protected them. They didn't know that he had started smoking in fifth grade. By that age, J had stopped praying to God for a miracle and had decided he didn't want to be a boy after all; he just wanted to hang out with them, look like them, be like them. After he could swallow the coughing fits and keep his eyes from burning, J practiced holding his cigarettes tough-style, like the older boys did, cupped in his fist, the other hand tucked into the pocket of his jeans. Hanging with the boys also meant fighting with them, and his parents didn't know how many fights there were, either, though J came home with bruises. The first big one was over a girl named Maria who was in special ed and was the butt of practical jokes. When three boys in the fifth grade stole Maria's nylon jacket and stuffed it down the toilet of the boys' bathroom, J became enraged and tried to fight them all at once. He whirled like a top, fists flailing, going for eyes, teeth, noses, and the kids tackled him to the ground, pinning him there, kicking him in the ribs and calling him a dyke until a playground attendant pulled them off.

That word came up again and again, marking time, breaking him down. Just last week, a few days before the party, he had been on the subway coming home from school when he heard it again. He was harassed by a gang of high school boys in enormous puffy coats and glinty fake-gold chains.

"Is that a guy or a girl?" one of the boys asked, jerking a thumb in J's direction. His friends laughed. The subway car was about half full; it was midafternoon, and there were moms with their kids, delivery messengers, businesspeople leaving work early. J glanced up but quickly made himself busy with the Japanese comic book he'd been reading.

"I don't think it's human," one of the friends

answered, lumbering up to J and kicking at his boot. J ignored him. The boy kicked harder.

"Are you a boy or a girl?" the guy asked. J turned a page.

"Or are you deaf?" another one in the group asked, coming up behind his friend. The four kids were now in a clump directly in front of J. One snatched the baseball cap off J's head and stuffed it in his back pocket.

"Hey!" J shouted. "Fuck you!"

"Fuck me?" the cap thief retorted. "Fuck me? What if I don't want to fuck you? I don't know what you got between your legs. Plus, you nasty."

"It sounds like a girl," one of the guys said. "Unless its voice hasn't changed. Unless it's a girly man."

"Are you a faggot?" the original instigator crooned at J in a high, sweet voice. J looked up, fury in his eyes. He saw that the guy had a gold tooth cap, that his chain had a dollar sign hanging from it.

"No, but you are," J said, standing up. With a quick swing, he punched the older boy in the gut and tried to squeeze past the throng and out the subway doors, which were just opening. The three other boys stopped him and shoved him back into a seat.

"Fuck you, bitch," one of them said, and smacked J upside the head, hard.

"The faggot hit me!" the first boy said, recovering.

Someone on the train muttered an uptight-sounding "cool it," but everyone ignored him. J, now pinned to his seat, kicked out at whatever he could, managing a hard jab at somebody's shin. Carolina hadn't sprung for the steel-toe boots J had begged for, but the sole was sturdy, and the boy yelped in pain. J was hit again, but he couldn't see who had done it; his head snapped back against the subway wall. J refused to make a sound, but he wondered, in an instant, if he was bleeding. He stayed in that position, catching his breath, closing his eyes, believing he was going to die, silently saying he was sorry to his mom.

"Oh, fuck, this is our stop," J heard over the rushing in his ears. "Leave the little bitch." When he opened his eyes, the boys were gone.

"Are you okay?" A mom with a toddler was squatting in front of J, tentatively reaching a hand toward his knee but not touching him. J looked at the woman, trying to focus, but he couldn't form any words. He got up, grabbed his backpack and his comic from the floor, and shoved his way into the next car.

And now Carolina had joined this league of boys, in her own way. She had joined everyone else in the world who misunderstood what J himself was barely grasping.

A dyke, J stormed. *My parents think of me as a*

dyke. And Melissa thinks of me as a monster. Well, maybe that's what I'll be, then. I'll become a real freak. Gen-u-ine freak. And it was there, in front of the deli on 170th and Amsterdam, that J hatched a plan.

CHAPTER
THREE

J hit the Google icon at the top of his screen and typed
women who want to be men in the search line. It was
morning again, and the apartment was quiet. His lies
were getting deeper; that day, he had pretended to dress
and leave for school. He bought a cup of coffee at the
Dominican diner and waited impatiently for an hour,
until he was sure his parents wouldn't come home for
anything they might have forgotten. He smoked three
cigarettes on the corner, then ran back up the stairs to
his apartment, thankfully avoiding Mercie, and logged

back on to the computer. *This is it*, he thought. *That which does not kill you makes you strong.*

The first time he had heard the word *transsexual* was on a daytime talk show, when he was eleven. Home from school for the summer, J was flipping channels when *Your Girlfriend's Really a Man!* flashed in yellow script across the screen. He stopped to watch several beautiful, scantily clad women traipse across a stage and kiss their unsuspecting boyfriends, who had been waiting in a greenroom. One by one, the women fell to their knees and confessed their "terrible secret"—they had been born men—while the audience gasped or laughed at the spectacle. That day, J learned the word *transsexual* and that, quite possibly, there were people in the world like him.

It took J only one day more to look up the word online, finding a time when his parents were asleep and wouldn't catch him exploring. The definition he found was "a person who self-identifies as a member of the gender opposite to the one assigned to them at birth." For a while afterward, when he wasn't too freaked out to think about it, he was comforted by the word *assigned*. If gender was an assignment, then someone had mis-assigned him. J had assignments in school; assignments changed all the time. The old fantasy returned, minus God: perhaps J could go back to the hospital where he'd been born and just get "reassigned."

Pretty soon, J was logging on to look at pictures every few days. There were literally thousands of websites that showed transsexual surgeries, before-and-after pictures of penises that had been reconstructed to become vaginas, and vice versa. The "after" penises were ugly. Too small, or huge and misshapen. J didn't like looking, because the more he looked, the more he thought his "assignment" couldn't be fixed. His assignment was a curse. "Down there," as his mother called it, J was definitely a girl. He had stopped going to websites in sixth grade.

There were 6,130 results for *women who want to be men*. J clicked on a site he'd been to a few times before. The FTM Path, it was called. *FTM* stood for "female to male." *Screw Melissa*, J thought. *Screw everybody*. He was going to be more than just a hovering brain without a body. He was going to be what he knew he was at three, at five. He knew he couldn't stay home sick forever. He was going to make himself a boy.

There was a link on the page to *Twelve Myths About Testosterone*, and one of them said *Will testosterone make me gay?* J clicked it. *Everybody thinks I'm gay, anyway*, he thought. *Things can't get any worse*. But here a world opened up—how had he not clicked on the testosterone links before?

Testosterone, he read, was a hormone that both biological men and women produced in their bodies naturally. Men just produced more. Testosterone was the reason men had lower voices and grew facial hair—and no, it didn't make them gay. It sometimes made them more horny. *Just my luck. I'll end up trying to kiss another girl.* But if biological girls took extra testosterone, they could grow beards and have male voices. *The voice*, J thought, sweat breaking out all over, making him suddenly cold, then hot. *I could talk; I could yell at assholes when they harassed me; I could sound normal; I could sound real.* They'd get bigger muscles. Their periods would stop.

"Oh, my God," J whispered. Everything at once. The voice, the muscles, the periods he hated almost as much as the shape of his body. First the low pull in his abdomen, reminding him of the endless betrayal, and then the bleeding, that spiteful, hideous crush each month. "Oh, my God."

Titi suddenly jumped onto J's lap, startling him. "Do you want some testosterone, Titi?" he asked her. "Should we do this together?" Titi purred and arched her back.

There was a link to some pictures, and J clicked. Suddenly, there was Mike, there was Ty, there was Tate, there were Flip and Mac and two dozen others, who all (well, except for Ty, really) *looked like men*. J stared at the screen until his eyes felt dry. He remembered to blink.

Where did these guys live? How old were they? Mac looked pretty young, and so did Tate. Mike looked fifty, and he was really fat. And bald! Would testosterone make you bald? Flip had tattoos and huge muscles. He also had no breasts. J flashed to the old thoughts of slicing off his breasts. *Did Flip have surgery for that? How much would it cost?* J's stomach was so tight with excitement or terror, he felt as though he were breathing from the top of his head.

Why had he spent so much time, years ago, looking at those dumb surgery pictures? Testosterone was the magic potion, a little pill that would change everything.

Testosterone is delivered through an intramuscular injection with a syringe. He had clicked on the link *T Basics* to find out more. He hated shots. *Damn*, he thought.

The initial elation shifted, became overwhelming. J got up for some water, gently tossing Titi to the floor. But dealing with shots was the easy part, he realized; sneaking the change past his parents was going to be the killer. His dad, maybe, wouldn't be so bad. J could just pretend to be sleeping whenever Manny was home, which was rarely. But Carolina noticed everything.

Maybe he could pretend to have a bad case of laryngitis and whisper everything at home, so when his voice changed she wouldn't know. His voice changing! J thrilled at the thought. And the facial hair. God, what to do about that? He could pretend to have a bad case of acne and have to wear a face mask all the time. Summer was coming; scratch that. He could switch to Islam and—no. That was stupid, too.

"This won't work, this won't work, this'll never work," J said out loud. Still, he sat down at the computer again and clicked on *Chest binding. One thing at a time*, he told himself. *Just take it slow.*

Here he found something he could do right away. It looked like a zip-up vest, black and tight, that you wore under your clothes and that made you entirely flat. It was called a chest binder, and it cost eighty dollars. That was nearly half his savings.

"Damn," he said again. Titi was back, now trying to walk across his keyboard. He pulled her onto his lap. He clicked on *Make your own.*

Here the site said you could just line up two Ace bandages, one above the other like an equal sign, and stitch them together. Then wrap the wide bandage around yourself, marking off the dimensions of your rib cage, and stitch it together into a circle. You shimmied into the thing like a tube top.

J decided to call Carolina at the hospital and ask her to bring home some bandages for an ankle he had twisted on the stairs at school.

Suddenly, the keys in the door rattled, and the door swung open. It was his father. Bulky and tired-looking, with loose skin like empty pockets under his eyes, Manny thumped his shoulder bag to the floor and said, "Whatcha doing?"

J quickly closed the browser window and swiveled his chair around. "Nothing. I'm still sick. I had to come home early from school."

"Umph," Manny said, pulling off his boots and tossing them next to J's by the door. "It's not that early. It's already after four."

Manny padded over to J in his socks and put his hands on J's shoulders. He squeezed, and J winced and slumped down lower in the chair. He didn't like his father touching him, didn't like anyone touching him, really, but especially Manny. His father was so rarely around these days, their interactions felt forced or staged, like two mannequins posed together in a window. Manny used to be playful and even roughhouse with him when he was younger, but when J had started to develop the curves he tried so desperately to hide, Manny treated him more delicately. J wanted the old Manny back.

"What? Now you don't even like my shoulder rubs?"

Manny asked, his enormous hands dangling in space. "You're too much, J. Go start some dinner. Mami's gonna be here soon." And he went into the bedroom to change.

The next morning, J pulled out three shirts and a bandanna for his head. He inhaled two bowls of Cocoa Puffs, ignoring his mother's "guess someone's feeling better," and lied again about leaving for school. Carolina hadn't even asked to look at J's ankle, just handed over the bandages while prattling away on her cell phone.

At the corner, instead of turning left for the subway, J turned right toward the twenty-four-hour drugstore. Drugstores carried thread, didn't they? The website said he needed heavy-duty flesh-colored thread.

"Whaddya need thread for, hon?" the tired-looking cashier asked J. It was still before eight in the morning.

J hadn't considered this, and he hated being called *hon*. "Um, I need to sew something for school."

"I figured you needed to sew something, but I think we only got those kits they sell for traveling. Aisle four."

J had no idea what kind of kits someone would need for traveling. He'd only ever been to Puerto Rico, and that was when he was a little kid. He remembered the beaches and the way his cousins were so much darker than he was, forever playing in the sun. There was always some aunt around, wanting to hug J, give him some soda or a sandwich. J had begged to stay in the ocean all day, where his body was light and buoyant and where, if he was very still, the sand-colored fish would swim up and kiss his skin.

There was no heavy thread in aisle four, just envelopes of multicolored string looped around a cardboard strip, with a few needles pegged to the side. No way would that hold two bandages together. J opted for a pack of safety pins. They'd be faster than sewing, anyway. After he bought the pins, a small notebook, and an energy drink, J had a half hour to kill before Carolina would be out of the house and he could make his first transformation.

He smoked a cigarette and leaned against a brick wall, wishing it wasn't so damn cold in New York City. The smoke gave him a headache this early in the morning, like a tar balloon expanding the inside of his skull, and J relished the pain, appreciating this small control over his body. He watched two men in suits and overcoats push their way into the deli across the street and jotted a note in the new notebook he had just purchased.

From here on out, J would be a spy. He would go undercover.

Overcoat: gray better than black, J wrote. He wondered if, when he was older, he would dress like these men. Would he go into some business that made him wear a suit? Would he coordinate his ties with his socks? Could he be a veterinarian, the white smock, the deep voice in the waiting room announcing "owner of Roscoe?" Yes, that last part he could do. For now he'd like to look like the three guys walking up the block, in their low-slung jeans and their oversize jackets. The boys were probably eighteen or twenty, and they walked as though they had nothing better to do, their eyes cast down before they glowered outward, their arms loose in their sockets, their gait wide and casual. *Don't be too tight*, J wrote in the notebook. *Walk like you've got a bowling ball between your legs.*

Carolina would be gone by now, so J trudged home slowly, head down against the wind. He practiced taking bigger steps, but he felt stupid and uncomfortable. He stopped and smoked another cigarette. That, he knew, he could do right.

The chest binder was harder to construct than J had thought; the safety pins wouldn't lie flat, and the material bunched and puckered and showed little ridges through his shirts. He ended up sewing the bandages together the way the website instructed, using some of his mother's skinny black thread he had found next to the nail polish in the bathroom. It was strong enough. The result looked like a badly sutured flesh wound, but the thing held together, and when J wrapped the binder around himself and marked out where the ends should be sewn together, and added an extra inch for tightness, he felt a kind of happy peace settle down on him. He whistled as he knotted the threads into sloppy, tangled balls, dolloping on some Krazy Glue for good measure. Squeezing himself in felt mentally like strapping on a seat belt in the car, only more painful; aside from the sharp jabbing sensation that was most acute under his armpits, J felt secure and protected, and once he layered on his three shirts, he looked as flat as any boy.

He deliberated for hours over which pair of jeans made his butt look most masculine, tossing one pair of Levi's after another on the floor, only to try them on again, twisting himself like a Slinky to get a fair appraisal. He wished he could wear them as low as other guys did, advertising the full expanse of his boxers from behind, but that would require having something up front to hold them up. He was not about to stuff socks into his shorts. So he settled on his biggest jersey over two thermals and his biggest jeans, which dwarfed him like a tent.

By the time he made it out of the apartment, it was one o'clock. School would be out in an hour. He ran so quickly out of the building, trying to avoid Mercedes, that he was almost startled to be on the sidewalk again. *You're a dude*, J said to himself. *You're a dude. Slow down.* He practiced the bowling-ball walk. He caught his reflection in the glass door of another apartment building; even with all his oversize winter clothes, he didn't look any different. Same face, same grungy cap, same coat, same J.

But no, J thought. *This time if somebody asks, I'm saying I'm a guy.* There was no going back.

J looked down the block. Was that lady with a dog staring at him? J tightened his jaw, jutted out his chin a bit, as though he was about to nod upward in a kind of tough hello, and squinted a little, too. The lady, only about twenty yards away, squatted to swipe up her dog's mess. The dog, though, did a double take. *I'm crazy*, J thought. *Now I'm thinking animals can see through me.*

Even though it was chilly outside, sweat had soaked through the sides of his binder. He wanted to go home, suddenly wanted to check his messages, wanted Titi. All the earlier confidence was vanishing. He wanted to talk to Melissa.

J was feeling better by nightfall. His chest binder was tucked away safely in the bottom of his trunk, and Carolina had just been paid, so she wanted to go out to dinner. They settled on Greek food, which J loved, the garlic lingering in his mouth all night.

After Manny griped about some union vote for the better part of an hour, Carolina turned to J.

"J, do you think you could take some nice pictures of your father and me tonight?"

"Why?" J answered, his mouth full of chicken.

"Don't sound so excited," Carolina answered.

"I mean, sure," J said. "But why?"

"You haven't shown us your pictures in a long time," Manny said, a little stern.

"I haven't been taking as many," J said, though this wasn't true. He'd been taking pictures of construction sites lately; there was so much of it going on in Manhattan, and he liked the way you couldn't tell whether the buildings in the pictures were being built or destroyed. There was something savage about the photographs, something raw and slightly embarrassing about construction sites that J liked—it was like catching a building in its underwear, before it had a chance to get dressed. Often J placed something entirely incongruous in the picture frame—something that you'd have to look hard to see, but once you noticed it, you couldn't take your eyes off it. One time he put his mother's Virgin Mary clock from home up on a half-built wall; another time he snuck in a stuffed elephant, just on the rim of a dump truck. He knew his parents wouldn't understand these pictures.

"You used to take such great pictures of animals. Remember when you wanted to be a wildlife photographer?" Manny asked.

Carolina shot her husband a look.

"Pops, that was, like, when I was ten years old," J said. His father was always reminding J of when he was younger.

"Anyway," Carolina said, "I'd like you to take a picture of me and Daddy so I can send it out in invitations. Our twentieth wedding anniversary is coming up."

"You want to have a party?" Manny said, his voice rising in concern.

Why did his parents always have their disagreements in front of him? J groaned internally. Manny hated parties; Carolina loved them.

"Yes. Twenty years with you? I deserve it."

That night, J set up the lights and moved the furniture around for a proper portrait of his parents. Carolina asked if J could set the timer so he could be in the picture, too. J refused, saying this should just be a special shot of the two of them, but really he hated being in pictures, and everybody knew it. He never looked the way he felt inside, and he hated being watched. Being behind the camera usually gave him a good excuse. Carolina wore her best blouse, the magenta one that looked like silk, and Manny covered up his growing belly with a tie. They laughed when J said, "Say Titi!" It was the friendliest J had been in months. He snapped the picture.

After his parents had gone to bed, J spent a long time staring at the photograph in the digital camera's viewing screen. They looked relaxed and happy, Carolina leaning slightly into Manny's shoulder, Manny's dimple showing plainly in his left cheek. *I want to remember them like this*, J thought suddenly, inexplicably.

Because what if Carolina and Manny couldn't take his new incarnation? They had already withstood so much. They witnessed the stares, the hostile glances, the young children tugging at their parents' hands and whispering, "Is that a boy or a girl?" And all Carolina and Manny wanted was for J to have a good life, to go to college; they'd forgone so much for this dream. J was close to tears thinking about it, the melancholy seeping in like a scent. But he hadn't let himself cry in a long time; it was as though his tear ducts had cemented shut in their sockets. His parents, J thought, had stayed in this rent-stabilized apartment his entire life, stuffed themselves into a one-bedroom, so they could sock away money for his education. And now here he was, skipping school, acting as though he didn't care. But he *did* care—he just cared about his own survival more. He hated himself, hated his stupid body. And if he went through with the change—if he took T, the testosterone, and lowered his voice, if he looked and acted more and more like a man, he'd shatter all his parents' dreams. They'd probably never speak to him again. Yes, he'd have to take this picture with him. To remember.

J went to the bookshelf where his parents kept the photo albums. He picked up the puffy one with the rose embroidered on the cover. He was four in these pictures.

There he was in the pixie haircut; there he was at the slides in the park. There was Carolina, with some woman J didn't remember, laughing outside on a picnic blanket. There he was, staring intently at a picture book, his face serious, the book upside down in his lap. He didn't know anyone was taking his picture then, wasn't aware of people watching him or, usually, what he'd looked like. He would miss his mother's laughter, though that was rarer these days; she was always so stressed and uptight. He turned the page: a birthday. Everyone was wearing party hats, even Manny. J had frosting on one cheek. Now he'd never let that happen; every small error was quickly scrutinized and fixed, every bit of frosting wiped away. Who would throw him birthday parties after he left?

J shut the album but then opened it again, near the back. He was older there, maybe ten. There was a photo of him with his parents at dinner; Manny must have set the timer. There was challah on the table—the ill-fated era when his dad had decided they'd all have Shabbos dinner every Friday night. Carolina had gone along with the plan, dutifully buying the bread and the candles, and Manny had tried to teach them the prayers, saying how that was his one good memory from childhood—the way his parents had stopped fighting for Friday dinners. But at that point, the three of them were still eating together most nights, anyway; the television and the computer had yet to make their noisy intrusions, and Manny hadn't been working so much, so Shabbos hadn't seemed so different from other times. Still, J liked the candles and the scratchy feel of a new language in his mouth. But Manny had given up on the habit before the prayers had time to set, and J was too young to ask him why. J slammed the book shut again and shoved it roughly onto the shelf. The pictures made him angry; he was so little then, so innocent. When had things gone so terribly, awfully wrong? Why was he being punished for something he'd never asked for in the first place? Why couldn't he just call Melissa and talk like normal anymore, listen to her chatter away about the symmetry of her dance turnout, how many calories she'd managed to consume, how her mother hadn't come home again last night? J looked around the room for Titi but couldn't find her. She was probably snuggled up with his parents, he thought. Even the animals were against him.

That night, J didn't even bother opening the couch into a bed. He just curled up under a blanket and fell into a fitful, angst-y sleep.

The next morning was Saturday, and J had to get through two whole days with his parents around, without touching the chest binder that still lay at the bottom of his trunk. For something that had taken practically the whole day to put on, he missed it. He fantasized endlessly about wearing it again, about being flat-chested, about leaving the house with it. This time, he thought, he would take the subway.

When Monday morning finally broke, bright and cold, J adopted the same routine. He sucked down some breakfast, went to the diner for coffee, and ran back home when he was sure his parents were safely gone. The binder, in all its sloppy majesty, was still there. He wiggled into it and felt the same peace, the same *rightness* he had felt the Friday before. To get in the mood, he put on Yankee's "Who's Your Daddy?" and danced around just a bit for Titi. He practiced looking angry in the mirror.

The No. 1 train was practically empty. J always tried to time his rides for such journeys, when he'd have to interact with the fewest passengers. He slipped on his headphones and tried to look disinterested when he plopped into the orange plastic chair in the center of the car, close to the doors. Slowly he spread his knees wider and wider, the way he had watched men do when they rode the trains. Nobody seemed to notice him. A man reading his newspaper didn't look up. A woman feeding her child french fries was busy cleaning up spilled ketchup. And two teenagers at the end of the car—the most dangerous of all—were cracking up over something they were texting into a cell phone. J made sure these girls weren't looking or laughing at him, and when it was clear that the phone was their central preoccupation, he went back to his music and even closed his eyes for a moment. Daddy Yankee just kept singing, no matter what.

Where should he get off the train? He hadn't thought this far. Probably the Village. Over the weekend, he'd read online that the gay and lesbian center on Thirteenth Street had support groups for transguys; he wasn't ready for that, not yet. But maybe that was a sign to get off. He stood up, shot a quick glance down his body, and stepped off the train at Fourteenth Street.

It was freezing outside, and J's headphones were blaring "Dale Caliente." *Irony is everywhere*, J thought. A school was letting out from somewhere, and teenagers were pushing each other and clumping on the corner of Fourteenth and Sixth Avenue, shouting "Marcus!" and "Shemeka!" and "You goin' to basketball?" as they dispersed like a thinning storm cloud. He kept walking. Finally a Starbucks materialized, and he went in.

It was so much warmer inside, the stereo playing some kind of girly hippie music. J ordered a cappuccino and was shocked when it cost him almost a quarter of his weekly allowance. Who could afford these places? He wished he'd brought something to read.

A knot of girls, possibly from the school that just got out, had followed J inside. They were giggling and blowing on their hands, staring up at the menu board and deciding what they could buy with their pooled cash. J noticed they were all clutching binders with cutouts of boy bands stuck inside the plastic sleeves.

This was definitely not Melissa's crowd. Plus, these girls were younger. Probably freshmen. J sat at a table by the window and took off his sweatshirt, leaving on only two T-shirts and a thermal. This place really cranked up the heat. He glanced down: no bumps. The binder was working. J looked more closely at one of the girls, who seemed to be the leader, a girl with short hair dyed pink at the tips. Suddenly, she turned and looked at J.

"You looking at us?" Pink Tips asked loudly, over the heads of her girlfriends. The girls, like a circle of birds, all tipped their heads up in unison.

"No," J said, and quickly stared down at his cappuccino.

"Yes, you are—I saw you," Pink Tips said, and moved closer, sticking her chest out slightly and dropping her binder down by her side. Even though it was cold outside, she was wearing only a thin, threadbare sweater with holes at the elbows. So this was the uniform of Village school kids—trying to look poor when they were probably rich, J thought. "You go to PS two fifty-two?"

"No," J answered, and put on his headphones.

"I think I've seen you before," Pink Tips kept going. One of her friends, a thin girl with dark eye makeup like a raccoon, handed her a steaming paper cup of coffee.

"No, you haven't. I don't hang out around here." J knew that girls liked the boys who were more aggressive and rough. It seemed, at least with Melissa and her friends, that although they pined for sweetness and consideration, what they responded to most was indifference.

The girls tittered. A few inched closer to J. "I'm Madison. What's your name?"

"J."

"Cool," Madison answered. At the same time one of the other girls, leaning forward in a dark skirt and combat boots, said, "Is that short for something?"

"Jason." As he spoke, J's heart skipped. Would the girls laugh? Would they call him out? *At least they won't beat me up*, J thought. And then, *I could never hit a girl.*

Ever since puberty, J had preferred the company of girls—not that he had much of a choice, outside of Melissa. When he was younger and life was about sports and tumbling around in the dirt, boys were his playmates. But then as limbs lengthened and voices deepened, J's old friends didn't have time for him anymore. They wanted to hang out on corners and catcall girls. They laughed at J, told him his mama was calling. Girls, at least, had been trained to be more polite. Maybe that was why the "Jason" comment worked. They were just being nice.

"What school you go to?" Combat Boots asked. She didn't give her name.

"I don't go to school," J said. At this, all the girls—J noticed now that there were only four of them—raised their eyebrows and bulged out their eyes in surprise.

"Why not?" Raccoon Eyes asked. "You run away or something?"

By now the girls had pulled up chairs and gathered around J. "Nah," he said, thinking fast. "I'm, um, between schools. I just moved here."

"From where?" Madison asked, her eyes narrowing. J thought she might be onto him, but then her expression softened, and she looked infinitely interested. Girls were so amazing this way, he thought. They always kept the questions coming.

"Philly."

"Oh, cool. I got family there." Combat Boots was suddenly intrigued.

Shit, J thought. *Caught.* J snapped open his cell phone, looked at the time.

"Crap," he said. "I gotta go."

"Okay," Madison said, shifting back her chair so J could pass. "Maybe we'll see you here again? We come here every day."

It worked! J was screaming inside his head, despite the half-lumber, half-swagger he carefully executed for his exit stage right. His mind was a blaze of colors and bursting; he had passed, he had flirted, he had passed, he had spoken to strangers, he had passed, he had bound his breasts, he had passed, he had passed, he had passed! He, J—yes—*he*, that glorious pronoun, *he* had been J on a new corner, in a new Starbucks, with a new name and a new body but the selfsame soul, talking—actually talking—to other people, who believed he was a boy. And getting more attention than he ever had at his stupid old school.

On the subway ride home, J put himself back in check. What kind of Puerto Rican guy hung out at a Starbucks on Fourteenth Street? Even half Puerto Rican. A pussy, that's who. A mama's boy. Nobody from his neighborhood. But in a way, J thought, hanging out downtown would keep him from getting spooked, discovered as a girl. *Who the hell am I?* J thought. *I haven't been to school in a week—so I'm no closer to college. I have no future. I'm a loser, a poser. I don't know who I am.*

In the bathroom at the diner on the corner of his block, J's mood grew certifiably black. Squeezing around the toilet as well as a bucket and a mop in a room the size of a place mat, J wriggled out of the binder, which was soaked in sweat but still stitched together. He put on the sports bras he had tossed into his backpack, avoiding looking at his breasts, trying not to touch them. If only he could slice them off, precise and neat as a rat dissection.

That night, there was a message from Melissa on the computer. *J—* she wrote. *Can we talk?*

No, we can't talk, J thought. *You don't know me anymore. You said it yourself.*

CHAPTER FOUR

The next day, right on time, J was back at the Starbucks. He was early, actually; it didn't take him as long to get ready, and he had wasted most of the day reading men's fitness magazines at a newsstand. At two o'clock, when school got out, J was standing in front of the Starbucks, tying his sneaker; he didn't want to spend the money on coffee. He practiced a bored expression, and when he stood up, as if on cue, there were Madison and another girl, this one with blue hair, walking toward him.

"Hey, J," Madison said, spotting him.

"Hey."

"This is Blue," Madison said. She gave her friend, who was wearing old painter pants and a tight leather jacket, a small push toward J.

"That's original," J said. What was with this group and their colors?

"So's that," Blue answered, squinting up at him. Blue was a white girl; she was short, with a tiny chin and wide gray eyes and an accent, something European. "Everybody has to say something about my name."

"So, is it real?" J asked, a little stung but showing nothing in his flat, withdrawn expression. His name was one of the only things he liked about himself.

"What, my hair?" Blue asked. And out came a tumble of laughs—bright and heavy, like polished apples.

This girl was snappy, J thought, standing up a little straighter. And pretty, too, in an elfin kind of way. Why didn't he ever have a clever comeback? Melissa knew what to say in situations like these. Melissa knew how to communicate "come hither" and "back off" with a phrase. But J couldn't think of anything. "No, your name."

"Of course not," Blue said, still smiling. "Do you think a Polish family with a name like Karasinska would call their only daughter Blue? My real name is Basia. But I hate it."

"Blue's a painter," Madison interrupted. "Guess what color she paints in."

J raised an eyebrow.

"You should see her work. It's amazing," Madison continued. "Whole landscapes and people and cities, only everything's blue."

"Why?" J asked, and then immediately regretted it. Showing too much interest was the kiss of death. He worried he might be giving himself away. He felt the sweat pool in his armpits.

"I dunno, I just like it," Blue answered, a little defensively. "Do you do any art?"

"I take photographs," J said before he could stop himself. *Don't give yourself away*, he thought. *Be a dude. Shut the hell up.* To change the topic, J pulled out a cigarette and lit it. He halfheartedly waved the box toward the girls, as though he didn't care whether they took one or not. Each of them did.

"What do you shoot?" Blue asked. Her lips, he noticed, were soft and pouty. But not in stuck-up way. In a way that might be nice to kiss. *Stop it*, he thought. *You haven't even gotten a whiff of testosterone. You have no right to be like this.*

"People," J said. "Sometimes with cameras and sometimes with guns."

Blue looked confused, so J laughed, a little half-laugh-half-grunt he'd been practicing.

"Oh," she said, relieved. Her eyes, he noticed, glittered with flecks of gold. This girl was actually hot. "What kinds of people?"

"All kinds," J said, though this was a lie. He hadn't ever shot portraits, other than the ones of his parents—he mostly felt too shy.

"Not much for conversation, are you?" Madison said. "Well, thanks for the cigarettes; we have to go. We have drama today. We'll see you tomorrow?"

"Yeah, maybe," J said, knowing full well he'd be right there, right on time.

While J worried that his school would catch on to his multiple absences and call Carolina or Manny, each day passed without trouble. The administration at PS 386 had enough parent calls to make, he imagined, with the petty thefts and fights that broke out each day, to concern itself with him. He left for "school" in the morning, his backpack full of comic books, his chest binder, and extra shirts. He spent the day roaming the streets, feeling a bit safer in his skin, and counting the hours until he could show up outside the Starbucks. He wasn't sure what people in stores or on the subway thought of him, but he knew that at least two girls on Fourteenth Street believed he was a guy, and he didn't want to miss a moment with them.

Wednesday afternoon went pretty much the same as

Tuesday, with Blue and Madison chattering at J, and him giving one- or two-word answers and offering up his cigarettes. He wasn't sure what they saw in him, didn't know if he would be considered "cute" or if he was just somebody new who could alleviate their boredom. On Thursday, he found out.

Standing at his regular spot by the tar stain outside the café, J was practicing his absentminded smoking look when Madison bounded out of school and snatched the cigarette from his hand. She took a long drag, smiling at him mischievously.

This girl is too forward, J thought. *Where'd she get such balls?*

"I know someone who likes you," Madison said, kicking the toe of J's boot with her sneakered foot.

God, not the footsie game. That's what led to trouble with Melissa. Still, he took the bait. "Yeah?" he asked, examining a scrape on his knuckle.

"Yeah," Madison said. "Gimme a cigarette and I'll tell you who."

"You're already smoking this one."

"Come *on*," Madison whined. "This is a trade."

J gave Madison a cigarette and lit it for her. Madison said, "I'll give you a hint. It's not me."

"You're not making it very hard," J said, his stomach leaping up toward his lungs.

"So, do you like her, too?"

"I barely know her," J said, taking off his cap, scratching his hair, and then quickly securing it on his head again.

"Yes, you do. You know her enough. She wants to know if you want to see her art and show her your photos."

"Why doesn't she ask me herself?" J knew the earlier quip about his photography was too revealing. What if she hated it?

"She's home sick today. She'll be here tomorrow." Madison stubbed out her cigarette. "Hey, did you get placed in a school yet?"

"Nah," J said, surprised at how quickly the lies came to him. "They're thinking of letting me wait out the school year and just starting me up again next fall."

"Why?"

" 'Cause I'm that smart."

These were the most words J had ever said in succession to Madison or her troop. He felt exhausted.

"Oh." For once, Madison seemed stumped. "Well, anyway, do you want to go over and see Blue's art? Her house is cool."

"That'd be okay."

"Cool! Lemme call her and see if we can come over. She doesn't live that far." Madison pulled a cell phone out of her bag. A plastic alien charm hung from the case, and it jiggled as she dialed.

"I thought Blue was sick," J said.

"She's not that sick," Madison retorted with an eye roll, and turned her back when Blue answered the phone. She talked quietly so J couldn't hear her. When she turned back around, J was smoking again and reading a comic. "She doesn't want us to come over. I think she's pissed I told you."

"Oh," J said, trying to look uninterested. "Well, I gotta go, anyway." And he sauntered off, his heart lighter, his head terrified.

That night, Melissa called J's cell phone. J didn't pick up, but he listened to the message right away.

"Come on, J," Melissa said into the voice mail, her voice whiny and impatient. "Call me back. I'm getting worried about you. You haven't been at school in over a week. Call me."

Good, let her worry, J thought. *I have a new life now.*

But did he? He had Starbucks, and some girl with a crush, and two flesh-colored bandages stitched together with some now-fraying thread. Not much of a life. He suddenly remembered one day at the East River, not long ago, when he and Melissa had sat on a bench and watched the tugboats after school.

"If I threw myself in the river and started drowning, would you save me?" Melissa had asked.

"Yeah," J answered. This was going to be one of

Melissa's heavy, nihilistic discussions. He lit a cigarette. She grabbed it from his mouth and threw it in the river.

"Why'd you do that?" J asked, his eyebrows knitting together.

"Because if you keep killing yourself with cigarettes, you're not going to be able to save me."

"You smoke, too."

"Not as much as you," Melissa countered. She kicked off her flip-flops and put her feet in J's lap. It was spring, and an ice-cream truck jingled from far away. "Can you give me a foot rub?"

J hated giving foot rubs; touching made him nervous. Melissa always wanted them, though, after all the dance rehearsals. He gingerly pulled at Melissa's toes, which were dirty from the city streets. Melissa continued. "I mean, what if I really did die? It's not like New York needs another dancer."

"Come on, Melis, don't think like that."

"Do you think they'd find my father for the funeral?"

J considered. Melissa's father had never shown an interest in his daughter, even when Karyn tracked him down to tell him she was pregnant, and a few times through the years when she was looking for child support. Karyn didn't like to talk about him, only said that he was a musician who was briefly in town for a gig.

"Your mom would be wrecked, for real."

"That's not what I'm asking," Melissa said, pulling her feet back and crossing them underneath her. "I'm asking about my father. Why are men such assholes?"

"Not all men." *Not me.*

"J, I know not all men. I'm not an idiot. God." Melissa fished in her bag for a hair tie and deftly pulled her curls back into a loose bun. "I just hate them. I think sometimes it would be easier to be with women."

J froze. What was Melissa saying? Crazy, *boy-crazy* Melissa could be with girls? God, he wanted a cigarette, but he didn't want Melissa to throw it away again. He couldn't look at her.

"Sometimes I think you're the only person in the world I trust," Melissa said. "Sometimes I just wish you were a guy."

I wish that, too, J thought before he could stop it. *You don't know how I wish that, too.* To change the channel in his brain, he thought of Titi at home. He thought of her getting run over by a car, finding her mangled and bloody in the street. J imagined a cat funeral, how he'd have to get a suit, a black one, and a new pair of black sunglasses. He changed the subject. "M, you can't kill yourself. Don't be throwing yourself into the river."

"I wasn't serious," Melissa said, flashing him one of her goofy grins. Her moods could change on a dime.

"Come on, let's get ice cream." And she grabbed his hand and pulled him up from the bench, running off toward the sound of the ice-cream truck.

Listening to Melissa's message again and thinking of that afternoon, something clicked for J. He hadn't kissed her that night of the party out of nowhere; Melissa had been leading him on. Yes, they were best friends, but Melissa had liked him, too, at least some days, at least on the days she let herself entertain the possibility. But J had been so busy hating himself that he couldn't believe someone would actually like him. Blue had a crush on him, J thought; why couldn't Melissa? He was a stud; he wasn't that bad-looking. Or at least he looked okay on some days, when he caught a good angle.

He sent her a text. "Can I come over?"

The reply came back immediately. It was yes.

"J, I don't like you going out so late on a school night," Carolina said when she saw J bundling up.

"Ma, I gotta go."

"Where do you have to be that's so important?"

"Melissa's. She needs something."

"J, no. It's late. You can see Melissa tomorrow," Carolina said. She was getting ready to feed the cat, but she stopped and gave J her serious face.

"No, I can't," J said. And he pushed out the door.

"J!" Carolina shouted, but he was already gone.

Karyn was home when J got there, so he and Melissa went to the corner for pizza.

"Okay, so where have you been?" Melissa asked, blowing on her slice, the grease dripping in fat drops onto her paper plate.

"Nowhere," J said. He had been so confident when he left his apartment, but now he didn't know what to say. He wished he'd worn the chest binder. He felt exposed, childlike. He tried to rouse his anger, but it was halfhearted. "Your e-mail was a bitch."

Melissa sighed. "Can we be a bit more articulate?"

Melissa had tromped out of the house in her pajamas, and J had to admit, she looked adorable sitting there in her parka and flannels with the stars and moons and fluffy sheep, pink Timberlands peeking out beneath. Here was Melissa, bossy as always, pushing J for the truth.

"You accused me," J said. And then, into his paper cup full of Coke, "I think you wanted it."

Melissa's eyes bugged out. "Wanted what? The kiss? No, J, you're my friend. I told you I'm not gay. But we can forget about it and move on."

"You said you think about me sometimes. You told me, that day at the river."

"J—" Melissa said, her mouth opening and closing like a fish. She sat silent for a while, her eyes distant. Suddenly they lit up, as though she had been scanning the horizon and had finally spotted a landmark. "J, everybody thinks about girls sometimes. It's a normal, healthy part of human sexuality."

Melissa sounded like she was quoting a textbook. J looked down, fiddled with his jeans. "Not everybody."

"What, J, you think about guys?"

"Don't change the subject," J said, proud he had a comeback for once. "Melissa, this is about you."

"No, J. It's about you. About how you kissed me. *When I was sleeping.*"

"And about you. You told me you don't want to be my friend anymore because I'm not as *serious about my art* as you are." J put on a mocking tone.

"I said I wanted to take a break, not stop being friends," Melissa said. She got softer then and tried to touch J's hand. He pulled it away. "I was scared. I didn't know what to say."

"Scared of what?"

"I don't know."

She's as scared as I am, J thought. J loved Melissa again in that moment, the fluorescent lights of the pizzeria making her face look yellow and alien-beautiful. *Girls are amazing. They can be so vulnerable.* He made his face more gentle. "Scared of what?"

"Oh, God. Don't get mad, okay?" Melissa snarfed down the last few bites of her pizza. "Five hundred calories before bed. And I've been so good about not eating after six."

"I'm not mad."

"J, I get confused. You're my best friend; you've always been there. You'd save me from the river, remember?"

J nodded.

"And I know you're a girl, but sometimes you seem more like a guy." Melissa started rushing her sentences, wouldn't meet J's eyes. "And when you seem like a guy, I am attracted to you. But then I remember you're a girl, and I just can't go there. I don't know. Don't hate me. I'm just confused. Do you want more pizza?"

Melissa jumped up and got in the line that had suddenly formed at the pizzeria. J hadn't even noticed people walking in. He gripped the edges of his plastic chair, watching her, checking his instinct to run out the door. The thoughts rushed in, like a fire.

I was right—she did like me. She saw me as a dude! Whoa, she saw me as a dude. Could Melissa be my girlfriend? No, you idiot. She doesn't want you. She sees you as a girl. But I'm not a girl. Should I tell her? Should I tell her I'm in love with her? No. She already knows that. Should I tell her about the chest binding, that I'm changing more? Fuck that! She'll really abandon you then. Don't say shit. What do I say now? She wants to be all comforted and shit, for her confession; girls always want to be comforted. Fuck Melissa and her honesty. Fuck honesty. Fuck everything. Oh, fuck.

Melissa sat back down, a Diet Coke in her hand. "J, what are you thinking?"

"Too many things at once."

"I'm sorry I said that thing about you taking advantage of me."

"That's okay."

"Are you freaked out I said I sometimes thought of you as a guy? I mean, don't worry, I know you're not."

"No." J felt like a hand was choking him. Tighter, tighter.

"Can you say something? I'm feeling really weird."

"Um, I don't know what to say."

"How about what you feel?"

J paused. There was so much to say, and no way to say it. "Can I take a picture, maybe, and show it to you? I think that'd be better."

Melissa smiled. "Yeah. Take a picture. E-mail it to me." She stood up. " 'Cause I have a feeling you're not coming back to school for a while. Am I right?"

J gave her one of his half smiles back. *Does she really understand?* he thought. *Does she really know why I'm not going to school?*

"I love you, J," Melissa said, giving him a hug. She smiled. "As a friend."

That night, on his bed, there was a note from Carolina. *J*, she wrote in her tiny, boxy script. *We have to talk. Before school. I'll wake you up.*

No we don't, J thought, his head swimming from the talk with Melissa. He couldn't handle any more interrogations; he'd used up all his words. This apartment was too small for three people; he needed to breathe. *I can't be myself here*, J thought. *How can I explain myself to you if I can't explain myself to me?*

CHAPTER FIVE

J spent the rest of the night roaming around his neighborhood. It was already two a.m. by the time he got home from the pizza place; he figured he only had to wait a few hours before it was light again. But it was late fall, and it was cold. *Better weather to focus my thoughts*, he said to himself.

J was glad he and Melissa were friends again, but he wasn't sure how long it would last. She was hinting, wasn't she, that she understood that he wanted to be a man, that he already was a man, that part of him was a man, or something like that? The conversation was already jumbling in his head, like pieces of a jigsaw puzzle when it scatters to the floor. Or had Melissa made the conversation all about Melissa, as she always did? Did she say that part about him being like a guy (Did she even say that? Was he making it up?) to justify her attraction to him? If he told her about the chest binder, about the testosterone idea that was slowly becoming more and more feasible—would he lose his only friend? J felt especially in need of a friend, alone and freezing on a side street in the middle of the night. *Get used to it,* he thought. *Welcome to the wonderful world of homelessness.*

He'd seen homeless teenagers on the piers when he was younger. Once he and Manny had gone fishing there, back when Manny was trying to spend time with him. Manny had taught J how to bait and tie a hook, and the two of them sat in the fading sun, waiting for fish that never bit.

From their spot on the bench by the water, J could gaze openly at the kids that his dad said had run away. Here were boys who looked like girls and girls who looked like boys, dancing to music on portable speakers, their hair all kinds of colors, their shoes bright and fantastic.

"Don't stare," Manny had admonished J, who was twelve at the time. "Don't ever stare at people with problems."

But J couldn't help it. A black girl with enormous breasts wore Ben Davis pants and two Hanes T-shirts and had her arm slung around another girl, skinny and loudmouthed in a skirt and rainbow bracelets up to her elbows. The loud girl kept shouting to other friends down the pier, a motley crew of teenagers who were repeating the steps of some kind of coordinated dance. "Show me the money!" the girl kept shrieking.

Finally J asked Manny, "Why does she keep saying that?"

"Because they're prostitutes," Manny answered. J looked back at the girl couple.

"Not them," Manny said. "Them." He jerked his fishing pole toward another group of teenagers, walking and laughing, pushing each other along the pier. They were black and white and even Puerto Rican, J noticed. One wore a Puerto Rican flag bandanna as a skirt. These kids were loud, too, and they made exaggerated faces with their lipsticked mouths. Two were boys acting like girls, and doing a pretty bad job of it, J had thought at the time; one hadn't even shaved her legs, and the other had her wig askew. But the other two were really girls, J thought. They wore tank tops and tight shorts and sneakers with no laces, their faces pretty and slender.

"They don't look like prostitutes," J said, thinking

of the movies he'd seen with women in red dresses, leaning into cars.

"They are, and they're all boys. You know that, right? It's disgusting," Manny said, looking back at the water.

At the word *disgusting*, J felt a flash of recognition. Hadn't his dad ever looked at him? He didn't look like the prostitutes, but he sure resembled the girl in the Ben Davis pants. What was his father trying to say? J almost couldn't muster the word, but he had to know. "Why?" he asked, his voice barely a whisper.

"Because they got no money," Manny answered, misunderstanding the question. "But they got no money out of choice. They're choosing to be freaks. Kids down here don't have parents."

J must have looked scared, because Manny suddenly offered to buy him a flavored ice from an old man who was pushing a cart down the pier. "Don't worry— you've got your parents," Manny said. And then, more quietly, "I shouldn't have taken you here. I heard the piers had been cleaned up."

But J wouldn't have his parents, not if he really fully transitioned, not if that's what Manny thought of kids like that. And now that he was on the street—J glanced at the clock on his cell phone—at three a.m., he'd be in so much trouble when he got home, he might as well go through with his plan. This wasn't a game anymore, playing boy at a silly café with silly girls downtown. This was his life, and he had to live it. Even if it meant living on a pier.

I can fight, he thought as a rat scurried across his path. In a way, he liked the thought of surviving on his own. *If people mess with me, I could kill them.* He ran through the countless fantasies he'd had in his head, of beating up people who humiliated him, of being the gangster his do-good parents had never let him be. Then he thought of the camera in his backpack, how he really wasn't tough at all, how he was a nerd underneath it all, how he didn't know what he was. *I need to take that photograph*, J thought. *For Melissa.*

J walked a few more blocks, his body so numb from the cold he almost couldn't feel it anymore. Near the hospital on 168th, some new construction was going up. The site was mostly just an enormous dirt hole, and J could see from the streetlight the outlines of diggers and Dumpsters and one giant crane. The fence was just cheap plywood, and J kicked at a section until it splintered and caved to his boot; glancing quickly over his shoulder at the silent street beind him, J dropped to his knees and crawled into the site.

A path had been carved into the dirt, a street of

sorts for the utility vehicles, and J made his way down the construction path and toward a yellow digger, bulky and eerie in the moonlight. Oddly, someone had left a jackhammer lying on its side, along with an orange vest, though J didn't see any cement to break up. *Maybe I can do something with this*, J thought.

The jackhammer was heavy as J dragged it toward a Dumpster about fifty yards away. The handles were thick and worn down, and the bit made a satisfying scraping sound as he lugged it along. *Like dragging a dead body*, J thought. He propped it upright against the bin, which was garbage-truck green. Nearby, J noticed, a security light was shining toward the bin, casting long shadows. He realized that if he lay down, just right, in front of the jackhammer, and set the timer on his camera, he could capture a picture of just his shadow with the jackhammer driving right through it. He worked quickly; the light was pretty bright, and he didn't want to get caught. J set his camera up on the back of an orange cone he found. He set the timer for thirty seconds, turned off the flash, and lined up the shot. Then he carefully lay down a few feet in front of the jackhammer, so the length of his body cast a shadow.

When he came back to check the results, he shivered. The jackhammer glowed an eerie yellow against the Dumpster, and the shadow of his face and torso was strangely clear, if a bit distorted; you could tell the form was human. The hammer seemed to be driving straight through the shadow's heart. Maybe it was scary and maybe it was cheesy, but if J had the courage to send Melissa the photograph, she'd understand what it meant.

Stuffing the camera back into his backpack alongside the chest binder, the comics, and the change of underwear he had grabbed before he left, J climbed back out of the construction site. He didn't want to think about what was going on at home if his parents had noticed he wasn't in bed. He had turned off his cell phone. It was four a.m. now, still cold and still dark. He needed a little sleep, but he knew the twenty-four-hour diner wouldn't let him rest his head on one of their Formica tables. They'd think he was on drugs and throw him out. Then he saw the lights of the hospital, the red sign of the emergency room beckoning to him from a few blocks away. He could sleep there, in the waiting room. *Waiting for an emergency*, J thought. *Perfect.*

Outside the Starbucks, J was nervous and exhausted. He'd changed into his chest binder at the hospital and gotten some coffee, but he knew he looked rumpled and worn. It had rattled him a little, sitting in the emergency room for hours, watching families struggle in with feverish babies, and homeless people coming off their highs. One guy had been shot, rushed in on a stretcher, and two different women were hyperventilating or having asthma attacks or something and were sent straight to the back for oxygen. A cop dragged in three scared kids in pajamas and diapers, followed by their hysterical mother screaming that she'd get a lawyer. He tried to watch the television running an endless cycle of weather reports and sports recaps, but the room was so grim that he couldn't focus.

He realized that no matter how angry or messed up he was inside, he'd have to come up with a better plan; sitting around in emergency rooms was no way to get one's head together. He decided to go back home for the weekend, take stock of his meager finances, get a few good nights of sleep, and then run away for real. He'd figure out a place where he could live for cheap, and he'd start his transition. Testosterone, ever since he'd read about it online, was burning a fierce tunnel in his brain. Everything else would have to follow that.

But right now there was Starbucks. His heart fluttered at the sight of Madison and Blue, flocked by three other girls who looked vaguely familiar. Amazing, the power of a little crush. The three other girls peeled away as soon as Madison and Blue got close.

"Hey," Blue said.

"Hey."

"What're you reading?" Madison asked.

"Just manga," J said, handing over his comic book.

"Do you like this stuff?" Blue asked, thumbing through the pictures. J felt stung; did Blue think comics were stupid?

"Not really," J answered.

"Hey, J wants to see your art," Madison said, hopping forward on one foot. Blue shot her a look that said *shut up*. Madison was so intense; he felt a little bad for Blue.

"Do you have anything on you?" he asked.

"No, not really. Just sketches. But they're lame. My real stuff is at my house."

"Her house is cool," Madison said. "Her mom is, too."

"No, she's not!" Blue said, looking incredulous. She was wearing what looked like a Brownie uniform, some kind of brown jumper, with black tights, and combat boots speckled in paint. J thought she looked hot. Blue glanced up at him.

"You could come over tomorrow. I mean, if you want, and see it," Blue said, half shy, half defiant. "I don't live too far. Just, like, five stops on the L."

"Um, tomorrow it's Saturday and I have something to do," J said, thinking of the shit that was going to hit the fan as soon as he got home. He hadn't ever stayed out all night before, hadn't done anything remotely close to that, and so far Carolina hadn't even called his cell; maybe she wouldn't let him come home. Blue's cheeks reddened with the rejection. J cocked his chin up. "Want to do it today?"

"Yeah, okay," Blue said, happier. "Lemme call my mom."

Blue's apartment was filled with toddlers. Her mother ran a day care out of the living room, and the place smelled like Play-Doh and diapers.

"Sorry," Blue said as she stepped over a Big Wheel and tousled a wailing baby's hair with her free hand. "The rats are running free."

"That's okay," J answered, amazed by the chaos. "I like rats." His own apartment was so quiet, you could hear the clock tick and Manny chew from across the room. At Blue's place, crayon markings tattooed each available wall, and toddler shrieks bounced off the endless surfaces of cheery-colored plastic chairs and toys. The Brooklyn brownstone's living room had once been grand, with its ballroom-style chandelier, but now the wooden floors were scratched and pockmarked, and the windows were cracked and taped and smudged with tiny noseprints.

"Basia?" A voice called from another room. "Come help me with snack?"

Blue rolled her eyes. "Want some delicious Goldfish out of Dixie cups? Or maybe some graham crackers and generic jelly?" Blue trotted off through what used to be French doors. J followed.

"Who's this?" asked a thin woman in jeans, her hair tied up messily in a bun.

"This is J. He's a new kid at school. The art teacher asked him to work on a painting project with me."

"Maybe you can get Basia to use some"—here Blue's mom gave an overly dramatic gasp—"colors!"

"Mom, don't bug him," Blue said, grimacing. She picked up a tray of fruit punch and baby bottles and took it into the living room. "Come with me."

Blue shared a bedroom with her older sister, the space divided with a piece of masking tape that snaked straight across the center of the floor. The sister's side was filled with books with titles like *Mission of the Apostles*; she was apparently studying religion, and there was a cross above her bed. Blue's side was crammed with paintings. Big ones on paper and cardboard and canvases, taller than J, and little ones the size of a postcard, leaned against one another. Madison was right, they were all blue, but J hadn't known there could be so many shades. There were night blues and day blues, cruel-looking blues, the blues of water, and the blues of sun-beaten wood porches. And Madison was right about another thing, too: Blue's work was amazing. The top canvas, the one Blue appeared to be working on now, was the face of an old man. His forehead was prominent and angular, as was his jaw, but his lips were loose and somewhat sexual. His eyes looked at J dead-on, like he was accusing and, underneath that, forgiving. The weird thing, which J hadn't noticed at first, was that the guy was missing his nose. In its place was a dark wedge of deep blue, swirled with an almost imperceptible blackness.

"Why doesn't he have a nose?" J asked.

"Um, I've been learning online about this thing called trepanation, where people drill parts of their own skull away to increase blood volume to their brains and make them more psychic," Blue said. "So I was thinking about this old guy who kind of wasted his life, and he wanted to see why. So he did trepanation, but he did it between his eyes and lost his nose. I guess it's about what you have to give up to gain something else."

J sat back on the bed. Did you always have to give something up for a gain? He looked at the old man's eyes. Now they were mocking and sad—two opposites again. "It's deep" was all he could think of to say. He knew it sounded stupid.

"Thanks," Blue answered. She saw J glance over at her sister's side of the room. "Oh, she's a religious freak.

Supersmart, and I love her and everything, but she's really into God."

"I hate that," J answered.

"Me, too. Is your family religious?"

"Sort of. I mean, maybe culturally my mom is—she's Catholic. My dad's Jewish, but he let her have all the religion in the family."

"Oh." Blue didn't seem to know what to say.

J didn't want her to stop talking. "Why blue? Why do you paint only in blue?"

"I don't know. I just love it. It's the only color that seems to make sense inside me. I like it so much, sometimes I eat the paint."

J imagined this. A plate of blue mashed potatoes next to a cereal bowl full of paint. Or a wine glass sloshing around with gloppy, gluey paint. And Blue licking her lips, the tip of her tongue blue as a plush Smurf toy. He laughed.

"You think I'm a freak, don't you?" Blue asked, looking closely at her cuticles.

"No!" *Freak* was a word J never used. It was a grenade, tossed from car windows, meant to land at J's feet and blow up in his face. He knew that Blue had no idea how many times he'd been called that word; J would never say it to a friend.

"You've probably never wanted to be anything different than what you are," Blue said. "You seem so, I don't know, confident."

Confident? J thought. *Confident?* And then, *I'd better kiss this chick before she changes her mind or figures me out. Or her religious sister barges in.* Suddenly J wanted to know, more than anything, what it would feel like to be a guy kissing a girl. Not a girl pretending to be a guy, as he had when he played "bar" way back when, or a girl kissing a girl, as he had with Melissa. Just a regular guy, on a regular day, copping the moves on a regular girl. He didn't want all this deep talk that made his head hurt, didn't want to think about his parents or shooting testosterone or getting kicked out of his house. He just wanted to get away with whatever he could, while there was still time.

But he said nothing and looked at the old-man painting again. He had to answer her question. "Of course I have."

"Like what?"

"I dunno." *Crap,* J thought. *What to say now?* "I guess I've wanted to be less shy."

"I like you shy," Blue said, picking up a pencil from a can full of brushes and pens on her desk. "It means you're not an asshole like other guys."

She knows, J thought with a sharp constriction of his throat. Blue was giving him a message. He tried to quickly make eye contact, but Blue had picked up a pad of paper and was sketching a cheekbone and what looked to be part of an eyebrow. Was she trying to communicate that she knew he wasn't really a guy or that he wasn't really an asshole? He suddenly felt that he was going to have a panic attack, like that one time when he was stuck in an elevator for twenty minutes with two families and three strollers. Too many people, too many chances to be watched. He had to switch the focus. *Back on the girl*, he told himself. If you ask women questions about themselves, he had read in a men's magazine, they'll be more likely to give it up. "What kind of paint do you eat?"

"I don't eat that much," Blue answered, tipping her head to see her sketch from a new angle. She started drawing an eye. "Watercolors are fine for you. So are tempera paints—they're made for preschoolers. Besides, I just need a few tastes to feel like I'm changing inside, like the color is moving me."

It was like hormones, J thought. He had read that testosterone had an effect on people before it even altered a hair on their chin. The hormones made them think somewhat magically, because they knew they were changing themselves—making them stronger, making them men. J asked, "What does it taste like?"

"It tastes..." Blue looked up at the ceiling. "It tastes like blue. I don't know. And like dirt. Like sky and earth maybe. I love it."

J laughed again but this time tried to stifle it with a cough.

"It's okay, you can laugh," Blue said. "I like your laugh."

They were sitting side by side on Blue's bed. *It's working*, J thought. *She likes me.* Blue looked at J's profile and tapped him lightly on the mouth with her pencil. "You want to try it?"

Blue looked like a picture-book drawing of a fairy, J thought, almost like a manga cartoon. But a sexy one. Her nose was narrow, with a little ball at the end, like a marble. Her eyes were wide set and gray as fog, with tiny flecks of gold in them, and her cheeks, which hadn't yet lost their baby fat, were peach-colored and got splotchy when she was embarrassed. Blue was curvy but compact, probably just under five feet, J guessed, and her hands were ink-stained, with pinkie fingers that bent slightly out from the rest of her hand, as if they were trying to escape. Because J had nodded to Blue's question, she was using a long brush to mix some water-color paint and some water in a shallow dish. With her fingers, she squeezed the bristles to a point.

"You first," she said.

"What do I do?"

"Just stick out your tongue. And, if you want, close your eyes."

J stuck out his tongue but kept his eyes open. Blue's hair, which had been dyed so many times it looked waxen and dry as a doll's, was pulled up in a high ponytail and made pointy blue dashes around her face. Her expression was serious as she leaned in. She touched J's tongue once with the brush, so lightly he could barely feel it. Still, his mouth watered in anticipation. "I don't taste anything."

"Let me give you more," Blue said, dunking the brush back in the dish. J stuck his tongue out again. This time, he imagined the paint was testosterone and Blue was giving him his first dose. The paint would make him more male; he would swallow it, and he would change. Blue drew a figure eight with the brush. It tickled, like an animal tail on his tongue. This time, he tasted it; the paint was bitter, like old almonds, and also earthy, like a dirty creek. *I'm a man*, he thought. *I'm a man.*

"How is it?" Blue asked, her hair bobbing around her like a star.

"It's weird…" J said. "And good. I like it. You eat it now." *And then I kiss you.*

Blue rested the brush on the sketch pad and picked up the dish of paint. She darted her tongue into the bowl like a cat, taking tiny dabs into her mouth. At first only the tip of her tongue was blue, but then the whole thing was a faded wash of color. Blue watched J carefully, then closed her eyes and lay back on the bed, the dish resting on her stomach. She breathed in deep.

"Aaaaah," Blue sighed. "I love that." She looked back over at J and sat up. "No one's ever been with me for that before. I mean, I've never shared my paint."

"Thank you," J said. He didn't know what else to say. His head was swimming again. Blue was his first hormone nurse, except she wasn't; this was only his second week being a boy, except it wasn't; Blue was really nice, and he just wanted to use her for hooking up, except maybe he could like her, too. Where did Melissa fit into this picture? Melissa was his friend—and, he hoped, would remain so after he sent the jackhammer picture. And Blue, this sensitive artist Blue, who was sitting on a bed—a bed!—and staring at him...oh, God, this could never work. They'd kiss, Blue would try to take off his shirt, and blam. *Think of a dead baby*, J commanded himself. *A carjacking, a knife wound.* Anything to take him out of this picture.

"I gotta go," J said, and stood up.

"Wait, why?" Blue asked, looking startled.

"I have a girlfriend. I can't do this," J said, thinking, *Stop yourself. Don't screw everything up.* "Back in Philly."

"You do?" Blue looked shocked.

J sat down on the bed again. "No."

"Wait—" Blue said, slowly setting the dish of paint on her desk. "Do you or don't you have a girlfriend?"

"I don't," J stammered. "I mean, I did. We broke up. I'm just freaked out being here with you, I mean, after that."

Blue's face softened. She smiled at J, looked at him full on, her eyes wide. "Oh, J, you're sweeter than I thought. When did you break up?"

"Um, it's hard to talk about."

"She broke up with you?"

J nodded. He was really working the sympathy card; maybe Blue would kiss him after all. *But that's it*, he thought. *Then you're bolting out the door.*

"I understand—you need time," Blue said.

J put his hand on Blue's knee. It was smaller than he'd expected, and bonier. He played with the ribbing on her tights. "You're shaking," Blue said. She leaned in closer.

J tried not to breathe. She was so close, he couldn't focus on her features anymore. His hand on her knee felt awkward, detached from his arm. *Do I squeeze her knee? Do I kiss her?*

"Nah," J said, deepening his voice, trying to cover for the tightness in his throat. "I'm just cold."

"Here," Blue said, taking off her thrift-store cardigan and carefully laying it across J's shoulders. She paused, looking at J's face, and then slowly wrapped the sweater around his neck, like a scarf. J stiffened, panicking. *Don't look so closely at my neck*, he prayed silently. *Don't look for an Adam's apple.*

"You have nice eyes," Blue said quietly.

"I do?" J blurted, too loud, relieved. Why was he so bad at this? He was supposed to be the one in control.

"Yeah, I like their shape."

"What's their shape?" He took a quick intake of breath and held it.

"Well, they tip down a little toward your nose, like boats, but they're big and round—like manga characters."

"I was thinking that about *your* eyes!"

"Like manga? That's funny," Blue said. The gold flecks in her eyes sparked. Then she looked serious, cocking her head to assess J's face more closely. "But mine aren't as beautiful a color as yours. The brown is almost like a henna, with some amber tones, and your irises are outlined in a dark brown, almost black."

J did like his eyes, that was true. But he'd never seen amber in them. He thought, if he passed, he might look like a regular Jewto Rican kid, kind of light-skinned, boring, plain. But Blue said his eyes were *nice*. Thank God she hadn't mentioned the lashes. That was nice, to be nice. *Nice* didn't mean *feminine*. A man's eyes could be nice.

"Basia!" a voice called from across the apartment. "I need your help in here!"

It was Blue's mom. It was time for J to go.

After Blue had pecked J on the cheek (*so much for hooking up*) and bustled off to help her mom, J found himself back on the cold sidewalk, staring at a dead cell phone. He hadn't packed his charger, had no idea if his parents had tried to reach him. It was after six; Carolina would be home by now, and worried. So what if he'd stayed out all night, he thought—that wasn't a federal crime. It wasn't like he was doing anything. Just thinking. Other teenagers did much worse things; J had been a good kid until now, and his parents should remember that. If his parents tried to punish him, he'd argue for his rights. At least until he got his phone charger, and some money stored up, a better chest binder, a real plan. If he was really going to become a man, full-time, he'd have to do it where his parents wouldn't see him. And to make a real getaway, he'd have to prepare—long, hard, and smart. And he would, just as soon as he got some sleep.

Back at the apartment, J heard Carolina before he saw her. At the turn of his key in the door, Carolina started screaming.

"Jenifer Juana Silver!"

Uh-oh, J thought. The full name.

"Get in here!"

J took off his shoes as slowly as possible. "Now!" his mother screamed.

"What the hell were you thinking?" Carolina demanded as J ducked his head into the kitchen. Carolina slammed a wooden spoon so hard on the stovetop that it bounced back up into the air and hit the floor with a *splat* sound. She didn't even bend to pick it up.

"I'm sorry, Mami," J said. He was prepared. "I just had a lot of thinking to do."

"Thinking?! Thinking?! What does thinking have to do with *truancy*, J? What does thinking have to do with screwing up your chance for *college*?" Carolina's face was bright red, her voice strained from the screaming. "Why are you doing this to yourself?!"

Huh? Had Carolina not noticed he'd been out all night? Had he freaked out for nothing? "What are you talking about?" he asked.

Carolina slapped him.

"You *liar*! You act like you go to school every day, and they call here to say it's been *two weeks*! Who are you, J? What have you been doing? Are you taking drugs? *¡Pendeja!*"

J widened his eyes.

Carolina took in a breath, very slowly, as though she were sucking it in through a straw. "I'm too angry. Go talk to your father. He's in the bedroom."

Manny was sitting on the bed when J walked in. He looked like he was expecting this. His face, like Carolina's, was strained, but he forced a smile.

"Come here, J," Manny said, patting the bed beside him. J sat. "We got a call from the assistant principal today."

"I know," J said. He hung his head. "I'm sorry."

"You know, J, when I was your age, I did the same thing."

J looked up. What was his father talking about?

"I was working at the racetrack at Belmont—" Manny put a hand on J's knee. J tried not to shift away. He'd heard this story before. "All I wanted was to be with the horses. I was just a stable kid, you know, cleaning up after the horses. But me, I wanted to be a jockey. When we'd have big races, and jockeys would come in from all over, I'd skip school to talk with them, find out how they built their careers."

J nodded. Where was this going?

"I knew in my heart, though, that I would never be a jockey. My body was too big. Look at me."

J looked. His father was over six feet tall; that's where J had gotten his height. Thank God for that height. "Even at seventeen, your age, I weighed one-eighty. I wanted so much to change my body, to be somebody different."

J stopped breathing. Did Manny know? Had he seen J leave the house and change in the diner bathroom? Manny squeezed J's knee, where his hand had been resting.

"I've seen you change, too," Manny said, and paused. J couldn't look at his father. "You've gone from swimming to lifting weights at night. I know you do that."

My God, J thought, *do you know why?* He started to shake. This was the most his father had said to him, alone, in over two years. Mostly Manny had acted nervous around J, or angry, or some twisted combination. Why now, when J was in such trouble, was Manny trying so hard to be nice? J thought he might be sick.

"It's okay, Jay-jay. You don't have to be scared. Being a teenager is hard." J could feel Manny trying to get him to look at him, but he stared at Manny's hand on his knee. The knuckles were wrinkled, his fingers thick and hairy, so much more masculine than J's would ever be. "Anyway, when my parents found out I was skipping school to hang out at the racetrack, they were very angry. Nice Jewish boys didn't become jockeys—even though there have been some great ones. But I just liked horses more than people. I didn't want to go to school. I didn't see why it was important."

J had never met his father's parents—they had had Manny late and had died before J was born. He had a feeling his dad never got along with them very well.

"But now I know why it's important," J's father continued. "You need school to get a good job. To go to college, to get an even better job. To figure out who you want to be. You're smarter than I am, J. You have your whole life ahead of you. And your mother and I—we've been saving money—you can go to almost any school you want."

J pulled his knee away from his father's hand. He had to. This was too much. Manny sighed. J risked a glance at his father's face, saw the anger flush his cheeks, saw him try to swallow it down. Manny had rehearsed this speech in his head; he was going to get through it.

"J, listen to me. I know you're changing. I've noticed you haven't been on the computer as much as you used to be." Here, Manny paused again. J could hear Carolina slamming pots around in the kitchen. "And that's okay. If you don't want to go into computer science, or even photography, like you've talked about, that's fine with me. You can be anything you want."

Here, J looked up and made brief eye contact. What was his father trying to say?

"Just be something, J. I know we used to put a lot of pressure on you for the swimming. And I wanted you to get A's in your computer and math classes, because programming and engineering are good jobs to go into. But if you want to do something entirely different with your life, your mother and I support you. If you want to be a DJ, or an architect, or, I don't know, an actress, we'd help you do that. Just go to college, that's all I ask."

Manny put his hand on J's back and gently rubbed it. "I didn't finish college, J. I was so busy getting away from my parents—and it's the biggest regret of my life."

He knew he shouldn't hate it when his father touched him, knew Manny was trying hard to bond and force his way through a heart-to-heart. But J had things other than school on his mind right now. Like Blue, and the kiss that almost was. And Melissa, and the photograph he might send her. And becoming a man. That was more important than school, surely. That was more important than everything. Wasn't it?

"If this is why you're cutting school, because you're changing directions and don't want to tell us…" Here, Manny faltered. J thought he heard some doubt creep into his father's voice. Didn't Manny know this was just wishful thinking, that he was sticking his head in the sand like always and pretending the real problem lay elsewhere? Manny, as usual, was years too late. "I just want you to know, we love you no matter what you do with your life."

Manny took his right hand back and clasped it with his left on his lap. "You're growing up, Jay-jay. Just stay in school. And go make up with your mother—she loves you."

Manny stood up and pulled J into a hug. "You're still my baby girl," he said into J's baseball cap. His voice was sweet and crooning. "You'll always be my baby girl."

J stiffened, resisting the urge in every one of his nerve endings to pull away. *What if I'm not?* he thought. *What if I've never been your baby girl?* He knew, for sure, his father would never accept him. He'd have to leave his parents' house. Now.

CHAPTER SIX

The pier down by Christopher Street looked the same as it had when he and Manny went fishing there so many years ago, only colder. Seagulls were squawking their morning rage at the wind, and J watched their slow swoops and dives, jealous. *If I had wings*, he thought, *and a way to catch my own food...*

I'd live on the water, too, be a waterbird. J took his camera from his backpack that was stuffed with clothes, some comics, and the gold necklace he had gotten for his First Communion, which he'd sell if he got desperate. He watched the gulls through the camera as they touched down on the surface of the Hudson River and spiked back up, airborne again. *Water's weird. All these animals down there that we can't see, that we can't cage up. They can't even live up here with us; we don't even breathe the same.* If he had a choice, J thought, he'd live back in Puerto Rico, right on the beach, right where the earth is on the verge of becoming something else. He snapped a picture of a gull flying, but when he looked at the image, it was only a blur, an indistinct smudge of gray against a gray winter sky.

J didn't see any kids like him on the pier, didn't see anyone at all, really, save for a man walking two big dogs, his collar turned up against the wind, and a homeless woman bundled on a bench, sleeping in her stench of stained coats and too-big shoes. J shuddered. He had to find somewhere to stay. He had to do this thing, even if this thing was still unformed in his mind. He had to find a way to be a boy. A man. A man boy? A transboy? J. He had to find a way to be J. And to do that, he had to get away from Carolina and Manny. And probably Melissa. And maybe Blue, too. Or maybe not. Or maybe for a little while. And then he could go home again. Or not.

Fear can't stop me. Don't be afraid, J repeated to himself like a mantra as he crossed the West Side Highway, the little red-hand crosswalk sign blinking at him as he hurried across. *Art is the lie that tells the truth*, he thought, remembering the first day he met Melissa. *I am the lie that tells the truth.*

The West Side Highway—unlike its cross streets, West Tenth, Charles, Perry—was not entirely gentrified. It still had its share of bars and triple-X video shops and, J discovered, one hotel.

"We rent by the week," the grizzled man at the desk told him. His old face was yellow, and his teeth were yellower.

"How much?" J asked, trying to sound as though he'd done this before.

"Three hundred forty." The man was reading the comics page of the *Daily News* and didn't look up. "Cash."

J had two hundred dollars in his front pocket, squirreled away from his allowance and from selling his old bike for forty bucks a few months back. All his money in the world.

"Could you just let me stay for the night?"

"Nope." The man didn't look up from his paper.

J looked at his feet, the laces still threaded in straight lines from Melissa. He turned and slowly shuffled away.

At the door, a woman was sitting in a battered armchair, also reading the paper. Her hair was dyed red and was flat and tangled in the back, as if she'd just woken up, but she had lipstick on. "Just show him some money," she said to J as he reached for the door.

"Huh?" J answered.

"He wants to see that you have cash on you. He'll let you stay. There are empty rooms; Greg's not a bad guy." She held out her hand. "I'm Marcia."

J took her hand and got a closer look. Marcia, which she pronounced "Mar-see-uh," had watery dark eyes and crow's-feet. Her hands were dry, and her fingers felt thick against J's own. J thought, just for a moment, that she might be trans, too. "Thanks," he said.

J walked back toward Greg's desk, fingering the bills in his pocket, but suddenly turned back around. "How much?" he asked Marcia. He didn't want to be duped.

"Just divide whatever he told you by seven, and go up from there."

Greg had moved from comics to sports, when J carefully laid fifty dollars above his paper. Greg gave a small head shake and licked his thumb, about to turn the page. J added a ten. Greg shook his head again. If J added more money and ate for the day, he could only last two nights. Still, J put down another twenty. Greg reached behind him, to a wall of keys hanging on hooks. "Room seventeen," he said, handing J a set. "Third floor. Be out by ten. Elevator's broke."

The eighty-dollar room had a painting of a ship bolted above the bed, and a small fridge that buzzed wetly in the corner. The blue polyester bedspread with its eighties floral design clashed with the blue carpet, worn in spots and burned with several cigarette holes by the window. J looked out on the West Side Highway, and the zoom of cars competed for auditory dominance with the fridge's buzzing and a man seemingly coughing up a hairbrush next door. He pulled back the bedspread, lay on the sheets, and lit a cigarette.

This was almost too easy. He never knew that a kid could just run away one morning and have a room within two hours. Greg didn't even ask for his name, though J had practiced saying "Jason Garcia" on the train and had made up a story about having just flown in, his luggage lost by the airline, all his identification with it. J assumed that adults who worked in hotels, even crappy ones like this, would ask for driver's licenses and credit cards, but Greg had cared only about the cash.

Maybe J could just keep going. He could sell the necklace and go somewhere cheaper, hang out for a while, get a job. Would New Jersey do it? How far away was Montana? He let his mind drift to a horse ranch, brushing manes and tails, nailing on shoes, somewhere in a pasture, beneath mountains. He'd sleep in a stable, and the ranch owner's daughter, who looked like Blue, would bring him a breakfast of coffee and toast, to eat sitting on a bale of hay. No one would believe that this mysterious city boy could be so masterful with the horses. Even the wildest would be tame under his command, and the ranch would become rich, offering rides and lessons to women and kids who would come from miles away to train on these majestic horses.

J had never been on a horse, had only pet the ones who pulled buggies through Central Park. But it seemed likely that he'd be good with them, since animals generally liked him more than humans did. Besides, this hotel room, for all its shabbiness, made J feel powerful. He'd never had his own room before, only his own corner, and never a door.

I could do anything if I had my own place, he thought.

But this place wasn't going to last him very long, not on the money he had. He couldn't lie around all day, daydreaming. He looked out the window; it had started to snow. He wondered when his parents would notice he was missing and who they would call.

T, J thought. *Focus on T.* Sadness had slowed him down before, and he didn't have time for it now. Before he lost his nerve or his money, J had to get to the clinic and get a shot of testosterone. He was ready. By the time he got home, with a new voice and bigger muscles, his parents certainly would have missed him so much they wouldn't care anymore about what he looked like.

Maybe T would work incredibly fast on J; maybe he'd get the voice in a matter of weeks. Maybe he could apply for jobs in camera shops; did all employers require identification? Everything was so complicated. But once he started T, there would be no going back; this was a decision he was, for once, making entirely on his own. His parents couldn't stop him. By the time he got back to his parents' apartment, the hormones would already be pulling their invisible threads, stitching him up tighter inside, making him tougher to all the world's threats and demands. His mother could be frightened, his dad could be angry, but they couldn't take this change away; he was nobody's little girl. J was nobody's pussy. He may have run away in a panic, but testosterone, he knew, would give him direction.

The snow was falling gently as J made his way to the clinic he'd read about online. It wasn't too far from where he was staying. He'd left most of the clothes from his backpack at the hotel, so now only his camera clanked against his lower back, and he'd carefully divided his money into three different pockets, one of which held the gold necklace. Now that he was on his own, he had to be careful. But the city looked softer in its snow dust, and the cars moved more slowly, making way for J to cross in front of them. *I'm ready*, he said again. *Give me that shot.*

But there was a line at the clinic. The waiting room was smaller than the one he was used to, at his pediatrician's office in the hospital where his mother worked. J signed in at a clipboard and looked around. Posters claiming HIV STOPS WITH ME and advertisements for medical trials cluttered one wall, and a few adults sat around reading magazines. J sat and jiggled his knee. He felt too young for this place; he'd never gone to a doctor without his mother. *Just stay*, he told himself. *Get the shot and go.*

J had read that testosterone took six months to really kick in, but some guys stopped their periods in three weeks. God, he hated those days. Stopping at the bodega to pick up tampons, saying "no, super plus" to the guy behind the counter, wishing he could just disappear. If T could just end the periods, that alone would be worth the sharp jab in the thigh every other week.

And maybe, because J was young, the testosterone would work extra fast on him. He could almost feel his shoulders growing, pressing up and out against the seams in his shirt, his neck thickening, his jawline jutting out into a tough, masculine edge. He knew facial hair took a long time to come in, but that was okay. If he could lose the baby fat on his face, he'd look a lot better. He imagined the fluid in the shot (it was probably gold-colored) zipping up through his flesh, under his skin, and eating up the fat, melting it on contact. Yes, the fat around his jaw would go first, maybe within a week. And then the magical gold would pour down his throat, lengthening his vocal cords, burning them,

stripping them into a raspy, deep bass. Okay, maybe not
with the first shot; he had to be realistic. But the first
shot would do *something* to his voice. It would kick-
start it, especially if he smoked more cigarettes to help
it along. His body was made for testosterone, he could
feel it; it was as if he had a million receptor cells, open
like hungry mouths, that had been waiting for the testosterone since the day he was born.

"J?" A receptionist behind a window called his
name.

J wiped his palms on his jeans and got up.

"We do testosterone on Thursdays, five to ten."

J tumbled down a few stairs inside himself. This
was Saturday; how could he wait that long? The receptionist had led him to a small room where he was meeting with a social worker named Janet. She was pretty,
in a wool skirt and high boots, and she twirled her pen
as she spoke. "Do you have a letter from your doctor?"

"A what?" J could barely get the words out, now
that he knew he'd have to wait nearly an entire week for
his shot. And he was so ready.

"Okay, let's start at the beginning," Janet was

saying, though now she sounded like she was in a tunnel, somewhere far away. "How old are you, J?"

"Eighteen," he lied. His birthday wasn't for another six weeks.

"Okay, that's good," Janet said. "Because you know you have to be eighteen to get started on hormone therapy, right?"

J hadn't known. He shook his head miserably.

"And you have identification, showing you're eighteen?"

J nodded. Things were getting worse. Melissa could maybe score him a fake ID; she was good at things like that. If Melissa was still talking to him. If doctors' offices would accept a fake ID; this wasn't a dance club.

Janet was still talking. "Okay, J, I'm going to explain how the protocol works at our clinic, and we can go from there." Janet handed him some kind of packet, which J automatically stuffed into his back pocket. He didn't want to look desperate. "Basically, you come in here and get an examination from one of our doctors to determine your general health and current hormone levels and to see whether you have any counseling needs we can meet. You can make an appointment with the receptionist to do that. In the meantime, you need to provide us with a letter from your therapist saying that you're in her care, you are gender variant, and she's willing to vouch for you being ready to undergo hormone therapy. Then—"

"You mean I have to see a shrink to do this?" J interrupted. "I can't just get a shot?"

Janet looked at him and shook her head. "Unfortunately, no. There's something called the *Standards of Care*, which most doctors follow. They require psychiatric evaluation before any gender reassignment procedures can be implemented."

That word again: *reassignment.* "But I don't need a shrink!" J protested. "I just need T!"

"A lot of people feel that way," Janet said, leaning back in her chair and twirling the pen again. She wasn't pretty anymore, J realized; she was very plain, and her lips were too thin. "But that's not the way it works. If you don't have a therapist, we have some excellent ones here, accustomed to working with the young transgender populations. Once they've seen you for an appropriate length of time—and this varies, but generally between three and six months—they can provide the requisite letter, and we can begin the hormone protocol."

Suddenly J hated Janet, and her skirt and her pen and her stupid prissy boots. Did she have to talk like a robot, like a white, dictionary-obsessed robot? Janet had the shots, probably filled and ready to go, right behind her in that cabinet, and she was babbling away in fancy words that just meant no.

But instead of blowing up Janet with the hand grenade J wished he had in his backpack, he just stood up to leave. "Okay," he mumbled.

"J," Janet said, "I know this can be terribly disappointing. But we're here to help. Even if you're under eighteen, you can sometimes get the treatment with a guardian's informed consent. I included information about all this in the package I handed you. Also, I don't know how you're faring on housing, but there are other brochures at the front desk, about shelters where you can stay for free. They're for youth up to age twenty-three."

J narrowed his eyes, which were finding patterns in the carpet. "I'm not homeless."

"I wasn't implying that you were. We just let everyone in your age demographic know the services that are available to them."

Thank you, Robotron, J said in his head as he turned to leave. Still, he took a brochure for the shelter before he slammed out the clinic door.

"Damn, damn, damn, damn, damn!" J shouted, kicking the wall, kicking the snow, kicking a hydrant, and jumping up to punch a bus-stop sign overhead. A lady with her arms full of shopping bags made a wide half circle around J to give him room on the sidewalk, and he shouted at her back. "Yeah, I'm crazy! They sending me to a shrink! You wanna take me home, lady?" The woman didn't look back.

On a weekend, Blue and Madison wouldn't be at the Starbucks. J was too pissed to be alone but too lonely to be pissed for long. He wanted distraction, and after kicking a few more garbage cans, he called Blue.

"How's the weather in Brooklyn?" J asked when she picked up.

"J!" Blue said into the phone. She sounded happy. "Where are you?"

They decided to meet at the corner of Blue's block, despite the snow; she didn't want her mom to interfere again.

"I was afraid you'd be mad at me," Blue said, running up to J and hugging him when she saw him turn her corner. It was their first hug, and J felt a heat rising up his neck, under Blue's cardigan, which he was wearing as a scarf. Blue jumped back and was hopping from one foot to the other to fight the cold. Ladybugs decorated her rain boots (ladybugs!), along with a generous amount of blue paint.

"Mad? Why?" J tried to swallow up the full, sweet sexiness of Blue in one gulp, as though she were a photograph, hopping there in her rain boots and old-man overcoat, a knitted scarf wrapped around her neck and head, blue hair poking out at her temples. He unwrapped the cardigan from his neck and handed it to her. "I brought you your sweater."

"No, keep it," Blue said. "It looks cute on you."

Cute. That word. Was J cute? He blushed. "Well, then, I have to give you something of mine." He felt around in his pockets. "I mean, I bought you something."

Blue blinked, a half smile making her cheek dimple. J loved the way she had to look up at him; Blue was so short.

"Close your eyes and take off your scarf," he said. Where was he getting this confidence? A few hours ago, he was being robotronned into therapy; now he was starring in his own romantic movie. Blue did as she was told, tipping her chin up toward his face. God, he wanted to kiss her.

J pulled the gold chain from his pocket. It took him a few extra seconds to untangle a knot and figure out the clasp, but finally he got it around her neck, the gold resting perfectly on Blue's clavicle. It was a simple chain, not too thick but not cheap, either, and it made the white of Blue's skin even whiter, almost fragile.

Blue opened her eyes and smiled. She felt the chain, lifted it in her palm, tried to see it, but it was too short to pull into her line of vision. "J," she whispered. "This is too much."

Was it? Had he screwed up again? Had J just scared

away his potential girlfriend *and* his backup savings in one dumb, spontaneous move? Blue was walking away, toward her house, but then she stopped in front of a drugstore. She looked at her reflection in the window. "It's beautiful," she said. "Oh, my God. It's so beautiful."

J walked over to her and looked at the reflection. Blue was touching the chain with one finger and smiling softly to herself. She spun and hugged J, the second time that day. "J, thank you, thank you!"

And then they were kissing. With the snow falling and the streetlights coming on, they were kissing. With Blue's knitted scarf tangled on the sidewalk, and J's hands fumbling to find a resting place on Blue's back, they were kissing. And there was tongue, and lip and a quick smile, and mouth and then puffy jacket pressed hard against overcoat, and J snuck a peek, but Blue's eyes were closed, those beautiful eyes, and they were kissing and kissing and kissing.

Back at the hotel, J spread his remaining money out on the bed. A laugh track from a sitcom blared from the room next door. A hundred sixteen dollars and some change. The cost of the room minus the pizza and candy he'd eaten that day.

"Hahahahahaha!" the wall to his right bellowed.

If he stayed again tomorrow and could eat for three bucks, that would mean he'd have thirty-three dollars left by Monday morning.

"Hahahahaha!"

Still, he wasn't sorry he'd given Blue the chain.

"Hahahahahaha!" A really big laugh this time. J banged on the wall with his fist. Someone banged back, and the TV volume went up. J put on his headphones. He could sell his iPod. That might get him another twenty. And his camera—no, not that. Not yet.

Think, J, he commanded. *Think.*

By now, Carolina would have returned from her shift at the hospital and found his note. He imagined her reading it, in the chair by the window, tears gathering in her eyes, suddenly sorry for the way she'd treated him last night. But why hadn't she called his cell phone yet? That part was weird.

Dear Mami, he'd written. *I can't live here anymore. I'm sorry. Please don't worry about me. I love you. J.*

J looked at his phone. No calls.

So thirty bucks by Monday, maybe fifty if he sold the iPod somewhere, and a hundred miles from starting T. It was nine o'clock; maybe his mother was relieved to have him gone. Maybe she and his father had talked about it and realized they could use all the college money they'd saved and throw a really big anniversary party, take a trip back to Puerto Rico, get a bigger apartment. J had already screwed up his chances for college, probably. His grades in junior year were good, and everybody said that was the most important, but this year he'd been a mess. And he'd missed two weeks already.

What was he thinking? He wasn't going back to school! Not PS 386, not anywhere. He had run away to become a man, and then maybe come back home, muscular, confident, solid in himself. But where was home if his parents didn't want him? Maybe he was being dramatic; he'd only run away for fourteen hours now. But the man part was slipping away, too. Damn, he'd been so sure he could get that testosterone, and everything else would just fall into place. He hadn't thought this through.

But now that he'd started, he also wouldn't stop. He couldn't go home, where his parents sometimes called him Jeni. Or school, where everyone knew he'd been born a girl. He had to find a way, with his last $116 on the bed, to make this work.

Suddenly, there was knock on the door. J froze. How had Carolina found him so fast?

Knock-knock.

J didn't move.

"J?" A voice said. "It's Marcia. Are you in there?"

Marcia! The woman from the lobby. J let out a long

breath of relief, scooped his money into his pocket, and went to the door.

"I was just thinking about you," Marcia said, brushing past J to stand and survey his room. "Oh, you got one with a view. My room looks out on a wall."

Marcia fluffed up some pillows and lay back on J's bed. She was wearing tight jeans and an angora sweater, cut low. "Sit down," she said, patting the space beside her.

"I'm okay," J said. Who was this woman? This was his room.

"Suit yourself. I need a rest." Marcia closed her eyes. J thought she had fallen asleep, when she propped up on her elbows and asked, "Where are you from?"

"Here," J said. "I mean, Washington Heights."

"So you run away?"

"No. I'm moving," J said, thinking fast. "I'm looking for an apartment."

"Mmm-hmm," Marcia purred. "Aren't we all."

"Do you live here?"

"Here? In the hotel?" Marcia asked. She laughed, a throaty, low chuckle, almost mean. "No, I just work here on the weekends. It's close to clients. I live in Jersey. I was about to leave for work now, but it's so nasty outside, I thought I'd stop by to say hello first."

"Hello," J said.

Marcia laughed again. "You're sweet. How old are you?"

"Eighteen."

"You look about twelve. Really, how old are you?"

"Eighteen." J was offended.

"Okay, well, I'm twenty-one," Marcia said, though she looked about forty. "Now that we're through lying to each other, how 'bout I tell you some truth?"

J sat down at the tiny table by the window. He'd never met anyone like Marcia before. Sure, there were plenty of bold and sassy women in his neighborhood at home, but he was pretty sure Marcia used to be a man. Was that the right way to say it? He was pretty sure Marcia was transgender.

"When you came in here this morning, you looked just like a scared little kitten," Marcia said, gazing at the ceiling. "I've seen plenty of kids like you."

"You have?" J asked. "Like what?"

"Like gay, and traveling down to the Village like it's a foreign country, trying to find their people, and then getting all mixed up in the scene, and losing their money, losing their parents, losing their way."

"I'm not gay," J said.

Marcia sat straight up and looked at him. "What are you?"

J coughed. This would be the first time he said the word, out loud, to anyone. "I'm transgender."

Marcia smiled. "Oh, honey, we're *all* transgender."

"We are?"

"Baby, there's a whole mess of us. The good, the bad, and the ugly. And the very beautiful, like me."

J laughed. Marcia was all right.

"Just don't waste your money on a hotel like this one. It's not a good scene," Marcia said. And then, "Do you really have the money to get your own apartment?"

J looked down. "No."

"Do you have kin?"

"Sort of," J said. "I mean, they don't understand."

"They might," Marcia said. "Just give 'em time. My mother didn't understand for the longest, and then, right around five years ago, she had some sort of visitation. She said an angel spoke to her, but I think it was the booze. Anyway, it doesn't matter. She decided she loved me, as her daughter, and now we have dinner almost every Sunday. All I'm saying is, don't give up on family."

"I'm not," J said. "I just ran away this morning."

"That's good. And where are you staying tomorrow?"

"Here?"

Marcia's eyes blazed. "I just *told* you, this hotel's no place for a kid. There's addicts all over the place, and the scene's no good. You're young. You can stay somewhere free, get your head together. There's Covenant House—I stayed there when I was young—and I think the center maybe has a place for gay and lesbian kids."

"I don't want to stay with gay kids."

"Your homophobia's *real* tired," Marcia said, exasperated. "We all gotta get along."

"I'm sorry," J said, embarrassed. He didn't want to make Marcia mad. "Why are you trying to help me?"

"I don't know," Marcia said, getting up. "I ask myself that every day. 'Marcia, why you gotta be so nice to everybody?' Lord knows, people haven't been nice to me. Maybe I'm looking for some karma; maybe my mama raised me right."

Marcia looked at herself in the mirror and smacked her lips together. She walked over to J and kissed him on the forehead. "But, honey, I won't be nice if I get up tomorrow and find you're still checked into this hotel. Get yourself a free bed. Stay there for a while."

J locked the door behind Marcia when she left, and looked at the lipstick on his forehead. It looked like a magenta heart. He didn't wash it off.

CHAPTER SEVEN

"Bitch, you take the bottom bunk, I need me some privacy!"

J had taken Marcia's advice and gone to the shelter for GLBT and "questioning" youth. By morning, nobody had called—not his mother, not Melissa, not even Blue—and J felt more alone than he had in all his seventeen years. Clearly, his parents didn't care that he had run away, and Melissa didn't understand the photograph at the construction site, or maybe she did, and she hated him now, too. And he'd spent four dollars at an Internet café downloading it from his camera to e-mail it to her. And now here he was at a shelter, where they'd taken his camera, his iPod, and his phone at the door and shown him to a room with two other girls, one of whom apparently thought J was deaf.

"You gonna take your shit off that bunk, or do I have to throw it?" the girl yelled, her thick hands on her hips. She was big, her face screwed up in fury.

J had come into the room only moments before and said hello to the one other person there, a skinny girl reading a hair magazine on the other bunk bed. She hadn't answered him. J had just put his backpack on the empty top bunk when the angry tank rolled in.

"Fine," J said. "Chill." He grabbed his bag and threw it onto the floor.

"You tellin' *me* to chill?" the big girl yelled, getting right in J's face. The skinny girl didn't look up from her magazine.

"Nah," J said, knowing that backing down was the kiss of death. "I gotta piss."

The big girl miraculously let J brush past, and J quickly locked the bathroom door, grateful the room was empty. What was he doing here? This place was probably more dangerous than the hotel. The kids he'd seen on his "intake interview" were seriously wild-looking, even compared to Melissa, with her wacky outfits. He'd barely listened to the counselor, who told him the rules—in by nine p.m., chores at seven a.m.—as he watched the stream of kids drop their electronics in a plastic bin and sign in with the guard, trying to out-holler each other as they pushed through the door. Now it seemed he'd have to fist-fight someone twice his size to even get some sleep. He'd never hit a girl before.

One thing the counselor said caught J's attention: to stay at the shelter, J had to go to school. Tomorrow. This place was worse than his parents: J had to show a signed slip each day proving his attendance.

But he could pick his school. He could either go back to PS 386 (*no way*) or show up at a school he'd never heard of—a special high school for queer kids. Apparently, this school had been around for years. The counselor didn't say any more than that.

J was scared. It was a feeling he didn't like having, but there was no getting around it now, locked in a bathroom, with a tank of a teenager about to kick his ass on the other side of the door. When had he run from a fight before? Did becoming a boy mean becoming a pussy?

But I've never had to fight for my bed before, never for my bed, J thought, rocking slightly on the toilet seat. *And I don't even like this place.*

In other places, other times, J always had a home to come back to, always had Carolina and Titi—and, even in his own distant way, Manny. He felt suddenly like a fake. Were these other kids really homeless? Had their parents thrown them out, while he had left of his own accord? Was the Tank so pissed because she had a life worse than J's? He didn't know.

I don't care about her, J thought. *I deserve to be here, too. Wherever here is.*

It was his body that had gotten him into all this trouble. And his idiot brain. Thinking he could just leave and get T and show everybody what a man he was. And money, and a house, and a girlfriend would all just magically fall into place. And everybody would love him. What a fool.

It wasn't just the Ace bandages that hurt his chest. The pain came from inside, deep and deadly.

J walked quietly back to the bedroom, where the door was partly closed. He could hear the Tank saying something, but softly now.

"I know, I know, baby, we'll get it tomorrow," she was saying.

Who was she talking to?

The Tank laughed. "You *know* I love you."

Was she on the phone? Phones were serious contraband; how had she smuggled it in? J peeked in the door. The Tank was on a cell phone, curled on her side on the top bunk, her face to the wall. J walked in and quietly climbed into bed; the Tank didn't even notice.

*   *   *

By morning, the Tank's threats seemed to have dissipated; she was up and showering before a counselor knocked on the door and told them it was time for chores. *School*, J thought, with a clench in his stomach. He'd been dreaming of it all night. Rat intestines were served on a lunch tray, someone threw a book at his head, a teacher who looked like Melissa called him Jeni. Nightmares, all of them.

Mercifully, J was assigned kitchen mopping, so he didn't have to interact with any of the other shelter kids, and when he passed by the Tank in the room later, she didn't say a word. Morning didn't look like her finest hour.

He got to take his phone and camera when he left, and there were three messages: two from Melissa and one from Blue. Blue's was sweet: she said she missed him and she hoped to see him at the Starbucks later, but Melissa's messages were worrisome. She said something had happened at home, and she needed to talk to him today. Could he meet her at the pizza place by her house right after school? Her second message said basically the same thing, but she added that she liked the photo. *Please, please be there*, she'd said. *I really need to see you.*

J wanted to see Blue today—he needed to see her, after all he'd been through, but Melissa sounded pretty bad. What could have happened? He was pretty sure most guys would have skipped the best friend for the girlfriend (he was fairly confident that's what she was), but for J, old loyalty to Melissa won out. He called Blue to tell her something had come up.

The "gay school" looked like a rainbow that threw up on itself. Everywhere J turned was another mural of bright colors, and faces, and buildings. Each door and doorframe and exposed pipe was a different color. J had arrived late on purpose, and a woman at the front desk asked if she could help him. J didn't see any kids. "I'm new."

"I know," the woman said, smiling. "Are you interested in becoming a student?"

J felt too small in his clothes.

The receptionist pointed him down a hall, where J met with another woman, who couldn't have been more than twenty years old.

"You'll like it here," the woman, whose name was Gabriela, assured him. "Aside from our classes, we have a lot of after-school programming, like transgender rap groups, tutoring, a drama club."

"Transgender rap?" J asked. "Like hip-hop?"

Gabriela laughed. "No. Like a discussion group. We have them for transboys and transgirls. Where you can talk about what's going on in your life, and coming out, and get information about hormones, and stuff like that."

"Oh," J said. This was school?

"What grade are you in?" Gabriela asked.

"I'm a senior."

"And how long has it been since you've been in school?"

"Two weeks."

Gabriela seemed surprised. "Oh, that's good. That's great. We'll get your transcripts transferred and see what credits you still need. Jim Rodriguez handles that, and the college counseling. You'll meet him. But for today, there are still English and math. Why don't you go to those classes, and we'll sort out where you are when I get the transcripts."

It turned out all the seniors took their classes together, no matter what level they were at, and some juniors were in there, too. Gabriela showed J the room, and he opened the door slowly.

Six kids were huddled over papers at four large tables. Six kids looked up at J when he walked in, then all looked down again. A man in jeans and a T-shirt with a bull's-eye across the chest, apparently the teacher, walked up to J with his finger over his lips. "Test," he whispered. "You can sit down."

Bull's-eye handed J a math textbook. J glanced mildly at the cover. It was algebra; at his old school, he was already taking trigonometry. J felt a sheen of sweat form across his forehead. He wiped it off.

"Mister! Mister!" a girl in cornrows and a sweat-shirt was shout-whispering and waving her hand madly in the air. "I don't get this!" J noticed she had a tattoo on her neck that said TRIX.

"Shadow," Bull's-eye whispered back. "This is a test. I can't help you. Just do the best you can."

"But I can't read the problem," Shadow protested, at full volume now.

Another kid, a boy, groaned and leaned back in his chair.

"Do the best you can," the teacher repeated. Shadow stood up, crumpled her test into a ball, and threw it on the floor. She marched out of the room. "Just keep going," the teacher said, as though nothing had happened.

J watched in amazement. For one thing, the class was so small, more like an after-school club than a real math class. And the teacher looked like a model for Abercrombie, all white and clean-cut and muscled, commanding a troop of mismatched teens. These kids looked like the kids he had seen with Manny at the piers. There were two boys who were likely born girls, like J, and these were the kids who were giving J the least attention. One feminine girl had half-smiled at him, at least with her eyes, when J walked in but was now biting her bright pink nails and staring at her test. Two boys, probably gay, had finished their test and were sharing headphones and seat-dancing at the back of the room, silently mouthing the words to some song. J never knew you could have music in class.

"Okay," Bull's-eye said. "Looks like you're done. Hand them up."

When he'd gathered the papers, the teacher looked at J and asked his name.

"J," J said softly.

"I can't hear you!" one of the dancers shouted from the back.

"J," J said again. The sweat was sogging up his binder.

"Okay, J, welcome. I'm Mike," the teacher said, shooting a look around the room. "We're studying integers."

"Intersex!"

"Integers," Mike said calmly, walking back to take the iPod and headphones from the boys.

"Oh, I thought you said *intersex*," the boy said, pulling a dramatic pout. "I thought you were trying to make the new girl feel comfortable." The girl with the pink nails giggled.

Girl! J thought indignantly. If only he were Melissa, if only he could think of something cruel enough to say back. Something that would make the other kids laugh, put that gay boy in his place. What the hell did *intersex* mean? But instead he scooted down in his chair and stared at the chalkboard, flat and gray as the sky outside. His first hour here, and he was being hassled already. He'd never have any friends at this school. He wasn't anything like these people.

You could smell the pizza place by Melissa's apartment before you saw it; it was famous in the neighborhood for its dollar slices and garlic knots. Was it really only four days ago that he and Melissa had their colossal talk here? It felt as though months had passed: the hotel, the shelter, the new school. The kiss. J slowed his pace; Melissa was from his old life—she didn't know anything of what he was becoming. She would be full of stories about her mom and Daniel, kids from their old school—J suddenly felt woozy, and he steadied himself against a building. Maybe he wasn't ready for Melissa, wasn't ready to defend the photo he'd sent her of the jackhammer and the shadow. Maybe he couldn't help her through whatever drama she had going on in her life, now that his own life was so different.

J felt that his very body was divided in parts. The top third, the third with his face and his brain and his shoulders, was the newer J, the male J, who lived in a shelter and went to a queer school and was going to get on T. Melissa didn't know this J. The middle third, the

one with his heart, that belonged to Blue. Melissa didn't
know this part, either. The lowest part of his body, the
part with his legs that could walk to this pizza parlor
and into his past, that was the old J, the J who had a
mom and a dad and a best friend named Melissa. He
didn't like this feeling of being so divided, and yet his
legs, ever devoted, pulled away from the wall and strode
toward Melissa, who was shouting his name.

"J!" Melissa yelled, running up the block. "J! I was
worried about you!" She grabbed him into a huge hug.

J pulled back and narrowed his eyes slightly. "Why
were you worried?"

"That picture!" Melissa said. "It was so violent! I
thought maybe you were going to hurt yourself."

"Oh," J said, disappointment registering in the crack
of his voice. She didn't get it, yet again. "I wasn't."

"Thank God," Melissa said, pulling J into the pizza
shop. "Let's go inside. It's freezing. And I have so much
to tell you."

J didn't want anything to eat, and Melissa was on a
diet, so they sat at a small table near the back. Melissa
seemed nervous and kept looking down to check her
phone.

"What's wrong?"

"Huh?" Melissa asked, looking up. "Oh, nothing.
I'm just waiting for my mom to call."

"What's going on?"

"Nothing," Melissa said, looking at her phone again.

"Well, why did you want to meet me here?" *I could be with Blue right now*, J thought.

"Oh, right. Well, things are weird with my mom."

"So?" J hated the way everything was a five-alarm fire with Melissa.

"So—let's talk about your photograph. It was good. I mean, disturbing, because the hammer was going through your heart—"

"It wasn't going through my heart," J interrupted. "It was going through a shadow."

"So what does that mean?"

J paused. "Like I'm killing off a part of me."

Melissa didn't flinch. "You've always been doing that."

"Now I'm doing it more," J said. He struggled to find the right words. "Now I'm—"

"Jay-jay!" A rush of air from the open door, and suddenly J's mother was upon him, hugging him, kissing his face, pulling back, kissing it again, and standing him up so she could hug him hard and long. "My Jay-jay!"

J was so startled, at first he didn't hug Carolina back, but then he said, "Hi, Mami," and let her smother him. He snuck a look at Melissa, who was feigning shock: J knew that face. It was Melissa's fake face, the one she pulled whenever she told a lie. She and Carolina had planned this!

"Why'd you run away, J? We were worried, so worried—your father was worried, I was worried, your cousins were worried—"

"In Puerto Rico?" J asked.

"Of course!" Carolina said. "I called everybody. Even Melissa didn't know where you were." Carolina started to cry.

"Why didn't you call me?" J asked. He touched his mother's hair, then pulled back his hand.

"The police—"

"You called the police?!" J noticed a cop standing at the door. Was this all for him?

Anger colored Carolina's cheeks, and she raised her voice. "J! I'm your mother! You can't run away from me!"

J was embarrassed in front of all these people; the cop, Melissa, a few customers, and the guy behind the counter were all staring. "I'm sorry, Mami," he said, shooting dagger eyes at Melissa, who looked back with a desperate *What else could I do?* expression.

"Let's go, J," Carolina said, hugging him again. "You can tell me everything at home."

At this, the cop got up and opened the door for them

and shuffled them into his squad car, which was waiting outside. Melissa reached out to touch J's arm, but he yanked it away. Melissa had betrayed him again.

In the squad car, Carolina wouldn't let go of J's hand. "Don't ever do that again," she said. "I was so worried."

Manny was waiting for them when they got home, stirring something at the stove. He didn't turn around.

"Hello, J," he said, irony thick and heavy in his voice. "Welcome back."

J could tell Manny was angry by the stiffness in his shoulders. How had J bargained for this? He hadn't asked to come home. "Hi, Pops."

"Where were you?" Manny asked, still not looking at them.

"Just downtown," J said quietly.

"And did you enjoy scaring your mother to death?"

"Manny—" Carolina began.

"No, Cari," Manny said, his voice steely. "I want to know. Did you enjoy *torturing* your mother, when she's done everything to raise you right?"

At this, Manny turned on J. He was huge, his eyes red and glaring. "Was it worth it, J? A weekend of partying, *downtown*, without even one phone call, and your mother's crying day and night?"

"Manny—" Carolina tried again.

"I wasn't partying," J said. *You don't know me at all.*

"I don't give a rat's ass what you were doing," Manny stormed. "You talk to her. I'm going out!" And Manny left.

"Don't worry about your dad," Carolina said once Manny was gone, but J could see she was shaking. "He was worried about you, too."

"You didn't have to worry," J said. "I was fine."

Carolina went to turn off the stove. "I don't understand, J. Why did you leave?"

Titi jumped up onto the arm of the couch and rubbed up against J's hip. J scratched her ears, and she purred. "I don't know," J said. Why couldn't humans be more like cats? No questions.

"No, J, that's not going to work this time. You have to answer me. Why did you leave?"

J didn't know what to say. Suddenly being a man seemed very remote, even impossible, in the face of his old sofa, and Titi, and his mother staring him down, soup spoon in hand. Oh, yes, this was why. He had to try to be himself. It just was going to take longer than he had planned. "I had to, Mami."

"Why did you have to?"

"Because I have a problem."

Carolina sat down. "What, J? What is the problem?"

J's phone buzzed. It was Blue. He put the ringer on silent. Blue was part of the problem. She believed he was a boy; how long would it be before she would want to meet his mother, his friends? See his school, see under his shirt? His mother was a problem; she believed J was a girl. How long would it be before she would need to know the truth? His whole life was a problem.

"Do you know what testosterone is?"

"J, I'm a nurse."

Of course she was a nurse; maybe she'd even heard of his condition. Maybe that was a good thing; maybe it was bad. J had started sweating. "I don't have enough."

"Enough what? Testosterone?" Carolina asked. "J, what are you saying?"

"I don't know, Mami, what I'm saying is hard." J lay back on the couch and put a pillow over his face.

"J, you have to try."

Through the pillow, J said very softly, "I'm a boy." But it sounded more like "Mmmghhouy."

"What, J? I can't understand you. Take the pillow off your face."

J suddenly had an idea. He had an information sheet about the effects of testosterone, from the clinic. He took it out and handed it to her. "Read this," he said. Then he went into the bathroom and shut the door.

Once again, J was faced with the prospect of surviving off water drippings from the bathroom sink. *Oh, God. Oh, God*, he thought as he lay his head against the cool porcelain of the tub. *I wasn't ready for this. Not yet.*

Blink, two, three, four, five, six, seven, eight, nine, ten, eleven, twelve. J's eyes started to strain. He could only go fourteen seconds between blinks, but he tried to stretch it longer each time. When that didn't distract him from the silence outside the bathroom door, he counted tiles. There were hundreds of them, tiny black hexagons, each surrounded by gray, dirty grout. The tiles must have taken some serious time to put in; why didn't they use bigger tiles back in the day? What was his mother *doing* with that testosterone information? J couldn't stand it anymore; he cracked open the door.

Carolina was sitting on the couch, her head cocked back, her eyes closed. The sheet was on the cushion beside her.

"Might as well come on out," she said, without opening her eyes.

J shut the door again.

"Don't be a baby," Carolina said. He could hear her getting up. Then she was knocking on the door. "Come out of there."

"I think I'm sick."

"You tried that already, remember?" Carolina's voice was thin and sarcastic. "When you skipped school?"

"I'm not going back to school," J answered defiantly, to the door. Who asked him to come back here, anyway? And he really did feel sick.

"Jenifer Juana Silver, you are not a delinquent!" his mother yelled. She rattled the doorknob. "Get out here right now."

The name! This was the second time she'd used it in many years. J felt his face grow red, knew he'd look splotchy and terrible if he stood and looked at himself in the mirror. "That's not my name!" he shouted.

"Ai, J! Your father was right! We've spoiled you!"

J watched the door shake in its frame as his mother gave it one more push. But he wasn't letting her get away with that one. He opened the door and faced her.

"Pops was right?" he yelled. He gestured wildly at the living room that was his bedroom, at the computer they all shared, at his two pairs of sneakers by the front door. Other kids had far more; she knew that. "How have you spoiled me?"

Carolina's voice deepened into a low hiss. "You run this house, J. Ever since you were little, you had to do your own thing, act your own way. And we let you get away with it."

J thought of his curfews, his cheap allowance, the

rules his parents set about grades. He'd never argued with any of this; until he'd run away, he was practically the poster child for restrained adolescence. "What are you *talking* about, Mami?"

"J!" his mother shouted, slapping her hand on the coffee table and startling the cat. "Other girls your age want piercings, want tattoos. You—you want *testosterone*? What am I supposed to think?"

"Think that I'm transgender!" J yelled back. "God, open your eyes!"

There was a knock at the door. J and Carolina looked at each other, frozen. The handle slowly turned, and a face peeked in. Mercie.

"Everything okay in here?" she asked, stepping in gingerly and glancing around. "I heard shouting."

"We're fine, Mercedes," Carolina answered, smoothing her hair and stepping toward the door. "We don't need your help."

But eagle-eye Mercie was scanning both of them up and down and shutting the door behind her. Mercie never missed a chance to partake in some drama; she was always in the front row of rubberneckers when a fire truck pulled up or when the cops shackled a kid on the corner. J stepped back into the bathroom and shut the door.

After a while, he heard the teakettle whistle. His mother must have surrendered to the battleship. In some ways, he was thankful to Mercie for breaking up the fight, but he was getting tired of these bathroom quarantines. He listened to them talking in low tones at the kitchen table. He scooted closer to the door to listen but couldn't understand what they were saying. And then, a laugh! Were they laughing about him? He could tell Mercie was doing most of the talking, his mother adding a few *sí*s here and there, but then silence.

J got up and slowly peeked out the bathroom door. His mother and Mercedes were sitting at the kitchen table, their heads bowed. Were they praying? His mother hadn't prayed in years. Mercedes popped her face up.

"Jeni! You finally came out!" she barked, heaving her jiggling bulk from the seat and limping toward J. He winced. "Give Mercie a hug!"

Mercedes smelled like bacon and sweat, but J hugged her dutifully. "Everybody was worried about you," she said. "You ran away and scared us all, you stupid kid." She took off J's cap and tousled his hair. Mercie held J by the shoulders and examined his face. "But you don't look too bad, for a runaway. Looks like you even had a bath or two."

J tried to force a smile. Then he noticed that Mercedes was clutching the testosterone sheet in her sweaty fist. Carolina saw him looking.

"Jay-jay, I showed Mercie the paper you gave me," Carolina said.

"This?" Mercie said, pulling it out in front of her. "I told your mom you shouldn't have run away over this. J, you remember Pedrito, right? We used to call him Tiny?"

J shook his head. What was Mercie talking about?

"He's my sister's kid. He used to live with me, when you were little. A few years older than you. Anyway, now he's Tina. She moved to California. I have pictures of her downstairs, if you want to see. It's not *that* big a deal. There was another person, too, lived in this building before your parents moved in—she was like a guy, with a girlfriend and everything, went by the name of Mac. Wanted us to call her *he*. Now even the soap operas got transsexual stars. *All My Children* had one—she was even pretty." Mercie paused to take a breath. She pulled a rag out of her bra and wiped her brow. "Wow, you keep your apartment hot. I was just telling your mom about my Tina when you finally came out of that bathroom."

J suddenly wanted to hug Mercie. He wanted to dance around the room with her, take her huge body in his arms and squeeze her with every ounce of gratitude he'd ever felt. Instead, he just stared at her.

"Close your mouth, honey," Mercie said, tapping J gently on the chin. "You look like you've never seen Tía Mercie before. You're going to be fine. My Tina takes estrogen pills, and she looks great. You want testosterone? So take testosterone. Just don't give your mother ulcers over it." Mercie wagged the information sheet in the air.

"I don't want J to change," Carolina said. J had almost forgotten that his mother was in the room.

"Well, not much you can do about that," Mercie said, pulling at her double chin. "Might as well try to stop the sun from shining. Or me from eating."

"But Tiny's not your kid," Carolina protested in a choked voice. "That's just your nephew."

Mercie looked as if she'd been slapped. J knew, from the countless Saturday morning complain-o-ramas, that Mercie had passed her prime. She'd wanted children, but since her no-good husband left her years ago she had nowhere to turn but the snack aisle for comfort. And other people's business.

"I know how to love my family. And that 'where your treasure is, there your heart will be also.' " Mercie stared Carolina down, her jaw solid. She could trump Carolina, quoting Scripture, since Carolina had stopped going to church, and Mercie was faithful, every Sunday.

Carolina averted her gaze and changed the subject. "What if the testosterone's dangerous?"

"It's not," J said. "I can show you websites—"

"Why, J?" Carolina said, tears filling her eyes. "Why do you want to be a boy?"

"I already am a boy," J answered, looking to Mercie for backup, but she was reading the testosterone sheet.

"No, you're not a boy!" Carolina said. "I gave birth to you. A lesbian, maybe—can't you just be a regular lesbian? Your father will deal with that."

"Is this about Pops?" J asked. He toyed with the teapot on the table.

"No, J, this is about you. You're the one that's making problems here."

"You're always worried about what Pops will think," J said. He knew he was hitting a nerve. "What about what you think?"

"I think you're being selfish," Carolina said, holding J's gaze, her voice shaking. "Your father and I have sacrificed everything for you. See that table there?" Carolina pointed to J's desk by the couch. "That stack is all college applications. I had to send away for them because you've been too preoccupied *with yourself* to remember. On your first birthday, we started saving for college, so you could have a good life, a chance to do whatever you wanted. We've saved everything, every year. And now all you want to do is hurt us with this, this *shit*, J. Leaving school, running away. All you care about anymore is what you *look like*."

"That's not true!" J said. It was so much more than that. He did care about college, about the sacrifices people made for him, but he'd already spent seventeen years of his life trying to make other people happy. Couldn't his mother see he was dying inside his own skin? There'd be no college if he shriveled up in there. He chewed on his thumbnail, muttered "damn" under his breath. His mother told him there was no need to swear.

"Why can you swear and not me?"

"Cari," Mercie said, softening again and coming up behind Carolina to rub her shoulders. "This isn't about what J looks like. Give the kid a break."

Exactly, J thought. *Thank you, Mercedes. Finally, someone with some sense.*

CHAPTER EIGHT

Manny called later that night to say he was going to crash at his friend's place. J was relieved: he knew for sure Manny wouldn't react to J's announcement as well as Mercie or even Carolina had. In the morning, J and his mother were delicate and careful around each other, politely offering up cereal or milk, J feeding Titi before he was asked.

"Should we take a drive?" Carolina asked.

"The car's working?" Their old Toyota, parked in a garage by the river, was like a cranky old man, wheezing and sputtering and complaining if you drove too fast.

"Daddy worked on it this weekend."

"Okay," J said. "Where do you want to go?"

They drove out past the George Washington Bridge, Carolina playing love songs on the tape deck and humming along. Cold air whistled in around the windows, and the heater blew in a comforting smell, like warm tar and caramel. J watched as the buildings went from brownstone to brick and then to ugly and industrial as they passed through Yonkers and then on to the smaller towns with their A-frame houses and their lawns. Finally, Carolina pulled over in Tarrytown and parked the car by the train station, with a view of the river. The water was slate-colored and flat, and together, in silence, they watched a red tugboat head back toward the city.

After several long minutes, Carolina spoke. "You know, I didn't love your father when I married him."

Of all things, J wasn't expecting this. "What?"

"He loved me, but I didn't love him."

J had been preparing for a lecture, maybe more of Carolina's tears. Through the night, he'd been gathering the courage to talk more about his body, which made him want to run into a cave somewhere very far away, like maybe Iceland. His mouth tasted bitter, as if he'd just woken up. He couldn't think of anything to say.

"It was a different time, J," Carolina said, picking at some leather that was fraying from the steering wheel. "I was new in New York. He had a good job, my mother wanted me to marry someone else and move back home, I don't know."

"Do you love him now?" The taste in his mouth grew stronger, and he peeked at her, quickly, through his eyelashes.

"Of course!" Carolina looked shocked. "That's the thing. You can learn to love the life you're handed."

The sun was breaking through the clouds and sparkling on the river in front of their car. So this was it. His mother was sharing an old secret to teach him a lesson. *Great*, he thought. *Screw me up even more.* "I've tried, Mami."

"J, you're only seventeen. I thought I knew everything when I was seventeen, too. But things change as you get older. You realize certain things in life are good for you, and others are not. You don't want to make an irreversible decision now that you may regret for the rest of your life."

J slumped in his seat. The car was getting cold. *We drove all this way so you could give me a lecture?*

Carolina continued. "J, listen. If I had done exactly

what I wanted when I was seventeen, I would have run away with a boy named Loco."

This part was funny: he couldn't imagine his serious, homebody mother running around with a kid with a street name.

"Don't laugh. He was loco. He was so handsome—and dangerous. He dropped out of school and already had a baby with somebody else. My mother hated him," Carolina said. "She wanted me to date a boy from our church."

This image was clearer. His mother with an altar boy, with crisply ironed pants and clean hands. "Did you?"

"Of course not. I didn't want a good boy. I wanted a bad one. If I had gone with Loco, I wouldn't have moved to New York, wouldn't have become a nurse, and wouldn't have had you," Carolina said, touching J's cheek. "So everything works out for a reason."

"But, Mami, this is different," J said. *Is she trying to tell me that mothers know best? That being trans is like being loco?* He didn't want to sort it out, so he changed the subject. "How did you meet Pops?"

"In college. You know that story."

J had heard the courtship tale but couldn't remember it exactly. Something about his father spotting the most beautiful woman he'd ever seen, in a college financial-aid line, and pursuing her for a date until she eventually caved. *But get to the part where you started loving Dad.*

"Abuelita is nice to you, J, but really she's a very selfish woman," Carolina said. "Your abuela wanted me to come home after I started college here, but I wouldn't."

More Abuela, J thought. *Where is this going?* He shivered. "Can we turn on the heat?"

Carolina started the engine. "I was very determined when I was young, too, J."

We're nothing alike, J thought, the bitter taste rising again in his mouth.

"And then I got pregnant."

J looked at his mother. She was staring out at the water, warming her hands on the vents. "With me?" he asked.

Carolina shook her head. "We lost that baby," she said, still not looking at him. "I think I thought if I got pregnant, I would have to stay in New York, and my mother would understand." She sighed. "The logic of the young."

"So, why'd you marry him?" This part of the story felt dangerous, as though he was betraying his dad, but he wanted to know.

"J, I'm Catholic. We got married as soon as I found out I was pregnant."

J tried to imagine his mother, young and frightened, trapped in a life she didn't plan, but the picture didn't fit with the responsible nurse-mom sitting behind the wheel. The image blurred.

"In the end, I was doing what my mother wanted. I married the good boy," she said. "He quit school and got a job to support me, and then I learned to love him. In my own way. Anyway, your grandmother was right about men."

"But Abuela was mad he was Jewish?" J suddenly felt that he wanted to defend his dad and malign his grandma; Manny was getting the short end of this story.

Carolina laughed. "Your abuela's always mad about something."

J was confused and a little stung by her laughter, by the ease with which she could turn his world upside down. His parents didn't love each other, he had a dead almost-sibling, his mom was a rebel, his dad was a pushover, his grandma was a shrew, his whole family history had been demolished in a car trip. Was she trying to get even, make him feel as rattled as she did? Or was she playing pastor, infusing a moral message in her sermon? He went for the catchall response. "Mami, this is different."

"How is it different?"

"It just is." J felt like his brain was a game show

where the words were all blank panels he had to some-how flip around to make his mother understand. If he turned the wrong ones, he'd be buzzed off the stage. "This isn't like falling in love. Or rebelling or whatever. I've known I was this way forever."

Carolina paused. "But you're still a kid, J. You don't know what you are yet. One day you want to be a vet-erinarian; the next, a photographer. How can you say you want to be a—a boy?"

"Mami—" How could he explain? It was like explaining the blood moving through his veins. It was constant, definite, nothing he controlled or chose. You could put all kinds of muscle and skin on top, and then add clothes and tattoos and makeup and hats, but noth-ing would change that blood.

"How can you say that you're a boy?" Carolina repeated. "I gave birth to you. I changed your diapers. I know what you are. You might dress masculine, but you're *not* a boy."

"There are other people like me," J protested. He thought of Marcia, of the Tank at the shelter, of all the kids he hadn't talked to at his new school.

Carolina looked at the water. She held her hands up in front of the car's heater and then lay her forehead on the steering wheel. Finally, she spoke. "What do you want to do?"

"I want to take testosterone so I look more male,

more like how I feel," J said, his voice even, his tone low. Aside from talking to the woman at the clinic and fighting with his mom last night, when he was all freaked out, this was the only time he'd spoken his desire aloud. Inside, a piece of him cracked; it was as though an emotion that had calcified into bone got tapped with a tiny hammer and splintered straight through. It was a small bone, made of equal parts shame and need, and it was lodged somewhere on the right side of his rib cage. He wrapped his arms around himself to steel against the pain.

"You still cold?" Carolina asked.

"No," J answered quietly. He focused inside. It felt as if part of the bone had broken free, its sharp edge scraping a piece of rib, then floating on, looking for a new place to root. Could it be that feelings actually did physical damage? Could he really have broken something? Did the pain stem from hearing his mother's words, or his own? He remembered what his old swimming coach used to say when the team was aching and groaning but still had more laps to do: "Pain is inevitable, but suffering is optional." *I won't suffer*, J thought. *This may hurt, but I won't suffer.* The bone settled.

Carolina tapped him on the leg. "What does testosterone do?" she asked. "I mean, Mercedes told me a little, and I tried to read that paper...."

J glanced up. Carolina's face was pale, her eyes even

darker than usual. The bone shard seemed to wiggle, its tip pointing toward the river. *Use the pain*, J remembered his coach saying. *Let it motivate you.* "It'll just deepen my voice," he said calmly, "and give me more muscles."

"Will it give you a beard?"

Yes, he thought. *This sharp little thing is a sword. I'll fight for what I need.* "After a while."

"Oh, God, J!" Carolina started to cry. "Why would you do that to yourself?"

J stared at the water. There was no answer to that question, really, none that his mother could understand. He wasn't doing anything to himself at his core; he was simply staying alive. But saying that was too dramatic, he felt; he didn't want to scare her. Carolina dug through her purse for a tissue. "J, you don't understand what this is like," she said.

"What *what* is like?"

"To have your baby change!" Carolina practically shouted. She sat still for a long time, and her words seemed to echo around the quiet car. Then she put her hand on J's knee. "I'm sorry for yelling."

"I'm sorry, too," J said stiffly, not exactly sure for what. And then he remembered. "I'm sorry I ran away."

"You should be!" Carolina laughed again, a kind of

sad little laugh. Then she pulled J into her arms. "Give me a hug."

They sat like that for a while, Carolina rubbing J's back, until J straightened up.

"Mami?"

Carolina pulled back and looked at him.

"I need you to consent, um, because I'm under eighteen." The piece of bone was a sword, though he couldn't feel it as acutely now; something had softened with the hug. He got the sense that he had to act fast, before he lost his courage, before whatever had cracked inside him sealed back up forever.

"Consent to what?" Carolina narrowed her eyes.

"It's just something called informed consent," J spoke quickly. "You have to write a note saying you approve me taking testosterone."

Carolina leaned her head against the headrest and closed her eyes. "Remember what I used to say to you when you were little?"

J did. He said the words in his head: *You just have to be yourself, because if you aren't, who else will be?* He couldn't find his voice; the shard was definitely gone, as quickly as it had come. Carolina blinked several times at the roof of the car.

Finally, she pulled out of the train station and headed back toward the highway. "I'll try to understand this thing, J," she said. "I can't make any promises, but I'll try."

On the way home, they decided Carolina would talk to Manny, but she warned J it would take some time. J told her about the hotel and the shelter and his new school, except he left out the part that it was a place exclusively for queer kids. He said it was a magnet school downtown, and Carolina seemed pleased enough. He felt oddly superficial as they talked, as if he and his mother were polite strangers and his runaway weekend was some kind of vacation. *I'm so exhausted*, he thought beneath the stream of chatter. And, *I can't believe she knows I'm trans. She really knows.*

"Maybe you could stay with Melissa for a while, just until your dad gets through this," Carolina suggested. She said she was worried Manny would tear into J for this one, maybe even want to send him to Puerto Rico to live with his abuela for a while. She argued that she didn't know how Manny would react, but she knew she needed some space to explain it slowly.

"Mami, Melissa lives in a studio apartment," J said. Leave it to his mother to jump into the practical details of sleeping arrangements. *Mami is three steps ahead, Pops is three steps behind, and I just need a long nap.*

"It would only be for a week or two," Carolina said. "I don't want you staying in a shelter. You're not homeless."

"But Melissa doesn't know"—J paused—"about me. Not exactly."

"She doesn't?" Carolina was surprised. "Well, then, you tell Melissa, and I'll tell your father. We each have a job to do."

J wasn't sure Melissa and her mom would go for the plan, but when he and Carolina pulled up in front of their building, Karyn was waiting outside.

"Hi, J," Karyn said happily as J stepped out. Did she know he was coming? "Glad to see you. We were all pretty worried about you this weekend."

"Sorry," J mumbled.

J brushed some cigarette butts off the stoop and sat down. Carolina got out of the car. "Karyn, thank you," she said, giving Melissa's mom an awkward hug. "I know this is last minute."

"Not a problem," Karyn answered. "We love J."

Wait, what? J thought. *Was this all plotted in advance?* How had he gone from being an independent guy this weekend, with his own hotel room by the pier, to a little kid being shuttled between mothers with psychic superpowers?

"Okay, J," Carolina said, motioning for him to stand up and say good-bye. "I'm going home. I'll bring you some clothes tomorrow. Be nice to Karyn."

As J hugged his mother, he whispered a quick question.

"I called her when you were in the bathroom at the gas station," Carolina answered, as if commandeering J's life like this was no big deal. "She said it was fine if you stayed with them."

As it turned out, it really was fine. Karyn put out a sleeping bag for J in the little alcove space off the kitchen, and Melissa was on extra-nice behavior, grateful that J wasn't mad at her for conspiring with Carolina to find him. After J picked up his clothes from the shelter, he found himself almost happy to be coming home to the studio apartment he knew so well, with the cat hair and the smell of candle wax everywhere, and the promise of some real sleep. At first, J was worried Carolina might have told Karyn about J's plans to take T, but Karyn wasn't acting any differently with him; she just cooked spaghetti and studied her psychology textbooks, leaving Melissa and J to watch TV like old times.

English class the next day went pretty much like math; these kids were way below his level. At his old school, they had been reading *Hamlet*, but inside the rainbow explosion, J found his peers irritating and slow. He recognized only one person from Monday—the feminine girl with the pink nails. And she was struggling through a Walt Whitman poem the teacher had asked her to read aloud.

" 'From pent-up aching rivers,' " the girl read, giving equal stress to each syllable. It was almost painful to hear. " 'From that of myself, without which I were nothing'—*wha?*"

"Go on, just keep reading," the teacher said, cutting her eyes at another girl rustling a potato chip bag.

"But what's he saying, 'with which, what'? You told us to ask questions if we didn't understand," Pink Nails whined.

"Ask after—just keep going, Blanca," the teacher said. She was short and stocky, probably in her forties.

Blanca kept going. *Just wait 'til she gets to the "phallus" line*, J thought, reading ahead. *We'll never get through this poem.*

"This dude was *gay?*" someone from the back of the room interrupted.

So you're reading ahead, too, J thought, and turned around to look. It was a girl in a tan skirt and combat boots, her straightened hair tucked behind her ears. *Maybe everybody's not so dumb.*

"Chanelle, please don't interrupt," the teacher said. "You know better. Blanca, continue."

Blanca marched on, torturing the poem with her monotonous drone. Her tone was so flat, the students almost missed the "singing the phallus" line, but it only elicited a few giggles. J's favorite line was "singing the muscular urge and the blending." He knew this was a poem about sex, but still: that line sounded like transitioning from female to male. He wanted to sing "the muscular urge" and to blend. He wanted to fit in; he wished this whole process were less like a battle and more like a song.

The poem was over. A slender boy raised his hand and spoke simultaneously. "Miss Charlie, Whitman was, like, with a prostitute?"

The teacher took a breath. "Okay, we can do a close reading of that section in a moment, but who can tell me what this poem is really about, overall?"

"It's celebrating the body and sex," Chanelle, the girl with the combat boots, said. Her tone shifted. "He's singing about his glorious phallus and the woman's glorious vessel. Very heterocentric. I always heard Whitman was gay."

Another girl chimed in. She looked pretty tough, J thought. She was still wearing her leather jacket in the classroom. "Yeah, and why the phallus always gotta be the center of everything? Why we reading this poem?"

"A poet was with a prostitute?" The slender boy was still fixated. "Was that legal in the olden days?"

The teacher, Charlie, waved her hands to gain control. "Chanelle's right. This poem is a celebration of the body and of sex—and it is somewhat heterocentric." She sat at the edge of her desk. "But it's also about loving your own body, and the pleasures it can give you. It's also about surrender and power, all sorts of things."

J was interested in these ideas, but Charlie was losing the other students. The kid with the potato chips was chomping away noisily. Charlie snatched the bag and continued. "And Whitman did also love men."

"You mean he was bi?" someone said. "Eww."

"That's nasty," the girl in the leather jacket agreed.

Why? J thought. He didn't expect this from queer kids.

"*Bisexual* wasn't a term widely used in Whitman's day, so we shouldn't ascribe language that isn't historically accurate," Charlie said. "But he did love both men and women."

J raised his hand, just a few inches from his desk.

"Yes," Charlie said. "Tell me your name again?"

"J," he said quietly. He didn't like speaking in class, but he was feeling less afraid of these kids. He'd already been hassled in the math class and survived. "If there isn't a term for something, then does it even exist?"

Charlie scooted back on her desk and looked at him straight on. "That's actually a very big and difficult question. Does anyone want to try to answer it?"

"What'd he say?" asked the slender boy.

Someone else shouted, "Tyrone exists, and we don't know what to call him!" Everyone laughed and looked at a chubby boy sitting by the window. Tyrone tried to smile, but J could tell he was stung.

Blanca, the girl who had read the poem, raised her hand.

"Blanca?"

"Well, this is hard to say, but—" Blanca was blinking her mascara'ed eyes and struggling to find words. "I think that everything's existed forever. Like, even before we had words, like, even in caveman times. Like, everybody be having sex with everything, and maybe they called it 'ugg' or whatever. But nothing's new no more."

"Ooh baby, I want to ugg you," the tough girl in the leather jacket said. Everybody laughed again.

"Shut up!" Blanca protested. "I'm tryin' ta say something real!"

"For reals, this poet shoulda picked men or women or prostitutes. Bisexual's nasty," the slender boy said.

Forget it, J thought.

After class, Chanelle stopped J in the hall. He had been texting Blue to see if they could meet later.

"Your question was good," she said.

"Huh?"

"Your question in class—very postmodern."

J looked more closely at Chanelle. She was light-skinned, with smoky eye shadow on her lids and a clear gloss on her lips. She was pretty, in a kind of angular way, with a sharp chin and bangs that cut evenly across her brow and then dipped down toward her ears.

"Have you read much Walt Whitman?" Chanelle asked.

"Um, I read some at my old school, but it was a while ago. Do you like him?"

"He's okay. I'm a poet. My favorite is Gerard Manley Hopkins. And Sylvia Plath. And Rita Dove. And others, too."

"Oh," J said. He suddenly felt stupid. "I don't know that much about poetry."

"Are you an artist?"

"Not really," J said. Why was this beautiful girl talking to him? Why did everybody think he was an artist? She really was pretty. "I take pictures, though."

"Cool. Do you want to get coffee after school?"

Blue. He hadn't seen her in four days. "I can't," J said. "But maybe tomorrow?"

"Okay," Chanelle said. "Tell me your name again?"

"J."

"I'm Chanelle," she said, extending her hand. When they shook, she seemed to hold on just a moment longer than was necessary. "Very pleased to make your acquaintance."

⚜

J met Blue at the Starbucks, like old times. She hadn't responded to his text message earlier, but he found her at the café, sitting with Madison by the window.

"Hey," J said, knocking on the table.

"Speak of the devil," Madison said. Blue didn't look at him.

"Wassup?" He tried to sound casual, but his voice came out cautious instead.

"We were just talking about the ways of men," Madison answered, sounding mean, stirring her coffee with a stick. Blue still hadn't looked up.

"Okay. Maybe I should go."

At this, Blue looked at him. Her face was a little red,

her eyes puffy. Had she been crying? She was wearing the necklace.

"No, I'll go," Madison said, scooting back her chair and standing up to leave. "You can have my seat, *Mister* J."

Oh, shit, J thought. *What's this* Mister *crap?* J picked at his cuticles, his heart racing. He didn't take off his coat. Finally, Blue spoke.

"J, what's going on?"

"What's going on with you?"

"Nothing," Blue whined. Her face was twisted into a sad scowl.

She looks like a spoiled brat, J thought. *I better get outta here.* He stared out the window; it was getting dark earlier and earlier each day.

"Why aren't you talking to me?" Blue's voice was small.

"What am I doing right now?"

Blue opened her eyes wide. "J, you're acting so different."

What am I, on trial? Suddenly J was angry. He gives this girl a necklace, manages to give her his time and attention when his whole life is falling apart, and she says he's acting *different*? *You don't know the half of it*, J wanted to say. *While you've been painting your pretty pictures and getting snacks from your mommy, I've been sleeping in four different places. My mom doesn't want me at home because my dad might hate us both, and you're the one who's crying?* Sitting with Blue and her petty whimpers made the full weight of what had happened with Carolina hit him like a full-body punch. Would he ever be able to go home again? How long could he really sleep on Melissa's floor?

"J," Blue prodded. "What are you thinking?"

"Nothing."

Blue's eyes filled with tears. She reached out for his hand, and he snatched it back. Why could everybody cry but him? His mother, Melissa, Blue—everybody was always bawling around him.

Blue reached around behind her neck and started to unclasp the necklace. "Here, I'll give you this back," she said. She was really crying now.

"What?" J said. *She doesn't even want my present?*

"It seems like you don't want me to have it," Blue said. She kept the necklace on and touched it carefully. "My mom said it was too expensive to keep, but she's from Poland."

J's pride was hurt. "You don't want it?"

"J, it's the most beautiful present I've ever gotten *in my life*." Blue stared intently at her coffee and then looked up. "I was shocked when you gave it to me. But then you didn't call me for four days. That was Saturday. Today is Wednesday. What am I supposed to think?"

"I've been busy." *What do you want me to say? I've been living in a shelter, then busy getting picked up by the cops? I had to deal with a new school full of freaks? Oh, and by the way, Blue, I'm a freak, too. I'm not what you think I am.*

"Busy with what? J, you don't even go to school. My mom said I shouldn't accept the necklace because I don't know you well enough. I don't even know where you live."

Bingo! "Blue, I gotta go," J said. "Keep the necklace." And he pushed out the door, thankful that the street noise drowned out Blue's voice, plaintively calling his name.

J decided to walk back to Melissa's place, even though it was cold outside. He passed a magazine stand; both the men's and the women's magazines boasted scantily clad women. *And here I am, singing the muscular urge like Whitman*, J thought. *And for what? All you do is piss people off.*

Stop feeling sorry for yourself, he scolded himself. Sometimes J wished he could just crawl out of his own head or borrow someone else's for a month or a lifetime. Once, when he was in the car with his mother, he heard a radio program during which the announcer asked people whether they'd rather be invisible or able to fly, given the choice. Practically everyone chose flight, and J was shocked. Of course he'd be invisible. Not only could he spy on people's conversations and watch how other guys had sex, but he could stop feeling so many things. That was the problem—these feelings. He felt angry and confused, and then lost and embarrassed, and all these emotions tumbled together like the bad murals at school, all the colors running into one another, making him lash out at people, like Blue. *Wait, did we just break up? Is Blue not my girlfriend anymore?*

Was she ever his girlfriend? Or did they just make out on a street corner? J didn't understand girls or relationships at all. And would being invisible mean he wouldn't have feelings anymore? Somehow, he thought it would. Like, if people couldn't see him and react to him in all their complicated and terrible ways, then he wouldn't have anything to feel *about*. And, of course, he wouldn't have this body that betrayed him all the time.

Human beings are a bad prototype, J thought. *God made us wrong.* But he didn't believe in God anymore, at least not the God his mother used to talk about when J was little, when she made him say his prayers. "Pray for your cousins, pray for your abuela and Papa and Tía Yola," she would say each night before bed, and J would try to picture his extended family in Puerto Rico. Back then, J had believed that wishes could make things come true. He would clasp his hands together and imagine a man in the clouds smiling at each person his mother named. And then he'd pray to wake up a boy.

J was getting closer to Melissa's apartment. He stopped to lean against a building, smoke a cigarette, get his head together before he went inside. It was fully dark now, and a street lamp cast a yellow glow over the trash can on the corner. People rushed by, talking on cell phones, carrying groceries; a siren wailed from a few blocks away. J took out his camera. He wanted to capture the sense of this street, this moment, and stop thinking of the past and of Blue and her tears. But there was nothing, really, that caught his attention.

Then he saw it. Someone had taped a flyer to a phone booth, advertising MANDY WILL TEACH YOU GUITAR! The word MANDY was in large block letters, and J covered the last two letters with his fist. MAN, It now said, and J clicked the shutter with his free hand. It was the first time J had ever photographed any part of his body not in shadow. From the angle he was shooting, his fist looked bigger than it really was, strong and defiant next to the word MAN. In the background, you could see a fuzzy outline of the phone booth's interior; it looked as if the fist were punching through to make a call.

I'm still visible, J thought. It wasn't a photo of his whole body, but it was a start. *I exist.*

CHAPTER NINE

"J, your mom dropped off an envelope for you," Melissa called out to him when he came in.

The informed consent for testosterone! J tried to sound nonchalant. "Okay, where is it?"

The envelope was big and much too heavy for a single letter. It was filled with the college applications J had left behind, along with a note. *You need to fill these out and write your essays*, Carolina had written. J's stomach turned a little at the sight of her handwriting. If he were at home, she would be helping him. *Some are due at the end of the month.*

There was no *I love you*, no word about his father, and no parental approval for testosterone. What was going on uptown? Had Carolina talked to Manny? Had his father disowned him? J shoved the envelope under his sleeping bag.

"Daniel and I broke up," Melissa said. She was doing her ballet exercises, using a bookshelf as a barre.

"That was quick."

"No quicker than usual," Melissa said, kicking out her foot in tiny sweeps. "I hate men."

J shot her a look.

"What?" Melissa said defensively. "You know that."

"Then why do you screw them?"

"J!" Melissa stopped her kicking and put her hands on her hips. "What's wrong with you? First you run away, and then you become a dickhead?"

J mumbled an apology. He couldn't withstand another fight. "So, why'd you break up?"

Melissa went back to her barre exercises. "He bored me. He only talked about himself."

J flopped back on Melissa's bed and watched her practice. He knew she'd have fresh razor cuts under the sleeves of her sweatshirt. She was way too calm for a breakup. "You were right; he was pretentious." Melissa smiled at J and brushed a curl out of her eyes. "I think I need an older man."

"How much older?"

"Forty sounds about right."

J laughed. Melissa had her batch of problems, too. She came and joined him on the bed, with a bag of cookies.

"Want some? Only ten calories each, but they give you diarrhea."

"Gross."

"J—" Melissa started, then stopped to examine her cookie. "Why'd your mom bring you here? She was so worried about you—she called me four hundred times a day. I thought that once you came back, she'd lock the door and never let you out."

"Why didn't she call me, then?" Saying it aloud made him realize how truly alone he'd felt over the weekend.

"I think the cops told her not to—they didn't want you to run farther away. They wanted to use me as bait." Melissa laughed. "Because I'm such a hot catch."

J didn't say anything.

"Really, J, why aren't you at home?"

"I think my dad's mad at me." J picked cat hairs off Melissa's comforter.

" 'Cause you ran away?"

"Yeah, and—" Was he ready to tell her? J took a giant swallow. "Have you ever heard the word *trans-gender*?"

Melissa looked at him blandly. "Yeah."

"That's what I am."

"Okay."

"*Okay?*" J said, astounded. Melissa looked as though he'd just told her his shoe was untied.

"Give me a minute to process," Melissa said. She pulled back her sleeve and prodded a fresh cut. When she saw J watching, she quickly covered it again. "I've never seen you naked."

"What do you mean?" J was startled.

"I mean, in all our years of friendship, I just realized, I've never seen you naked, and you've seen me naked hundreds of times."

"Yeah?"

"Yeah, well, it's not really fair. I think you should let me see you naked."

"What?" J scooted back against the wall and pulled his knees up in front of his chest. "I'm not taking off my clothes for you!"

"Why not?" Melissa asked, her voice rising. "Don't you trust me?"

J felt like a rat in a cage. The apartment was so small and stuffy, and he was literally backed into a corner. Had his best friend lost her mind? "M, what are you doing?"

Melissa had jumped off the bed and was removing her dance tights and sweatshirt. J was right; there were fresh cuts on both arms. Then off came the tank top and bra, and she was standing in the middle of the room stark naked, arms outstretched.

"J, here's my body, every inch, and yes, I cut, so what?" Melissa was practically shouting now. "You've seen it before. If your body's so different from mine, I want to see it!"

J hung his head, dropping his forehead into the crook of his elbow. "My body's not any different from yours," he said softly. "You don't understand."

The tears, so long in coming, suddenly choked at the back of J's throat. His body trembled, and he cried softly into his crossed arms. Melissa didn't understand, his mother didn't understand, Blue didn't understand, even he himself didn't understand. No matter what, no matter how many photographs he took, or T-shirts he piled on, or attitudes he adopted, underneath it all his body would look just like Melissa's.

He felt Melissa gently stroking his back. "J, I'm sorry," she said. "I thought you said you were transgender."

J sniffed. He wiped his nose on his sleeve and nodded into his forearm.

"Doesn't that mean your body is different?"

"More like my brain," J said. He felt exhausted.

"I don't think I've ever seen you cry before," Melissa said. She was still stroking his back.

"Lucky you."

"And you've seen me cry so much." Melissa sat back and put her hands in her lap. "It's almost shocking to see you cry."

"Can we stop broadcasting it?"

"Sorry," Melissa said. She had put her sweatshirt back on, along with a pair of sweats she'd grabbed from the floor. She maneuvered around so she was sitting behind him, gently pushing him forward on the bed. "Move over," she said. "I want to spoon."

J scooted a few inches and let Melissa hold him. He shut his eyes and almost wished the tears would come again, if only to drain the grief from his body. And, besides, Melissa was behind him and couldn't see. But the tear ducts were sealed again, so he took a deep breath and tried to relax into her warmth. A twitching in his belly made him want to jump up and pee or smoke a cigarette or something, but another part of him wanted to forget everything that had just happened and simply be four arms, four legs, and two bellies, all curled up together, breathing in sync.

"Melis?" he asked.

"Yeah?"

"Can you remember being a baby?"

"Ummm, I don't think so." Melissa tucked her feet around his. "Why?"

"I just want to go back and start over."

Melissa ran her hand over J's forehead, slowly rubbed his temple.

J was so tired, but he continued. "I think it would have felt like this, being a baby."

"Maybe. If you were a twin."

J didn't say that Melissa seemed more like a mother to him right then, as she pulled the down comforter over them both. He couldn't say how much he missed his own mother, even though Carolina was more of a "do your homework" type mom than a tucking-in type mom. He was sure that Carolina had held him when he was little, and he wanted to go back. Back before he had anything to explain, before best friends couldn't understand you, before the stakes were all so high.

And yet as Melissa continued to rub his head, he remembered that she could, at times like this, give him precisely what he needed. Sometimes, when she didn't pressure him to talk or when she was especially contrite after one of her crazy outbursts, Melissa was the best sanctuary he knew. Melissa, with her gross bag of cookies and the cuts on her arms and her big dreams of dancing, was just as broken and hopeful as he was, and here they were, marooned in a sea of goose feathers, up against the world.

"J," Melissa whispered. "I have to go to rehearsal. But you can sleep in my bed."

J didn't know what Melissa was rehearsing for, but

he watched her throw leg warmers and an iPod and the rest of the cookies into her backpack, fumbling around in the dark. He nodded when she told him Karyn wouldn't be home 'til late. Once the door clicked shut, J crawled into his own sleeping bag on the floor, shut his eyes tight against the darkness, and fell asleep.

School was getting easier, in its own way. J had decided to view his classes, and his classmates, as an anthropological study. He would be the neutral, silent monitor sent to observe a strange planet of noisy misfits. He'd watch the mating rituals of *Homosexualis homosapianus* and report back to the fans in his head with fake Latin and a bad British accent. That was the plan he made with himself as he walked to school, stopping only to gaze at the expensive cameras in an electronics shop window. In the reflection, he thought he saw a person with blue hair across the street, watching him, but when he turned she was gone. It wasn't Blue, couldn't be. He was imagining things. He felt bad about their argument in the coffee shop but didn't know how to make things better. There were just too many things Blue would never understand about him, too wide a gulf to cross with language. When he was buying a pastry at a coffee cart, it happened again, though: he thought he saw a flash of blue whisk around a corner. He knew, from his experience with his own body, that a wish was powerful, but this was weird. Was he wishing Blue would show up in his life, the way he showed up in hers? Maybe that was it. He wanted her back, but he didn't want to work so hard for everything all the time.

J forgot about the imaginary Blue sightings as he settled into his life skills class, the most boring one of the day. He tuned out his teacher's voice and stared instead at the students. "The male of the species performs an unusual mating ritual," J said to himself, imagining a nature channel filming his classroom. "Ignoring the elder's attempts to teach him the survival technique of filling out a job application at Wendy's, the male stands up and swivels his hips. Note the elaborate dress: multicolored bracelets, and pants low on the buttocks that reveal expensive undergarments.

"Look! The male has caught the attention of a potential mate! The subordinate male stays seated and imitates a female dancer popular with other young *Homosexualis homosapianus*. Our young males make eye contact, which means the mating ritual will continue with a hand job in the fifth-floor bathroom. Very rare footage indeed."

A note landed on J's desk. It was from Chanelle: I'M DYING HERE. COFFEE LATER?

J turned and nodded. Nature documentary to be continued.

Chanelle and J walked to the coffeeshop near the school.

"What do you think of Rivera?" Chanelle asked J once they'd settled with their drinks.

"The school? It's okay."

"It's ri-tit-ulous," Chanelle answered. "But I'm starting college classes soon."

"Ri-*what*?" J asked.

"Oh. Ri-tit-ulous," Chanelle said, tucking a stray hair behind her ear. "I don't like how the dick gets so much play, even in language, so I don't say *ridiculous*. I'm a feminist."

J chuckled. He thought Melissa and Chanelle would probably get along.

"So, have you started your transition?"

Wow, this girl was forward, J thought. He wanted to tell her that was kind of personal, but Chanelle pushed on.

"I mean, are you taking hormones?"

"No."

"Do you want to? I've been taking hormones forever. I mean, like since I was sixteen."

"How?" The question came out like a pistol shot.

"What do you mean, how? I get a pill, I swallow it. I get a syringe, I shoot it."

J shifted in his seat. "I mean, how can you get the hormones if you're only sixteen?"

Chanelle rolled her eyes. "I'm not sixteen *now*. I'm twenty. I used to get my hormones at parties, but now I get them at the free clinic, legally."

"Where are the parties?" J imagined the apartment where Melissa kissed Daniel, but instead of being filled with typical New York City teenagers drinking themselves into stupors, transgender men and women sat around magically growing beards or breasts while nurses poked them with syringes.

"Oh, they were just dance clubs, where you could pay someone for a shot. But they were for the girls. I don't know where the boys go." J's face fell, along with his fantasy. Chanelle continued. "I hate it that the transwomen and transmen are so separate all the time. That's why I talked to you. You seemed different."

J didn't know about this gender separation, or about dance clubs for transgirls; he didn't know very much at all. If Chanelle recognized his ignorance, she probably wouldn't think he was so cool anymore, so he just nodded in agreement.

"Do you think the estrogen's working well enough?" Chanelle asked, turning her body to the side and sticking out her chest. "I've been doing this for almost four years, and I'm still barely a B."

J felt embarrassed to cast his eyes so blatantly. Why would anyone want the damn things? Chanelle could have his. "You look good," he mumbled.

"I wish my boyfriend thought so," Chanelle said, facing forward again and dramatically casting her palm to her forehead. "Don't look so surprised!"

"It's just—" *I thought you were flirting with me.*

"You don't think I'm pretty enough to have a boyfriend?"

"No!" J said. "Why doesn't your boyfriend like your—them?"

"Honestly? I think it's about his own self-loathing. That's what my therapist thinks. And my moms. Well, my foster moms. He's insecure because he needs a woman to validate his masculinity. Bigger boobs would make him a bigger man. It's rititulous."

"Whoa."

"I know. Everybody thinks I should break up with him. But we love each other, you know?"

J didn't.

"Are you seeing anybody?"

"Sort of." J tried to explain his situation with Blue, but when he got to the part about their argument in Starbucks, he couldn't remember why or how it had all unraveled. The story seemed petty and childish in front of Chanelle, with all her sophistication and experience.

"You should just call her, tell her you love her," Chanelle said.

"I don't know."

"Don't know if you love her or if you should?"

"Both."

"Does she know you're trans?"

J shook his head.

"Well, don't tell her." Chanelle straightened her back and made her mouth a straight line. "That always messes things up. A lover will drop you in a quick minute if she knows you're trans. Unless she's a lesbian. Lesbians love their transmen. Gay men hate transwomen, but gay women love the daddies. It's really not fair."

J liked that word, *lover*. It sounded so adult. Would he be able to be Blue's lover and keep his clothes on? And how did Chanelle know so much, how were her categories so clear and well defined? Maybe she was running her own nature documentary, too, and was just a better observer. J thanked Chanelle for her advice and went outside to call Blue.

Blue didn't pick up, and J didn't know what to say into her voice mail. *By the way, I love you?* He had never been good at messages. He wished he could go home and hang out with Titi for a while, space out on the computer, make himself a bowl of cereal. After yesterday's episode with Melissa, he wasn't eager to go back to her place, and he found himself walking aimlessly for a while. After about ten blocks, he realized where his legs were taking him: back to the clinic, where he'd gone asking about testosterone. Today was the day they were giving out shots.

J hoped Janet the pencil twirler wouldn't be there when he walked into the waiting room. He needn't have worried; the place was packed with men. *Blending with the muscular urge*, J thought. He pulled his cap lower to shield his eyes, picked up a magazine, and proceeded to stare around the room.

Some of the guys looked younger than he did, with the soft, chubby faces of childhood and clothes even baggier than J's. These kids sat far apart from one another and texted into their phones or fiddled with their iPods. Two guys who looked slightly older sat next to each other and were laughing about something private; one had a bike wheel in his hand, and the other had thick tribal tattoos snaking up both forearms. There were black, white, and Latino men in the room, and two Asian guys—one fat and one skinny. A few were businessmen straight from work, with their shirt-sleeves rolled up and briefcases nearby, but most were dressed casually. There was one full-on cowboy, with a hat and a Western shirt; he seemed to have fallen asleep.

I wouldn't spook one of these guys, J thought. *Nobody looks like he was born a girl.* The laughing teenagers in the back were talking about some TV show, and their voices sounded deep and authentic. Something ached in J's stomach—it was like a clench and a pull at once. *I need you,* he thought. But who was he talking to? No one in the room particularly caught his eye, though each man was interesting in his own way. *I need you,* he thought again. The voice was insistent. *I need.*

J wanted to run away and also to stay and stare and kick something. These men weren't pictures on the Internet; they were breathing, talking, reading, living. What if Carolina really did write him a letter? He would be a man in this room, he would be a man.

I hate her, J thought, suddenly vicious. *She stops me from everything. I was probably born female because she wanted a girl. She probably prayed for it.*

J knew he was thinking crazy, but this room was so overwhelming. What was a girl, really? It was just a word, one stupid, horrible little word. If there wasn't a word for male and female, would everyone just be a person? Would that be easier?

"Ian?" someone called from the corridor. The cowboy shook his head from his nap and got up.

J watched him walk. His stride was loose—not quite the bowling-ball look of the guys from his neighborhood but, still, this guy had a definite bulge beneath his silver belt buckle. Was that a sock? A fake penis? Had Ian had surgery?

Is that what made a guy? Chanelle thought dicks were overrated, but then again, she probably had one. *When I was a baby, I didn't hate myself. I only started when I learned I was a girl.* A sadness trailed through J's belly like a thick steam; he felt queasy. *I learned to hate my body because of other people.* And then that implacable thought again: *I need you.*

What if, on his own private nature channel, breasts were suddenly male anatomical parts? If all the guys on his corner strutted around showing off their chests as though it were manly to have big titties? Would he want to destroy his breasts then?

Then we'd walk on water and fish would fly. I'm definitely crazy. Chanelle had a therapist; she'd mentioned it earlier as though it was no big deal. He didn't know anyone else who saw a shrink, but so what? Maybe someone here at this clinic could help him sort out whether he had to change his body or his brain. Neither one was cooperating very well anymore.

J managed to stay out late enough to avoid talking to Melissa for a few days, but by the time the weekend hit, Melissa jumped on his sleeping bag and rolled him around like a trapped worm.

"Ow!"

"Get up; it's already ten!" Melissa was wearing J's favorite pajamas, and she'd tied her hair into about thirty tiny ponytails springing out of her head in all directions. "I'm making you pancakes."

Melissa was a terrible cook; even when she boiled eggs, they tasted burned. "I'm afraid," J said. He sat up and pulled a sweatshirt from his bag.

"Good morning, J," Karyn said brightly, emerging from the bathroom and swiping on some lipstick. "Aren't we looking gorgeous this morning?"

J managed a smile and glanced at himself in the alcove mirror. He had an imprint from the sleeping-bag zipper cutting across one cheek and drool crusted around his mouth.

"Want pancakes, Karyn?" Melissa called out. She never called her "Mom."

"No, I'm meeting a study group. Don't burn the place," she said. Karyn grabbed her bag and keys and was turning the doorknob when she spun back around. "Oh, and, J, I'm so proud of you."

J looked at Karyn, surprised. Karyn took a few steps and held J's chin in her hand, as if he were a misbehaving dog. But she was smiling. "It's because you're a Capricorn. You're so determined, but vulnerable underneath. It makes perfect sense." She patted J's cheek and left.

"What was that about?" J asked, though he had a feeling. He couldn't trust Melissa to shut up about anything.

"I had to tell her, J; she studies psychology. And she was totally cool. Obviously." Melissa was using a turkey baster to squirt pancake batter into a pan. She shaped out the letter *M*, but it quickly dissipated into a batter blob. The kitchen was filled with smoke from her earlier attempts, now piled in the trash. "I hate cooking."

"Let me do it." J turned down the flame and used two spatulas to flip Melissa's giant pancake. He added some butter, which he found at the back of the fridge.

"Do you know how many calories that is?" Melissa shrieked.

"You need something to keep it from sticking," J said calmly.

Melissa covered her eyes. "I can't watch."

*   *   *

The pancakes were disgusting; Melissa hadn't used sugar or butter and had substituted water for milk. Batter was all over the counter and stuck in Melissa's hair, and she picked at the tasteless cakes, made somewhat more palatable with sugar-free jam.

"I'm sorry these are so gross; I wanted to make you something special," Melissa said, spooning out more jam.

"Why?"

"Because! You totally saved my performance. We're going up in three months."

"What are you talking about?" J poured himself some coffee. At least that tasted normal.

"I told you. I got a solo with Becky's performance group. She rented out a space in Bed-Stuy, and everyone is dancing their own work."

J had no idea who Becky was, but he let Melissa ramble on.

"Anyway, it's for one night, and it's called 'Threshold.' Everyone interprets that in their own way. I'm interpreting you. Isn't that perfect?"

"Perfect." J was designing his pancake remnants into a smiley face on his plate.

"No, J, listen. I talked to my mom. She'd read all about you in psychology class."

"About me?"

"Not about *you*, about transgender, fool. And it's

really cool. Think about it—a girl becomes a guy in a dance. At the threshold—I think the music will stop—this boy comes out of the girl's body and is free. It's totally threshold. And the costumes could be amazing."

J was silent.

"Becky thinks it's a great idea. She's helping me with the choreography, but I want it to be really mine."

"Who's Becky?"

"She used to dance with Sisyphus—that company I took you to see, when you fell asleep?" Melissa picked at the pancake batter in her hair. "J, are you okay?"

"It's just—you're talking about my life."

"I thought you'd be honored." Melissa looked hurt. "Doesn't this show I'm fine with you being transgender? I mean, I messed up the other night. I thought you meant intersex—but I read all about it, and I know the difference now. I was stupid. J, I'm sorry I took off my clothes and everything."

"It's okay." As usual with Melissa, he felt the conversation going in too many directions at once.

"But now I get it—I get the photograph you sent me. And I'm going to use it in my dance. I'll project it onto a big screen behind me."

Melissa continued, but J stopped listening. His photograph of the jackhammer would be seen in public? He barely showed anyone his photos, let alone something so private.

"And that's the threshold, right?" Melissa asked. "Isn't it, J?"

"Um, I wasn't listening."

"J! We're talking about my art! This is important!"

J looked at his empty coffee cup. "Why don't you dance about your cutting? That's a threshold."

Melissa pouted. "Why? That's stupid."

"It's a threshold between life and death. Cut deeper, and you'll die."

Melissa got up from the table and started splashing dishes around in the sink. He could tell she was angry. "Why when we're talking about *you* do you always have to turn it around and talk about *me*?" she asked.

"Okay, let's talk about me," J said, standing up. "Do you really understand transgender, M? Are you really cool with it? Or did you just read about it in a book and think it would make a cool dance? Have you asked me anything, like how it feels to be transgender, how it feels to be me?"

"Fine, J," Melissa said, shaking soapy water from her hands. "How does it feel to be you?"

"Like shit."

"Articulate, as usual," Melissa shot back.

"I know you couldn't dance it," J said.

"Yes, I could," Melissa said. Her voice softened, and she wiped her soapy hands on a towel. "I don't want to fight. I'm proud of you, and this will be a beautiful dance. I've known you for, like, a third of my life. That's a long time. But everything you've ever done is on the inside of you, inside your own head. Your photography is amazing, but you don't show it to anyone. I'm different; I need to express." Melissa paused, trying to get her thoughts in order. "This boy or transgender or whatever part of you makes sense to me, because I know you so well. But that's been inside of you, too, deep inside, for a long time. So I'm the one who can express it for you, onstage. See?"

J took a long breath. "Can I smoke in here?"

Melissa opened the window, and a gust of winter air blew in. J lit a cigarette. "Thank you."

"You're welcome," Melissa said. Her eyes were glittering. "See, you're like my muse. And I'm the artist. You're the model, and I'm Michelangelo."

J felt like throwing up, Melissa could be so obnoxious. "I meant thank you for letting me smoke."

"Oh."

How could he explain to her that he was not somebody's muse, or a puppet, or a toy? How could he explain that she couldn't begin to understand his life if most days even he couldn't understand? And he was pretty sure Melissa didn't understand herself, either. Nobody did. Except for, maybe, Buddha or something. Being trans wasn't special, and yet it was. It was just good and bad and interesting and fucked-up and very human, like anything else.

J couldn't get any coherent words out but, as usual, Melissa still could. "Okay," she said, squaring her shoulders, "if you were choreographing a dance about being transgender, what would you do?"

"I'd probably just sit there."

"Why? I mean, I was looking at you sleeping this morning and I had this idea for a butterfly, except I guess it would have to be more male. Like, first you're in a cocoon as a girl, and then you emerge as a boy."

"It's not like that," J said. *I'm not a bug*, he thought. *No matter how much you want to dissect me. And who does that? Just* poof! *Becomes himself in one day.* Still, Melissa was trying. He didn't want to be a total jerk. "I mean, for me."

"Why?"

"I've kind of already emerged," he said. *Why can't you see what's right in front of your face?* "I'm staying here, aren't I?"

"But my mom said transgender people have surgery, and then they become the other gender." Melissa looked genuinely confused.

"No," J said. He balled up his fists and rubbed his eyes. "It's harder than that. It's like I've always been male, I think. Surgery's just one part; it doesn't fix everything." He sighed, trying to find the words to make her understand. "Does cutting change everything for you?"

"It helps," Melissa said, getting red. "Why are you so obsessed with that?"

"Okay, so surgery helps. But that's not the threshold. I'm, like, at a fucking threshold all the time."

Melissa stared at him. She seemed to be adding something in her head. "Well, then, what's the point when you become male?"

"Melissa, don't you listen? I always have been!" He stubbed out his cigarette and got softer. Maybe she'd understand if he mentioned her romantic side; girls got that. "That's why you liked me sometimes."

Melissa looked stumped. "Crap. Now I don't know what to do with this dance."

"Think about the cutting," J said. *Focus on yourself. You do all the time, anyway.* "Maybe if you make a dance about it, you won't have to do it anymore."

"God, J, you're always talking about the cutting," Melissa whined. "It's just not that easy."

"Neither is being trans."

"Okay, J," Melissa said. "Point taken." She balled

up her tights and her leg warmers and left for rehearsal without saying good-bye.

J sat for a long time on Melissa's bed, petting one of the cats. She purred when he rubbed behind her ears, tilting up her chin, directing him. He loved animals; they never judged, never threw you out, never wanted to dance your life story on a stage. He leaned back into Melissa's pillows, smelled her cinnamon-ish Melissa smell. Why had he been in love with her for so long? Yes, she had protected him when he was younger, and, true, she was loyal, but a real girlfriend has to understand you. Melissa was more like an older sister, a nosy, bossy one, even though they were the same age. There were things he couldn't tell her. Like, he couldn't tell her about Blue.

Blue had understood him. She hadn't known he was trans, but so what? She had drawn his portrait, asked him important questions, looked deep into his eyes. She saw him as a man, so she really saw him. Nobody else had done that. Why had he screwed everything up? Blue wouldn't try to choreograph his weirdness; she would just paint him as he was, and he would take her picture. They would have a good life together, get an apartment in Brooklyn, go to the same college. They would have some cats, name them Green and Red, for variety.

He'd called her so many times since Chanelle gave him her advice. He'd left one message, a stupid one, saying, "It's J, call me," but she *knew* by now he wasn't great with words. And she never picked up. He couldn't call again; how desperate could he look? Still, he knew, if only he had a girlfriend right now, if only he had Blue, his life would be okay.

CHAPTER
TEN

J had been staying with Melissa and Karyn for five full
weeks before Carolina called, saying she wanted to see
him and take him out for an early birthday. She had
phoned a few times, now and then, to ask if he needed
fresh clothes or money, but they didn't talk about anything real, and neither of them mentioned Manny. J
told his new shrink about the call.

The shrink's name was Philip, and he was a dark-
skinned man in his late twenties, with glasses and wrist
braces on both arms. It was Chanelle who had made J
go. Even though J felt at times that his brain was just

as duplicitous as his body, talking to a stranger about his problems seemed idiotic. Still, Chanelle promised him, there was no way around the psychiatric requirement.

"Biological women can get titties out to here," Chanelle had said, waving her arms in front of her chest, "and nobody will tell them they're crazy. But a transperson needs a few little hormones, and we've gotta sit in a chair for three months."

Chanelle and J had taken to climbing the stairs in the school building after class, five flights at a time, and then a cigarette break on the roof. Chanelle called it her "exercise." J said he'd just wait until he turned eighteen, then; it was coming up the next month.

"Doesn't matter," Chanelle said, peeling off her sweater and tying it around her waist. "Everybody has to see a shrink. They're the gatekeepers."

J worried that all this stair climbing would give him a bigger butt. He stopped on a landing. "Can't you fake a letter from a shrink?"

Chanelle kept climbing. "If you're too chicken to see a shrink, you're too chicken to get on T," she said. He couldn't see her anymore, but her voice echoed through the stairwell.

J told himself he wasn't afraid, exactly, but he felt embarrassed when he made the appointment at the clinic, embarrassed when he first walked into the office, and embarrassed when Philip asked J to tell him something about his life during the first visit.

How'd you injure both wrists? J wanted to ask, looking at the braces. *Were you strangling a patient?* J didn't know what to say.

"Let's start with why you're here," Philip prodded. He sat back in his chair and brought his fingers to his chin. Poking out from the braces, they looked like lobster claws.

"I just want testosterone," J said.

Philip looked at him.

"I mean, I want to get shots here." J thought of the transmen in the waiting room. He worried about how long it would take before he could get all the people to sign the right forms and start the damn shots. Sitting in front of Philip, J felt sure of his decision again, almost desperate for the hormones that would change his voice, his face, his muscles, his life.

Philip explained the process. He said every patient was different, but once he got to know J and could determine that hormones would indeed be appropriate, he could write a letter that would approve him for testosterone—likely in about three months.

"But," Philip said, settling a lobster claw in his lap, "testosterone is not magic. It doesn't fix your life. That's why therapy is a good idea—to help you with everything else you have going on."

Three months! J hadn't wanted to believe that terrible number when he'd heard it originally; he thought somehow with him it would be different. The first day with Philip, the timeline was all J could focus on, and it took most of his energy not to run from the room and kick over some garbage cans outside. Philip asked him questions about his mom, his dad, his childhood, and J was resolutely mum: Lobster Man was a gatekeeper, and that was it. J wouldn't spill.

Over a month of sessions, though, J started to tell Philip little things. Stupid things. Like the fact that Blue still hadn't returned the messages he'd left asking if he could see her. And he told Philip when Carolina wanted to take J out to dinner before his birthday.

"Do you want to go?" Philip asked.

"She's my mom; I have to."

Philip had a way of making J feel that he had more options than he really did. This just pissed him off.

"How do you feel about not celebrating your birthday at home?"

How do you feel about having claws for fingers? J glared at him.

"She doesn't want me there," J said finally, thinking, *All of this for hormones? Isn't there something called cruel and unusual punishment?* "Is that what you want me to say?"

"You don't know that," Philip said. "How would you feel if you went home?"

"A mess, Philip," J said, looking at the clock. "I'd feel a mess."

They met at a Chinese restaurant near Melissa's place. Carolina hugged J quickly; she still smelled like the hospital.

"You look...different," Carolina said, staring closely at J's face. "You're growing out the razor stripes?"

J had taken off his cap in the restaurant, before his mom even asked.

"How's Pops?" *Damn*, J thought. He had meant to wait until Carolina brought him up.

"Let's order," Carolina said. She picked up the menu and scanned it. "You're still good with mu shu pork?"

J said he wasn't hungry and, really, his stomach was a slick and tangled rope. His mother looked different, too—more tired, maybe, her hair pulled back into a sloppy bun at the back of her neck.

"We've missed you, J," Carolina said, finally, once the food had come and they'd made their way through the "how's school, how's Melissa, fine, fine, fine" babble that J couldn't stand. "Your dad and me both."

"I miss you, too."

"J—" Carolina put down her chopsticks. "Your dad's not ready."

"Ready for what?" The rope in his stomach tightened.

"I tried to explain, and he just can't hear it. He's angry right now."

"At me?"

"Oh, Jay-jay, at himself, I think. He thinks we did something wrong raising you."

J felt mean, cruel even, the rope inside rising up into a noose around his neck. Who was his father to say he couldn't come home? It was his apartment, too. When J took T, he could fight his father. J was younger—his muscles would be younger, too, and more resilient. "Maybe you did."

Carolina's eyes bulged. J pictured Manny sitting there in his mother's place. What kind of wimp was he to send Carolina as his mouthpiece? His father couldn't even speak for himself? "You don't own me, you know."

"J, I am your *mother*. Don't use that tone with me." Carolina's voice was strong, but she looked as though she'd been slapped.

"I'm just saying," J said, backing down. He looked at his plate. "That maybe some of this is your fault."

"How?" Carolina's eyes were fierce.

"Maybe you weren't home enough." J knew he was lying, but he had to lunge at something. How could Manny be mad at *him*? J had done nothing wrong. The food on his plate smelled like sewage.

"All those swim meets, J? That wasn't enough? And the math competitions in New Jersey? And the new cameras? And the computer? And driving you to that camp? And taking you to Puerto Rico? And washing your clothes, buying your food, *giving you life*? This is not enough?" Carolina's face was red, and a family at the next table was openly staring. "J, until you're a mother yourself, you won't understand."

They both sat with the weight of Carolina's mistake.

"Or a father," Carolina finally said, weakly.

"Fathers suck," J said.

"J!" Carolina said, slapping the table. "Do not disrespect your father!"

"Okay," J mumbled, miserably tying his napkin into a knot. But how was he supposed to respect Manny when Manny didn't even give him a chance? He remembered a night in the kitchen, not too long ago, when he and his father were home alone. Manny had been drinking and, for some reason, felt like talking. He was complaining about the union members, how they didn't show up for meetings anymore, how he couldn't get them excited about the things that really mattered. He'd turned on J, asking him what he would do in his shoes.

"Bring food," J had suggested, thinking of the activists at his school. They always ordered pizza if they wanted people to join their groups. He thought it was a good idea.

But Manny scoffed. "That's such a woman's response! Cook something. Food doesn't get us pensions, J."

He'd been deeply stung, but of course he couldn't tell his father why. He didn't think pizza had a gender, but he watched his words more carefully, testing his sentences before he spoke them, for any whiff of femininity. And he knew his father didn't really care about his thoughts or feelings, anyway; for Manny, J was just a blank wall for him to splat his rage against and see what it looked like hanging there.

At least Carolina tried. She listened to him. He looked at her watching him expectantly from across the table. Her face was strained.

"So, what do you want me to do?" J asked. His mother, he decided, he should try to respect.

"Just wait," Carolina said. "We'll all get used to this."

I've been waiting my whole life, J thought. *Pops knows who I am; he'd have known a long time ago if he'd taken the time to notice.* "So I can't come home?"

"It's not a good idea, not yet," Carolina said. "Things are still fine at Melissa's, right?"

J didn't answer. He just shook his head when the waitress asked if he wanted to take his leftovers home.

"Happy almost-birthday, J," Carolina said, brightening her tone. "This is the big one."

J nodded.

Carolina rummaged through her purse. "Buy yourself something special."

She pulled a fifty-dollar bill from her wallet. This was normal; ever since middle school, when his parents could no longer decipher his musical or clothing tastes, they'd given him money for his birthdays. But usually there was a card. And cake. And Manny. His absence felt physical, like a thick weight hovering nearby. J and Carolina stared at the cash. Finally J pocketed it and stood up. He thanked her, gave her a quick kiss on the cheek.

"And, J?" Carolina reached into her purse again. She handed him an envelope: here was the card. "Be careful."

J knew what it was before he opened it, but still he waited until he was back at Melissa's before he broke the envelope's seal. Melissa was at dance rehearsal, and Karyn was at a night class, so J turned off all the lights and wriggled into his sleeping bag. He felt somehow that too much illumination would make the envelope's contents crumble. It was like a whisper or a secret—better done in the dark. And he could still see enough from the street lamp outside.

And suddenly there it was—folded up inside a card that said *You're Special* (they must not have had any birthday cards at the hospital gift shop) was a note from his mom, saying he could take testostoerone; she gave her full permission. And her signature, clear and clean at the bottom, in dark blue ink. J breathed in deeply and touched his mother's signature with the tip of his finger.

You're too late, J thought. *I'm almost eighteen. I don't need this anymore.*

He gently folded the letter and put it back in the envelope. Then he found his cell phone and dialed his mother's number. She didn't pick up. So he texted her. *Gracias.*

When J was younger, he hated that his birthday fell so close to Christmas. His parents never had much money at that time of year, because they were busy buying Christmas presents for all of Carolina's family in San

Juan, and it seemed silly to throw a big celebration three days before Santa would come and they'd have to do it all again. This year, though, J was grateful. While the rest of the city was consumed with the twenty-fifth of December, J could quietly slip into adulthood without fanfare. It seemed nobody but Melissa knew the occasion.

School was out for winter break, and J woke up to Karyn and Melissa whistling "Happy Birthday" above his sleeping bag. He rubbed his eyes and sat up. Melissa was holding a cupcake with a candle stuffed in it, and Karyn was grinning.

"Make a wish!" she said.

Testosterone was the first thing he thought of. *Let them approve me for my shot.* He blew out the flame, and Karyn and Melissa clapped.

On the kitchen table were three presents, all the identical size, wrapped in newspaper.

"We didn't have anything prettier," Karyn apologized, handing him a cup of coffee.

"That's okay." He was touched she was home, and a little embarrassed.

"Open them!" Melissa said, plopping into a chair and tucking her legs beneath her.

J carefully untied the first present, setting the red ribbon on the table next to the messy pile of college applications that he was sure, by now, was getting in the way. He peeled back the newspaper to reveal the edge of a black picture frame.

"Just rip it," Melissa said.

He did, and there was his photograph of his shadow and the jackhammer—framed, matted, and professional.

"Wow," he breathed. He'd never framed one of his pictures before.

"We thought we could hang it up here," Karyn said. "Until you go to college and want to take it with you."

J looked at her. There was so much to think: Melissa had, once again, broadcast one of his private messages to her mother; his photo looked, well, it looked beautiful, almost spooky-good, matted and framed; and Karyn was talking about him staying for a really long time. Had she spoken to Carolina? Did his parents really not want him back?

"Thanks," he mustered.

"The other presents are the same—they just don't have any pictures in them," Melissa gushed, bobbing up and down.

"Melissa!" Karyn said, popping her daughter lightly on the head. "You're not supposed to give it away."

She was right; the other two gifts were empty frames—perfect, Melissa said, for showcasing more of J's work. "You can't just keep your pictures stored on

CDs," Melissa said. "You're an adult now. Time to act like a professional."

J cut his cupcake into thirds, and they ate. He wanted to ask how serious Karyn was about staying until the fall, but, as usual, she had to rush to class.

While Melissa was in the shower and J smoked his first cigarette as a true adult, his phone rang. Carolina.

"¡Feliz cumpleaños!"

"Thanks," J said, taking a long drag. He was sitting outside on the front stoop, and his butt was freezing.

"Are you having a good day?"

"I guess."

"I can't believe you're eighteen, Jay-jay," Carolina said. "I remember the day you were born."

J looked at the icicles that had formed on the tree overnight; Carolina went through this every year. J had been such a big baby; she and Manny were so excited; there was so much ice on the sidewalk, Manny didn't want her to slip walking to the corner for a cab, but the car service took half an hour to get there, blah, blah, blah.

"Your father wants to wish you a happy birthday."

What? J's cigarette froze in space, midway to his mouth.

"J, are you there?"

He mumbled out a "yes," and took another drag. He wasn't ready for this.

"Hi, J." His father sounded funny. His voice was deeper than usual—stern, serious. And the accent wasn't right. He lingered on the "J" a bit too long.

"Hi."

"Happy birthday."

It had only been a little less than two months; could a person forget his father's voice in such a short time? A terrible thought scuttled through: *this wasn't his father.* Carolina had asked a favor of someone—a friend, a coworker: "Just say 'happy birthday.' J will never know the difference." Was Carolina capable of such deception? Did she think J was a fool, a baby?

"Thanks," J said.

"Here's your mother."

Where was *Mami*? His father always called her *Mami.* If that was Manny, he would have said, "Here's Mami." What the hell was going on? J felt a kind of panic rise in his throat. And his mother was back on the line, happily asking him how he was going to spend his day.

"I want to talk to Pops again."

Carolina paused. "He just left for work."

"He can't have left that fast," J said. Was she lying to him? "He was just there."

"He was walking out the door, J. He just wanted to

tell you 'happy birthday.' " Now Carolina's voice sounded defensive, clipped.

J lit another cigarette. "When am I going to come home, Mami? What's going on over there?"

Carolina sighed loudly into the phone. "J, I told you at the restaurant. Your father's not ready."

"Not ready for what?"

"Not ready for you, J. You're the one who decided to do this." Carolina hesitated a moment and then said, "I don't want to talk about this again. It's your birthday."

"I do. What is Pops saying?" *And who was that guy on the phone?*

Carolina's voice got softer. "He thinks I'm coddling you."

"Coddling *me*?" J felt his face grow hot. "You're the one who kicked me out!"

"You ran away!" Carolina yelled back. "You started this whole thing."

J wondered when his mother had become such a child. There was something she was hiding; he was sure of it.

"J, look," Carolina said, softer now. "You're fine where you are. I've worked everything out with Karyn."

"What do you mean?"

"With rent. She's a student, she needs the money, she—"

J stopped listening. So this *was* going to be a long-term thing, and Karyn was boarding him because she needed the cash. He was just a puppet. His mother wasn't budging on his father's real perspective (maybe he'd disowned J; he'd never know) and she was hiring stand-ins to deliver birthday greetings. Pitiful, he thought, plain pitiful. He hung up the phone and didn't pick up when Carolina called back.

J spent Christmas indoors, feeling sorry for himself. Karyn was a pagan, but she made a ham for dinner before scuttling out the door to study, and Melissa had a rehearsal. *Who has a rehearsal on Christmas?* J had grumbled. But Melissa had said that the Bed-Stuy space was empty over the holidays and they could book free hours. He tried calling Chanelle, but she was in New Jersey visiting her foster mom's family.

Chanelle called him back and said she was sad, too. Her boyfriend, Bonez, hadn't gotten her anything for Christmas. For someone who claimed to be "over men and their superiority complex," Chanelle certainly seemed to be obsessed with her boyfriend. She talked to J about him practically every day. She wrote poems about him, worried that he was seeing other girls, and mulled over his text messages and e-mails for hours, trying to decipher secret meaning.

"Do you think we're meant to be together?" Chanelle asked J over the phone. "Me and Bonez?"

J didn't think someone as smart as Chanelle should be dating someone with a name as stupid as Bonez, let alone imagining a future with him, but he didn't say anything. Chanelle was brilliant, actually—J didn't think there was a book she hadn't read. She had been teaching J about poetry, which mostly felt fairly abstract but occasionally hit a nerve. Once she wrote a line from Rita Dove, one of her favorites, in J's notebook. It went, "Any fear, any memory will do; and if you've got a heart at all, someday it will kill you." J didn't know whether it was the heart or the memory that was the monster for Chanelle, but despite her fierce attitude and her optimism, he had a feeling it was both. It was a sadness that showed in her eyes. He wanted to photograph her eyes.

"I told Bonez about you, and he got jealous," Chanelle said. "So I was thinking maybe we should go on a double date once this stupid holiday's done—you with your girlfriend and me and Bonez, so he can see he has nothing to worry about."

J hadn't mentioned Blue in weeks, and since she hadn't returned his calls, he'd pretty much given up. Sometimes he'd wonder what would happen if he just showed up in the Starbucks, or he'd fantasize about how much more secure he'd feel with a girl to call at night, but that was lame. He wasn't like Melissa or Chanelle; he didn't *need* romance to validate his existence. He'd been doing okay without her, and the bruise to his ego had started to fade.

"Have you written her an e-mail?" Chanelle asked. "Sometimes that works better. The power of the written word, you know."

J wasn't the greatest writer. He'd always done well enough in English class at school, but when he wanted something badly and had to write to get it, he usually messed it up. He remembered his old photography teacher recommending him for an exclusive photo class at a museum. J sent two of his best pictures, of a chicken in a cage and a chicken playing chess in Chinatown, but he waited until the last minute to write the essay. All he could think to say was, "Pictures are worth *more* than a thousand words, so I use as few as possible." He didn't get accepted.

"I could help you," Chanelle suggested. "I could be your Cyrano!"

J didn't know who Cyrano was, but Chanelle was hooked on this idea of a double date. She thought that Blue would come running back if J sent her a poem, especially one he wrote himself. Or that Chanelle wrote for him.

"Except I would never write poetry," J protested. The whole idea made him nervous.

"She doesn't know that!" Chanelle was excited. "Trust me. We'll do it as soon as break's over."

True to her word, when school started again, J found himself with Chanelle in the computer room, surrounded by poetry books he didn't understand. Chanelle believed in borrowing liberally from published poets in order to "inspire her muses."

" 'I wake and feel the fell of dark, not day. What hours, O what black hours we have spent this night! What sights you, heart, saw; ways you went! But where I say hours, I mean years, mean life.' " Chanelle was leaning back in her plastic chair, reading from a book. She was practically swooning. "I skipped some parts, but isn't that amazing?"

"Chanelle, you're weird," J said.

"No, it's sprung rhythm! Hopkins invented it. You can feel it in your whole body if you read it right. Here, look at it." Chanelle tried to push the book on him, but J shook his head. " 'The black hours.' We'll use that. You have to show her how depressed you've been without her. What's Blue's favorite color?"

"Blue."

Chanelle nodded and rummaged through her books.

"How'd you learn so much about poetry?"

"My mom used to work in a bookstore," Chanelle answered, flipping pages. "My real mom."

"What happened to her?"

"Died. Here's one. I thought I remembered that 'Ash Wednesday' had a lot of colors in it! Does Blue like rocks?"

"I guess." Maybe this would work, J thought. It would be nice to have a girlfriend again. But he wouldn't hold out too much hope.

"How's this?" Chanelle cleared her throat and read: "'This is the time of tension between dying and birth, The place of solitude where three dreams cross, Between blue rocks.'"

"What does that even mean?"

"We can make it mean whatever we want. God, T. S. Eliot was a genius. Listen to this ending! 'Suffer me not to be separated, And let my cry come unto Thee.'" Chanelle sighed. "We have to use that line."

"'Unto thee'? Chanelle, she's never going to believe I wrote this."

"She'll think you're a closet genius!"

"She'll think I'm a closet something."

Chanelle picked up an enormous book. Shakespeare's collected works. "I think we should add a line or two from one of the sonnets for romance. We don't want it to be depressing."

"Chanelle, isn't this plagiarism?"

Chanelle put down the book and looked at J as though he were very young, or too stupid to understand. "Think of it like being a poetry DJ. We're just mixing music here to make something original."

J sighed and looked at the ceiling.

"How's this? 'Love alters not with his brief hours and weeks, But bears it out even to the edge of doom.'" Chanelle was unstoppable. "That's perfect, right? You're saying love endures, even though you've had a rough spell."

"Why do you like all this old poetry? It's all from a different century."

Chanelle looked hurt. "I don't. I told you, I love Rita Dove. I showed you her stuff."

"Yeah, but even her poems are about really old things."

Chanelle considered this. "Sometimes I think it would have been better to have lived in a different era."

"Because of what happened with your mom?" J asked. Maybe Chanelle had weird fantasies, too— like a different era would have produced a different outcome.

"I don't know what happened to my mom," Chanelle said quietly. "They didn't let me go to the funeral. She left me with my grandma when she went on a trip, and then there was a funeral that I didn't go to. That's the end of the story."

Rough, J thought. "How old were you?"

"Ten."

Chanelle didn't want to elaborate about the several years she said she spent with her grandmother before she ran away to New York and ended up in foster care. She just said she didn't know whether her grandmother was dead or alive, and she didn't care either way.

"So why would another era have been any easier?" J had imagined swapping genders but had never considered time travel or escaping his entire generation.

"I don't know. I'd just like to start over. With a different life and fancier clothes."

J wasn't buying it.

"You really want to know?" Chanelle picked up a book and touched the inside cover. "A hundred years ago, children weren't really children. I've read about it. People thought of them as little adults. They had to work, like in factories or whatever. But they weren't so protected."

"It sounds awful." J tried to imagine his childhood

without Carolina's buying him things, without his manga, without even his camera.

"Not really. It's like your question in class. Before there was a word for childhood, there weren't really children, you know? So kids grew up fast. They went to funerals. They lived where they could, where they wanted to. I think they had more of their own minds."

J wasn't sure; he had a lot of questions. How could you be transgender in a time like that? Could you go to school? Weren't the girls treated as subservient to boys a century ago? But Chanelle was still talking.

"People have controlled my life too much," Chanelle said. "That's why I'm taking control now. I put *myself* back in school. I'm going to put *myself* in college. I'm going to make *myself* a famous poet. Whether Bonez becomes my husband or not."

But J was still stuck on this idea of living in another century. "Could you have been a poet if you were a girl back then?"

Chanelle closed the book she'd been stroking. "I haven't figured that part out yet."

The poem Chanelle came up with was "brilliant," in Chanelle's estimation. J made her kill the *thee* and a few other lines he found obnoxious, but still the poem made him anxious. Aside from the fact that it was almost entirely lifted, it felt awkward to read it, like the way he felt when he was younger and his mother made him wear a more feminine shirt, or when he had to sing the soprano parts in chorus. It was just not him. Still, Chanelle was so excited and so sure this would bring Blue back, and then they could go on their double date. He owed Chanelle that; she had been his one real friend in this crazy school.

Chanelle asked for Blue's e-mail address, and J mechanically spelled it out. *Just don't think about it*, he told himself. She called the poem "Deep Blue" and pressed *Send*. She printed out an extra copy of the poem for herself, and handed it to J.

The paper read:

What black hours I have spent
But when I say hours, I mean years, mean life—
Without you.
In my solitude, my dreams cross between blue rocks.
Love is not altered by brief hours or weeks
But it is borne out to the edge of doom.
And back.
Suffer me not to be separated.
Hear my cry.

"It's great, right?" Chanelle gushed.
J tried his best not to groan out loud.

Even without the testosterone, J was passing as male more and more on the streets. Before the chest binder, before he'd moved out of his parents' apartment, strangers would look at him quizzically and only occasionally "sir" him. That was when he was trying to be a brain without a body, and he tried to not let anything stir him up too much. Except, of course, it did. Now, though, almost nobody did a double take, girls on the subway met his eye, and cashiers regularly called him "sir."

J didn't really know why. Maybe it was because he'd been practicing his walk; maybe his voice had deepened just because he dreamed about it so much. Could it be that a person became more male by wishing it so?

Philip was still encouraging J to go to a support group for transboys, but J resisted. He had already figured out who the transguys at his school were. There were two of them, at least, guys who were on T, and they were both aloof and distant. J didn't want to go to a meeting full of jerks.

But Philip persisted. He told J he didn't want him to go through his transition alone.

"Are you gay?" J asked during one of their sessions, to throw Philip off track.

"What do you imagine I am?" Philip asked. He seemed entirely unruffled by J's question.

"I think you are."

"And what would it mean to you if I were?" Philip asked.

J stared at Philip's wrist braces. "Nothing. I mean, I don't care." *Lobster Man.* "It's just, maybe you find men more fascinating than I do, so you think these meetings would be a good idea."

Philip thought it would be a good idea to examine J's aggressive feelings a little more closely. J got mad. "I hate the word *aggressive!*"

"And why is that?" Philip spoke so calmly, it aggravated J. It was like a fly buzzing against a screen.

"I'm not an aggressive! And why do you have those things on your hands?"

Philip burst out laughing. He said he had carpal tunnel syndrome, from too much typing, and that the braces eased the pressure.

"But this is progress, J," Philip said. "You're bringing some of your anger out, where we can deal with it."

That day J wrote in his notebook, the one he used for reminders about men. *Stay calm,* he wrote. *When someone pisses you off, laugh. Head back.* And then, *Don't wear wrist braces.*

*   *   *

He decided to go to a transgender meeting, just to show Philip he wasn't afraid, and so they'd have something to talk about besides his stupid anger. Why did everyone think he had so much turbulence going on inside? Melissa had said that to him, too.

The meeting was for people along the "masculine spectrum." *Díos mío*, J thought. *Can't escape the rainbow.* But the flyer Philip handed J included everybody: transboys, transmen, transsexuals, trans-identified, gender-queer, and exploring. J figured everybody would be on T already. He just wouldn't talk.

"We have a few new faces," a man in jeans and a skullcap said, smiling, as J walked in. He was arranging folding chairs and encouraging everyone to make a sort of circle. *Don't make me talk, don't make me talk*, J thought. "Why don't we just go around the room and introduce ourselves again."

J didn't hear anybody's name, but he memorized the tops of his sneakers. He needed new ones. He could barely keep the white parts white anymore. He'd nearly convinced Carolina of the critical value of shoes, especially because he didn't spend much on shirts and he got his hair cut at the Dominican barbershop for ten bucks. Really, he was saving her money. Someone nudged him. "J, I'm J," he said reflexively. He didn't look up.

The name game was endless; there must have been a hundred people in the room. When J cautioned a quick glance at the other feet around him, though, he saw maybe only ten other pairs of shoes, mostly sneakers.

"We-Pee is a stupid name; wasn't that what they called Popeye's kid?" This was a voice from across the circle. Definitely on T. Christ, were they making fun of people's names in here? In a support group? J would kill Philip.

"It wasn't Popeye's kid; it was Olive Oyl's. She was an unwed mother. A hillbilly ho."

As people laughed, J snuck another look. He made it as far as the knees all around the circle, and up to the face of the guy in the skullcap, who was laughing, too, but motioning for order. He had broad shoulders and muscles, J could tell, beneath his black sweater. He was South American, J thought. Maybe Ecuadoran? No accent. He wished he could stare.

"Zak, We-Pee is important. Can we please talk about this?" This came from a new voice, a higher one that squeaked and dropped like a thirteen-year-old's.

So Skullcap's name was Zak. That sweater was tight enough to show his pecs; this guy definitely worked out. Would he have scars under there? J had read something about "keyhole" surgery, where you could just remove breast fat from under the nipples and get practically no scarring. But you had to have a really small chest for that, and J was pretty sure he wouldn't qualify. Besides, he'd have to produce a mountain of cash. At this rate, he could barely afford to buy Blue a slice of pizza. *If* she'd see him again. J wondered if Zak had gone to college; he certainly spoke as if he had. He was talking about the "gender binary" and "those of trans-masculine identification" as easily as reciting the alphabet. If J went to college, he wondered, would he be able to afford surgery? He wanted to study photography; he wanted to be really good. Maybe he could look like Zak one day *and* sell his pictures for thousands of dollars.

"Colleges are getting better," someone in PUMA sneakers said, as if reading J's mind. "It's the high schools that are still a problem. Did you know you can get kidney problems from holding it all day?"

"My kidneys must be dead, then," someone answered. "I piss like twice a day."

"At my job, they make me use another floor."

J started paying attention; pissing was a problem for him, too. He knew all the public places that had unisex restrooms—Starbucks was one of the few, and the diner by his old apartment. If he was desperate, and stuck somewhere where he had to pick, it could be embarrassing at best and threatening at worst. In the women's room, they stared, and one time a lady ran out shrieking for management. That was in a freeway rest stop on a swim meet trip, and then J had rushed back to the bus without relieving his bladder. A men's room was scarier; there wasn't a word for his terror of getting jumped with his pants down.

Zak could go into a men's room without worrying, J thought. His body was amazing; even though he was sitting down, J could tell he barely had hips.

J remembered the first time he had trouble in a bathroom. It was a night with his father, when J was in first grade. They had gone to see Mexican wrestling that was in town, that J was dying to see. At the intermission, all the other little boys jumped into the ring wearing plastic wrestling masks and leaped on top of one another, shrieking and tumbling and punching, hyped up on sugar and soda, imitating the wrestling maneuvers they'd just witnessed. J wanted to join them, but Manny said such behavior wasn't for girls. J pouted until Manny promised to teach him some boxing moves later, when they got home.

At the stadium bathroom, Manny waited patiently by the concession stand while J hopped from foot to foot in the women's line. He remembered wishing he could just go into the men's room, where the line was shorter. J looked at all the little girls in their headbands or Disney T-shirts, holding their mothers' hands while he stood alone.

In the stall, J tried what he had mastered at home—

the art of peeing standing up. He had watched his father do it a few times, when he forgot to close the door, or when J was in the bath and his father really had to go. But J couldn't do it as Manny did—standing away from the toilet. When he'd tried this behind a locked bathroom door, the pee didn't arc up and out, like his father's, but rather trailed down his leg and into a puddle on the floor. Countless cleanups later, J had found a way. He could lift the lid, straddle the bowl, and pee straight down while standing. It wasn't perfect, but it worked.

But in the stadium stall, something went terribly wrong. The toilet there was wider, or somehow different from the one at home, and his practiced straddle was off balance. Instead of landing in the bowl, the pee veered down his right leg and onto the jeans bunched around his ankles. He desperately mopped at the darkening denim with toilet paper, but it was too late.

At the concession stand, he'd asked for a Mountain Dew, which Manny said was too expensive. J begged and when Manny caved, J promptly spilled the whole thing on his pants, covering the stain and the smell. Manny was angry, and J had tried hard not to cry about the whole sorry mess.

Still, that night J did learn some boxing moves—the

hook, the uppercut, and the jab—that Manny had learned in the Bronx. Manny wore a pillow stuffed up under his shirt and got on his knees so they'd be closer in height, and he let J pop him as many times as he wished, until Carolina shouted from the kitchen that she couldn't stand the noise any longer. J crawled into bed that night with his right shoulder sore and his knuckles raw from hitting the buttons on his dad's old workshirt, but he felt a kind of happiness, too, that almost erased the bathroom debacle. He'd forgotten about that night until now. Manny had been good to him once.

Someone in the support group was passing out stickers. WE PEE, TOO, they said. GENDER-NEUTRAL BATHROOMS FOR GENDER-VARIANT PEOPLE.

"You can just stick these over the men's or women's bathroom signs wherever you go," a white kid with red spiky hair was saying. "It's part of the new We-Pee campaign. It's cool because with their own signs covered, cisgender people don't know where to go, either."

Cisgender, J thought. *What the—?* But everyone else seemed to buzz right along.

"Is that safe for women, though?" J looked at the person who'd said this. He was a serious-looking guy in glasses. This room had all kinds. "I mean, bathrooms can be a safe space for women."

"We don't have a safe space!" This was from a younger, grungier-looking guy. J thought he probably worked in a health food store, like the one that Melissa liked, the one that smelled like sweat.

J had never thought about space being safe before. Space was, well, just space. People were unsafe. Sometimes the thoughts he had weren't so safe. Was the mind a space? Was Chanelle's idea of living in a different era a safe space for her? He thought his sleeping bag was, maybe, a safe space, and wherever Titi was, that was safe, too. And the space he saw when he looked through his camera and framed a really good shot.

And maybe this room was a little bit safe. He'd never been anywhere where people talked about bathrooms before, and how something so pedestrian could feel so menacing, could pose a problem every single day. These guys knew what he'd been through, and he didn't even have to tell them. Even though J didn't speak, even though he felt jealous of Zak's muscles and ease, it was as though he'd found some clan of cousins he never knew he had, or needed. The support group wasn't like finding a home, exactly, as Philip had espoused, but more of a garage next to the home—somewhere kind of offset and funky, where you wanted to hang out and explore what was inside.

The guys milled around after the meeting, but J didn't have anyone to talk to, so he pretended to be busy with his phone and slipped out the door. Once outside, though, he heard his name.

"J!" It was Zak, pulling on a leather jacket and jogging to catch up.

J hoped his grin didn't look too goofy.

"How'd you like the meeting?"

J told him it was good. He wanted to ask what *cisgender* meant, but he felt too shy.

"Will you come back next week?"

Is this his job to ask me? J wondered. "Sure," he said. He lit a cigarette.

Zak gave J his phone number, in case he had any questions.

"Where do you work out?" J asked. That wasn't the question he was expecting. His mind was getting ahead of his mouth these days.

Zak chuckled. "Just a Y in Brooklyn. And I have a chin-up bar at home. Three sets of ten each morning."

"Wow." J could barely do one, and he had to jump. *I need,* J thought. *I need, what?* He suddenly had an urge to wrestle with Zak, just knock him into the pile of dirty snow and roll around like kids. He stubbed out his cigarette with his sneaker, ground it hard into the concrete.

"Well, see you next week," Zak said, and jogged back into the building.

It took Blue a week to respond to J's e-mail. There was nothing in the subject line, save for a series of question marks. "Call me," she wrote inside. Nothing more. Not even her name.

He did, and got her voice mail. He left a mostly incoherent message, apologizing for the poem. He knew it was too much—he'd been a fool, he knew it when Chanelle started busting out the Shakespeare, but still he tried to sound casual on the phone, normal even, except he wasn't that, never normal, and couldn't they meet in person, maybe just for coffee?

He called Chanelle for advice.

"Bring her flowers," she said authoritatively. "Women love that."

"But what if she's still mad at me?" He was beginning to doubt Chanelle's quick answers for everything, her rigid definitions of what women and men did or enjoyed, when she herself so clearly fell outside the boundaries.

"Am I not the one in a successful relationship?" Chanelle shot back. "Believe me. A poem and flowers fix everything."

J kept his thoughts to himself and hung up the phone.

"I liked your poem," Blue said when she called back. "I didn't know you wrote."

"I don't," J bumbled. "I mean, only sometimes."

They met outside Blue's school, J skipping his last class to make sure she wouldn't have to wait. He didn't bring flowers.

He wanted to tell her how sexy she looked, in her old-man overcoat and her pom-pom hat, her cheeks all flushed and wintry, but Blue's hands were shoved deep into her pockets, and her mouth turned up only the tiniest smile when she said hello. There was something both grave and watery in her eyes—was it anger? Betrayal? He couldn't tell. But he didn't dare reach to hug her or say anything beyond a quick hi.

"Let's walk," Blue said when he offered to buy her a cappuccino, the kind Blue liked, with the whipped cream and the caramel drizzled on top.

And so they did. Three long blocks east, before Blue said anything. "I've been painting monsters."

J felt trepidatious. "What kind?"

"Little ones. In windows, and in hair, behind buildings. Places you can't see unless you really look."

J thought of the Virgin Mary clock, the stuffed elephant that he used to stick in photographs of construction sites. "Why?"

"Monsters are interesting. They're like demons but

more childlike. We only choose to believe in them." Blue quickly glanced at J.

"What does your sister think of your paintings?"

"Jadzia?" Blue scratched her nose, looked up. "Jadzia's complicated. I don't know what she thinks of my paintings, really. She wants to be a nun."

"Whoa."

"Jadzia tries to be kind to everybody, but it's like she's in a kind of trance. Mama will die if she goes to a convent, but she has one all picked out. It's super-strict, in Spain."

How could a parent be upset that a daughter was too religious? J wondered.

"Mama wants grandkids," Blue said. "And I don't want children, I don't think. I just want to paint. And Jadzia, if she's a nun—we'll both just disappoint her."

Maybe all kids disappoint their mothers in the end, J thought. He'd never considered this before. Well, except Melissa. Karyn would be proud of Melissa forever. "You don't want kids?"

"Kids are annoying. I can't even paint when the day care is open," Blue said. "What did you mean by 'my dreams cross between blue rocks'? In the poem?"

J tried to remember the poem he sent, and he felt his cheeks flush. "I don't know. Because Blue is your name."

"But why rocks?"

Damn, J thought. He knew this poem would come back to bite him in the ass. *Why rocks, why rocks?*

Blue stopped walking. They were in front of a pet store, where white puppies tumbled and jumped in a cage in the window. "That's so mean, how they keep them locked up like that," Blue said. And there it was, that softness in her eyes, that same tenderness she had shown when she looked at J as she sketched him that afternoon. But then her eyes glinted with something harder, more inscrutable. "Did you really write that poem?"

J shifted, kept his eyes on the dogs. "I borrowed some lines."

"Hmm," Blue said, but her face was unreadable. "Let's go in for a minute. It's freezing out here."

The pet store was warm and smelled like wood chips and dog kibble. They looked at the fish, a large tank filled with tetras, and then the turtles, slow and sleepy under their heat lamp. Blue asked J if he really did ever have a girlfriend back in Philly.

Where'd that come from? J thought. He tried to remember what he'd made up about the phantom Philly girl. "Of course," he said, sounding offended. "You don't believe me?"

"There are just little monsters we all have in our hair," she said, forcing a smile.

J looked at Blue's hair, messy from the hat she'd taken off. Her blond roots were showing, and the blue had faded to a washed-out denim color. She'd removed her scarf, too, and J noticed she wasn't wearing the necklace. He followed Blue to the hamster cages.

"So tell me about her," Blue said. "This old girlfriend."

"Um, I don't feel like talking about her," J said. His stomach was going soft and quaky.

"Did she look like me?"

"No."

"Did she look like...Kobe Bryant?"

What?! Meaning, did she look like a man? Was she black? Was she insanely tall? Did she have tattoos everywhere? J started to laugh, but the look on Blue's face stopped him cold. She was completely serious.

"J, please don't lie to me."

J watched the hamsters. He didn't know what to say. *Kobe Bryant?* "You know, some mothers eat their children."

"The females of some species can be pretty aggressive," Blue answered.

She knows, J thought. *That's it.* He traced his finger along the glass of the hamster cage. That word—*aggressive*—she definitely knew. And now she was just toying with him, the way an animal toys with prey.

Why did I ever think I could get away with it, before T? He caught his reflection in the glass—that jaw too soft, that neck too thin. *But Kobe Bryant?*

"So there never was a girlfriend?"

J slowly shook his head. He felt sad. There was no relief, just a heavy sadness—the kind that comes when you realize that people die and they never come back, or your father just may never love you again.

"But—" Blue paused. "A boyfriend?"

"What?" J was genuinely surprised. Never in his whole life had he been attracted to guys—except, maybe, for Zak. He didn't know what that was about.

"Don't mess with my head, J. We've been through enough," Blue sounded like a very old woman, and J might have laughed at the telenovela sigh coming from her pixie face, except he knew he shouldn't. He felt that he was in trouble for something he didn't understand. Blamed for stealing the cookies when he really drank the milk.

"Why would I have a boyfriend, Blue? I'm not gay." It was so hot in the pet store, and J could smell animal urine faintly soaking in the wood chips.

"Okay, bi, then."

"Why would I be bi?" He felt caged. He decided to try a tack his mother always used. "Is there something you're not telling me?"

Blue didn't answer, but then she, too, looked caught.

Her eyes welled. She really wasn't good at arguing. Suddenly J got it.

"You think because I wrote you a poem that I'm gay? That only gay guys write poems?"

Blue looked confused for a moment, and then she nodded.

"That's idiotic." J had never felt particularly defensive of gay people before, but now, suddenly, he did. The stereotypes of gay men being more sensitive or more feminine—J thought of his classmate Tyrone. Tyrone didn't fit any gay stereotype; he was just awkward and uncomfortable. And the other kids at school, there were so many "types"—there were aggressives and femmes, but there were also nerds and goths and punks and athletes, and every one of them queer in some way. *"Don't tell her."* Chanelle's words rang in J's head. *"A lover will drop you in a quick minute if she knows you're trans."*

So she must not know, J thought.

"I need to think," Blue said, wrapping her scarf around her neck.

"So do I," J answered. "So do I."

As she ducked out the door of the pet store, Blue looked back over her shoulder. She was crying again. "Boyfriends don't ignore girls for two months, J. And boyfriends don't call girlfriends 'idiotic.'"

The door shut with a jingle. *And girlfriends don't*

call boyfriends gay, J thought, zipping up his jacket. *Just because they wrote a poem.* He looked at the puppies trapped in their cage. How were puppies born in winter? *Or didn't write a poem.* Some miracle of science. *And boyfriends don't lie to girlfriends about their gender.* Weren't puppies born in spring? *Or didn't lie, not exactly.* My God, they're trampling on the littlest one. *My gender's not a lie. I am not a lie. Art is the lie that tells the truth. You should know that, Blue. You, especially. I don't need a girlfriend so badly that I'm willing to settle for such madness.*

J wasn't looking forward to telling Chanelle that the poem had bombed. She'd had such high hopes; why was he always letting everybody down? He caught her at the elevator before school. She asked him how it went yesterday, her eyes eager and almost hungry.

"Sorry, Chanelle. I suck at this."

"What happened?" She pushed the elevator button for their floor.

J adjusted the straps on his backpack. "It's 'cause I'm trans. Blue doesn't understand me."

"Bullshit!" Chanelle turned on him. "That's a tired excuse. Didn't I tell you not to tell her? What's going to happen with the double date now? I needed you for this, J. Things are bad for me and Bonez."

J felt his mouth open in protest, but no sound came out. They'd reached their floor. How was he supposed to help her? The poem was rititulous, anyway. And he wasn't used to being needed by anyone. That was new.

"Chanelle, wait!" She was striding across the reception area toward their classroom. There was still twenty minutes until class. She turned, and her eyes had filled. J caught up. "What's so bad with you and Bonez?"

Chanelle jutted her head toward the EXIT sign and the stairwell, where they could hide out. When the door had safely closed, they plopped down and each lit a cigarette. It reminded him of the old days, with Melissa.

"The question is," Chanelle answered, "what's good?"

J inhaled some smoke and waited.

"Men have it easy," Chanelle said, pulling back her bangs. "They can just give flowers and be done with it. Women, we have nothing to give but our feelings, and men don't want that."

"What do they want?" J asked. Chanelle's internal book of rules was getting weirder and weirder.

She looked at J like he was patently stupid. "Our bodies! God, J, where have you been?"

Did he just want Blue's body? If that was all, he

could have probably made it beyond a snowy kiss. He wanted to be understood, underneath it all, and he was a man. Maybe Chanelle sort of hated men, if she thought they were so simple. He took a risk. "Do you hate men?"

J was prepared for one of Chanelle's quick bites, but instead she just sat there, thoughtfully blowing smoke rings. "Probably," she said quietly. "At least I hate the man in me."

J extinguished his cigarette with a hard stomp of his heel. The *man* in Chanelle? How could she say that? There was no woman inside of him, not even one ounce; how could there be any man inside of Chanelle? He noticed his hand was clenched into a fist; he breathed and stretched his fingers. "You're not masculine, Chanelle."

"I didn't say I was masculine. I said I hate the man in me."

"I don't have any woman in me." J's voice sounded petulant rather than firm and assured, the way he wanted it to.

"Of course you do," Chanelle said. "You're just still afraid. You're newer at this than I am."

He wanted to tell her to fuck off; who did she think she was, telling him about his feelings, patronizing him like this? But he'd come into the stairwell to help her;

she'd said she needed him. Even Melissa had never admitted that.

"Maybe I'm dating the most masculine asshole to try to conquer what I hate," Chanelle said. "Or to change him—or—I don't know. I can't figure it out."

J softened a bit. Chanelle was so smart, he thought. So able to look at herself. One minute she was making categories for other people that seemed almost comic-like in their simplicity, and the next she was analyzing her own character better than even Philip could do. "Is Bonez really an asshole?"

Chanelle nodded her head miserably. "He only cares about tagging. And even that he misspells." She gave a little laugh.

J thought about having a woman inside, or a man, about having different parts. Was it like being Jewish and Puerto Rican? His dad was Jewish, and he himself always felt more Puerto Rican. Did that mean he was sort of feminine, like his mom? If he felt more Jewish, would he be even more like a man? He didn't know much about Judaism; Manny hadn't taught him enough about it. And besides, that wasn't what Chanelle was talking about. And what was a person, anyway? The sum of the parts? Some of the parts? That was a good pun. Was a person just the things he said he was, or also the things he denied? J felt confused; he couldn't hold on to a singular thread. He knew one thing: Bonez only made Chanelle feel bad about herself, and that wasn't worth it. "You deserve somebody better, Chanelle," he said.

"Yeah, sure," she answered. "All the good ones are taken."

Another line. And then he suddenly got it: Chanelle made up all her rules about other people to prepare herself for rejection. If she could simplify everyone into categories, she could brace herself for their predictable responses. Like everybody else, Chanelle was afraid of getting hurt.

"No, they aren't," he said. He thought of the way his feelings had shifted toward Blue; how at the beginning he believed he wanted her back no matter what, but then when his fantasies about her were bigger than who she really was, he could let her go. "You could get somebody great."

"How?" Chanelle looked skeptical.

J said he didn't know; he obviously wasn't a relationship expert. "But if you dump Bonez, I'll help you be less lonely, or whatever, until you find a better one."

"So you'll be my stand-in boyfriend?"

"Something like that."

"Great," Chanelle said, laughing. "You'll scare all the guys away cause they'll think I'm with you."

"I'll sit at another table and be an asshole meter. A wink means he's all right; a cough means run away."

"So, now *you* can judge men?"

"Been studying them all my life."

Chanelle smiled and kissed J on the cheek. "Thanks," she said, and they both stood up for class.

CHAPTER ELEVEN

Dear Pops, J typed into the computer at Melissa's house, knowing he could erase it later. This was another one of Philip's ideas—to write a letter to his father just to see what would come out. *How are you?* No, that was dumb. He backspaced. *Dear Manny*. More man to man. *How are you doing, living in the apartment where I used to live?* That sounded bitter, pitiful. *Dear Pops*, he tried again. *I'm fine, going to school, living with two women on the Lower East Side, working on my career in photography. How's your life in the subway?* Crap, he thought. Philip and his ideas.

One of Philip's ideas had been a good one—joining the young transgender group downtown. J had gone several times now and was invited to join the We-Pee organizing committee. Technically, everyone was invited to join We-Pee, but J was happy the redhead in charge had remembered his name. And then Zak, looking as muscled and confident as the last time, had invited J to his apartment, since he was "new to the community."

But for now he had promised Philip he'd write a letter. It was important, Philip thought, for J to express his feelings about Manny, since every time his name came up in therapy, J changed the subject. So they struck a deal: if J wrote the letter, Philip would drop the subject. For a while.

Dear Pops.

I wanted to be like you when I was little. This isn't your fault. It's just who I am. I hope one day we can talk again. —J

It took J the better part of an hour to work out those few lines. Despite Philip's instructions, J couldn't help but imagine his father actually reading what he wrote. And each time he struck a key, it was like tapping a memory—watching cartoons together when J was little, buying J's first bike, their special trip to the horse races in Saratoga. Manny screaming from the bleachers when

J won a swim race, that unmistakable shout of Pops-pride.

On the table next to the computer sat J's stack of college applications. A few were past due. They all required essays. *Describe an important event that changed your life.*

J called Chanelle. "Where are you going to college, again?" he asked, even though he knew. She had one more year of high school to complete, but then she was going to go to NYU, she knew it, on a full scholarship, and would be accepted early admission.

"What if my dad won't pay for school anymore? Now that..." J asked, trailing off.

"Ever heard of financial aid?" Chanelle was snippy with J again; maybe she was really considering a breakup with Bonez. "And go to a SUNY school. They have late admissions."

Chanelle knew all the policies and programs of the local schools by heart; she'd been scouring college web-sites for the past several months, eager to start her life as a capital-p Poet.

"But what about my transcripts? Do they need them for photography?" J was flipping through a brochure for a SUNY school upstate where, it seemed, he could major in photography. He'd need to pull together a portfolio.

"What about them? I thought you said your grades were good." She was definitely in a bad mood, J thought. Maybe she was jealous that he'd get to go to college before she would. "Everywhere needs transcripts."

"But"—J paused—"my transcripts all say my other name. By the time I start college—I mean, if I start college—I'll already be on T. I don't want anybody to know I've been a girl."

"Hmm." Chanelle sounded stumped. She said she'd meet him after school in the computer room the next day, and they'd figure it out.

All night long, twisting in his sleeping bag like an oversized worm, J fretted. Going away to college sounded better and better: he'd get to start over, as a boy, in a place where no one knew him. He'd learn more about photography and probably get to use nicer equipment than he could ever afford. Carolina would be proud of J in college—all his life, she'd talked about how important that was. She'd signed the testosterone form behind Manny's back; maybe she could sign over some of the college money, too. Maybe some of that money was hers alone.

But what if no school would let him in as J? They'd see *Jenifer* on his transcripts and think he was a girl. Which gender would he check off on the forms? What kind of dorm could he stay in, with his bound-down chest and his (he hoped) masculine voice? Where would he shower?

He couldn't stay at Melissa's forever; she'd be leaving to teach at a dance camp in the summer, as she did every year, and then go off to college herself. Karyn wouldn't want a roommate whose mother wasn't slipping her rent, and obviously he couldn't go home.

And even if he could, what would he do there? Play with the cat all day? Get a job at C-Town, bagging groceries? He wanted to be a real photographer; he wanted a chance.

In the college brochures, groups of kids clustered under trees laughing or studying, and not one of them looked trans. *What does that even mean?* J thought. *What if they are?* The girls had long hair, and the boys wore caps, and they all seemed to be happily settled at their campus, showing off team logos on sweatshirts or bags.

"Let's just call them," Chanelle said the next day. They were in the computer room where they'd written the poem for Blue. Chanelle had the website for the SUNY schools up on the screen, and she'd pulled out her cell phone.

"Wait, stop! What're you going to say?" J tried to grab the phone from her, but she was already dialing. "Don't tell them my name!"

"I won't. But they have a GLBT center on campus; it's a good sign." Chanelle's eyebrows furrowed and she sat up in her chair. "Hello? Yes, I was thinking of applying to your school."

J pulled his cap over his eyes. Sometimes Chanelle reminded him of his mother. No time for negotiating.

"But I've had a name change, and I was wondering if that would be a problem...." Chanelle paused, wrote something down. "Right, and where would I put that on the form?"

Chanelle looked at J with a grin—like, *See how easy this was?* "Right," she said. "And if I've changed my gender?"

J groaned.

"Uh-huh," she said, entirely businesslike. She dropped her voice to a lower register. "See, I was born a girl, but I live as a man. My older transcripts will say *female*, but the ones from my school now will say *male*. Will this be a problem?"

J felt a sudden flood of love for Chanelle. She was dropping her voice for him, acting like a male, which he imagined she hated. She seemed fine, though, prattling on with the person on the phone as if they were old friends.

"Really? And where can I shower?" J felt like Chanelle had been in his brain last night. He flashed to Marcia, in the hotel near the pier. *"Honey, we're all transgender.*" He wondered what had happened to her, her fuzzy sweater, her kindness. The paper Chanelle was writing on was filling up, and apparently she'd moved on. "So, how many photographs do I need for a photography portfolio?"

When Chanelle hung up the phone, she smiled smugly. "That was easy." She handed him her page of notes. "J baby, you're going to be old news at that school. Nothing special about you."

There had been others, Chanelle said, and the university was used to it. He could check the *M* box on the forms and just attach a note explaining he was transgender. The dorms wouldn't be a problem; most likely, they'd just assign him his own room.

"My own?" J interrupted. "With a door?"

"No, you'll have to hang a flag from your doorframe and hope nobody peeks."

I could do anything if I had a room with a door. Chanelle laughed. "You look like somebody went and bought you a car."

"It's better," he said, and reached into his bag for his camera. Even when she laughed, Chanelle's eyes looked sad. He adjusted the lens.

"You want to take my picture? Now?"

"Just your eyes. Look natural," J said.

Chanelle started pulling makeup out of her bag— mascara, an eyeliner, and an enormous powder brush.

"I said natural."

So J got a picture of Chanelle looking into the camera, her bangs pulled back behind her ears, one eyebrow raised slightly, like a challenge. Her brown eyes were open and unafraid, but if you looked closely, there was something searching in them, too—something lost and long ago. *Maybe she does belong in another century*, J thought.

"Thank you," J said.

"It was easy. I just sat there."

"No, for making that call." He knew if he did get into a school outside the city, he'd come back and visit Chanelle. He'd help her through if she got sad about her mom or if Bonez broke her heart. There was more to life than the struggles with Blue or his dad, or even getting T. There was family, and this was it.

Zak's apartment was a mess. He tried to pawn it off on his three roommates, who weren't home, but J could see that even Zak's bedroom was a hurricane of books and running shoes and sheets that appeared to be less than clean. The chin-up bar Zak had mentioned was in the doorframe to this bedroom, and as they talked, Zak absentmindedly did reps.

"Sorry there's not much room to sit," Zak said, hoisting himself up to the bar. He wasn't even out of breath. "Just shove some stuff off the bed."

"When did you finish college?" J asked. He wondered how long it would take him to afford a place like this—a place of his own, with his own room.

"I don't think I'll ever be done with school. I'm working on my doctorate." Zak dropped from the bar to swig from a Gatorade bottle that was nestled in a laundry basket. "In gender studies."

J didn't know what to say.

"It's partly why I'm running the group. It's material for my dissertation," Zak said. He had invited J over to hang out before they'd head to the support group together. "It's called 'Male-ancholia: Depression and Grief in the Transitioning Male.' Sometimes I call it 'Even Transboys Get the Blues,' but I don't think my adviser would go for it."

"You think transguys are depressed?" J looked at the chin-up bar and wondered if he could even do one. It had been so long since he'd tried.

"Ever look at a transguy's forearms? So many of us cut."

J thought of Melissa. She was the only one he knew, and she was far from trans.

"And then there's the depression that comes when

testosterone doesn't solve everything, or when we mourn after surgery."

"What?" J was incredulous. "I can't wait to get rid of these. I hate them."

"I did, too. But sometimes there's sadness. You do lose a part of your body."

Zak took off his sweater and did a few more chin-ups in his tank top. J stared at Zak's chest; he couldn't help it.

"I had my surgery two years ago. Want to see?"

J was sitting at the edge of the bed, his elbows on his knees. He nodded mutely. Zak peeled off the tank top and tossed it into the laundry basket, revealing a perfectly toned chest with a small tattoo of a dragon above the left nipple.

"That's my year," Zak said, flexing his pecs. "The year of the dragon. Healthy, sensitive, and brave. Plus, I think the tattoo distracts the eye from my scars."

J didn't see any scars, but when Zak motioned him to look more closely, he saw two pale lines below the pec muscles. Nothing you'd notice on a beach.

"Did it hurt?" J asked. He sat up a little straighter, jutted out his chin.

Zak said he'd had the surgery in San Francisco, one week apart from a friend who did it, too. They'd made a vacation of it, seeing the Golden Gate Bridge, riding cable cars, so the healing didn't seem so bad. The surgery itself, Zak didn't remember.

J suddenly felt annoyed. *Oh, sure*, he thought. *Major surgery, and you didn't feel a thing.* "That's cool," he said. "I'm pretty good with pain, too."

Zak raised his eyebrows and gave a sly grin. He was still doing the chin-ups. "You'll need to be. Sometimes your muscles get sore even after the testosterone shots."

Really? Like a tetanus shot? "I know," J said, looking out the grimy window so Zak wouldn't think he liked watching the workout. "I have lots of friends who have done it."

"Oh, yeah? Where? Maybe I know them."

"No. They're in Philly." *Why do I always say Philly? What is it with that city?*

Zak didn't know anyone in Philly and asked J if he wanted to do some pull-ups.

"Nah," J answered. "I'm tired from the weight lifting I did last night."

"Okay," Zak said, smiling again. "You don't want muscle fatigue. But if you need a bench partner, let me know."

J thought Zak's world was so much bigger than his parents', in their little apartment up in Washington Heights. A shiver of guilt went up his spine, and he tried to squelch the feeling.

"You look good. The surgery, I mean."

Zak looked down at his chest. "Thanks. I've got to get some new pictures, though. I posted my transition online, and the ones I have up are really old."

"I could take them," J said. And then he coughed. He didn't want to seem too eager. But, artistically, taking pictures of Zak would be cool. First there was Chanelle, and then Zak—maybe this could be a project, taking pictures of people who had transitioned or were in various stages of transition. It was like the photography term he loved, *parallax*, where what you got in the picture was more than what you saw through the camera itself. And what you see depends on where you stand. That was so true with transpeople. All people, really. He could really get into photographing "live subjects," as his old photography teacher would say—much harder than construction sites, which held still.

As it turned out, Zak was a better subject than Chanelle; he liked having his picture taken. He posed doing a pull-up, and J got a close-up of Zak's bicep, round as a tennis ball, his face a strained but smiling backdrop for the flexed arm. He posed, shirtless, sitting on a stack of books, pretending to read, and again standing, hands in his pockets, looking straight at the camera. Pretty soon they were laughing.

"I feel like I'm taking beefcake shots for a calendar," J said.

"Yeah, there's a huge market for topless tranny academics. Right up there with the firemen."

A few weeks later, when J got home from his trans group meeting, Melissa was waiting up for him. "Your mom called," she said. She was lying on her bed, flipping through a dance magazine.

J checked his cell phone—no missed calls from Carolina. "Why'd she call here?"

"I think she wanted to talk to Karyn, but she wasn't home," Melissa said, sitting up. "I told her about the dance performance, and I invited her. It's in two weeks. J—"

"Yeah?" He was about to go into the bathroom to change into sweats, for bed.

"At the performance space, where the dance is going to be, there's this long hallway, and Becky and me—we wanted to have some visual art there." Melissa looked at J, long enough to make him uncomfortable. "I told her my best friend was an amazing photographer, so we booked you for that space."

"Emmmm!"

"What, J? You can put it on your résumé that you've

had a gallery show in New York." She put on her defiant face, with the pouty lips and the flared nostrils.

"I don't have a résumé," he said. He hated Melissa's pretensions. "Unlike you, I'm not trying to pretend like I'm thirty-five when I'm eighteen. And it's not a gallery. It's just some warehouse place your friend rented for a night."

J could see the sting register in Melissa's eyes, but she didn't rise to the bait. "Unlike you, I'm trying to make something of my art," she said. "And, unlike you, I think about more than just myself and my gender. I think about my friends, and I try to help them out."

"Fuck you, Melissa."

"Fuck you, too."

J went into the bathroom and washed his face. How did everything with Melissa deteriorate so quickly into a fight? They were like an old married couple, knowing each other's wounds so well, knowing just where to press. How dare she say he didn't think about his friends? He'd helped Melissa so many times. Just today, he'd taken pictures of Zak for his website. And he was forever listening to Chanelle blather on about Bonez, whom she hadn't even broken up with yet. He brushed his teeth.

Maybe he could hang some pictures at the performance; it wasn't like people would have to know they were his. And he already had three frames, from his birthday. The problem was getting the pictures—all of his good ones were back at his old apartment, and the new series was just an idea. He spit toothpaste into the sink.

The room was dark when J came out, and he could see that Melissa was under the covers. J unzipped his bag and climbed in, turning from one side to the other, trying to find a comfortable position.

"Melis?"

"Yeah?" She obviously hadn't been sleeping.

"How many pictures would I need to have?"

"Five," she said. "Well, maybe four, but five would be better."

"I'll do it."

"Good," she said. J could hear the grin in her voice. " 'Night, J."

" 'Night."

J called Carolina on his way to school the next morning.

"Hi, m'ija," she said, a little too brightly. "Melissa told me you're showing your photos in a gallery?"

Oh, God, J thought. "It's not a *gallery*, Mami. It's just a dance Melissa and her friends are doing. And I'm gonna put up some pictures."

"That's good, Jay-jay. You can put that on your college applications."

J hadn't thought of that. Carolina asked when the show would be, and J's throat constricted. Through the night, he'd been considering the photos he had stored in his camera, most of which he wouldn't want his mother to see. He considered hanging up, feigning a bad connection.

"Two weeks from today. Friday," he said.

"Oh, J, that's what I wanted to talk to you about," her voice suddenly wavery. "That's the night of your father's and my anniversary—remember?"

J didn't. He didn't have a calendar to write down important dates, mostly because he didn't have any. Still, his stomach sank. How would he explain this to Melissa? He couldn't miss her performance; she'd already accused him of being a bad friend.

"We decided to make it smaller. It's not a big party, just a small party, just our close friends who really know us. We don't want to spend the money." Carolina always said too much when she was nervous, filling up every corner of space with words. "And it's going to be kind of an adult party. I mean, there'll be alcohol there."

Since when had alcohol been a problem? There had been beer and wine at every barbecue, birthday, wedding, and quinceañera J had attended with his parents since he was two years old.

"Where are you having it?" J asked. He bent to tie his shoe. A gust of wind hit J's face, and he watched a candy wrapper scuttle across the sidewalk.

"At Martino's. We're reserving the back room."

It wouldn't be the best place for taking pictures; Martino's had fluorescent lighting and no windows in the back. "Maybe we can bring some lamps from home," J suggested.

"What?"

"For the pictures."

"Oh, Jellybean, I don't want you to worry about the pictures. I'm looking so old, anyway, and your father's gotten so fat, and you have Melissa's dance that night—"

J interrupted. "You don't want me to take pictures? At your anniversary?"

"It's not that, J." Carolina paused. "It's just going to be an adult party. It won't be fun for you, anyway. And you have your other photography event; you have to go to that, J."

"Okay, Mami," J said. He got it. "I'm at school now. Talk to you later."

They don't want me there. J hung up the phone and shoved it in his back pocket. He wasn't at school; he'd started walking in the opposite direction as soon as his mother mentioned the back room at Martino's. *They're embarrassed of me.* Oddly, this realization didn't make J mad, just more resigned to what he already knew. His mother had been protecting Manny for months now, speaking for him, and protecting J, as well, from whatever Manny thought of him. How long could she last, sandwiched as she was between them?

J stopped in a deli and bought a coffee. It was too hot, but the burning soothed him. It let him focus on his tongue for a moment, and the numbness that spread after the first shocking sip. It would be like that with Manny after a while, too; J would grow cold to his father's disdain, J's emotional sensors thickening until there was nothing more to feel.

J imagined Carolina and Manny talking about the party. Without him around, they wouldn't have to close their door. His mother would be crying, begging Manny to let J come. "It's our anniversary," she'd say, tears in her eyes. "And J's our only child." The dishrag in her hand would be twisted into a soggy knot. In his mind, his mother looked like a soap-opera character he remembered—the wayward nun, clumpy mascara streaking her face, pleading for mercy.

Manny would slam his hand on the bureau, making the loose change jump. "Cari, no!" he'd say. Manny looked like Manny, only bigger, his face splotchy with rage. "If J wants to run away and then act the fool, let her do it on her own dime. I'm not taking responsibility anymore." As J imagined the scene unfolding, his father's words grew more clear and realistic. How many times had he called J a fool in the past?

"But what will we tell J?" In J's imagination, his mother was whimpering from the bed. "And what will our friends think if she's not there?" Manny grabbed his keys and turned to leave, just as J had seen him do countless times before. "I don't care what you tell her, Cari. She's your daughter now."

J knew this scene was made up, but it seemed so plausible and rang so true that he could barely light a cigarette. His hands shook, and the lighter sputtered before the flame finally caught and J could take a long, calming drag. *It's just your own messed-up head*, J told himself. *You don't know what he really thinks.*

J knew he shouldn't indulge in this abandonment illusion for long. He had to clear his mind for something more important: the clinic had called. They were ready to give him his testosterone shot.

J was scared. So scared, he'd even told Melissa. And Chanelle. And a few guys at the group the other night.

After all the buildup over T, J couldn't believe it was actually going to happen. The guys at the group congratulated him, and Melissa and Chanelle each asked if he wanted them to go with him to his appointment, but he'd said no: this was something a man had to do alone, like running away, or like—well, like what? There really was nothing like it. It felt momentous and impending, an ending to something, and a beginning. What was it that astronaut had said? One small step for man, one giant step for mankind? Something like that.

Plenty of people had done this before, J knew, so why was he so afraid? As soon as he'd brought it up in the group, he didn't want to talk about it anymore. It was the same way with Philip, who said taking testosterone would feel like going through a second puberty. It would be slow, oily, with pimples and emotions, sexual urges, and a new, curious relationship to his body. Talking about it made him queasy, so with Philip he'd changed the subject. The doctor had talked about the psychological responses, too. He told J that everyone reacted to testosterone differently: some people did feel more aggressive with the hormones, but some felt more at peace—calmer than before—and others didn't notice any difference at all.

But everybody got the voice. The voice that squeaked at first, like the tentative turning of a rusty bike, but then loosened and tumbled into the darker timbre that

J craved. With a new voice, J wouldn't have to answer in single-syllable murmurs, his chin bowed down toward his chest; he would be marked unmistakably "male" as soon as he ordered a slice of pizza or called a stranger on the phone.

J felt as if he were at the edge of one of his construction sites, staring at the deep hole in the earth that always came before the building. People forgot about the excavation once the building went up, once the shiny windows and elevators and rooftop terraces made the edifice seem so permanent, so entitled to its height and stature. But beneath the building was still the deep cut in the land that allowed for its growth, the hollow space that was once mulchy and dense. And where did all that dirt go, once it had been dug up and hauled away? J didn't know.

The thing about testosterone, J realized, was there was no turning back. The doctor had told him that some things would revert if he ever decided to stop taking T; his ovaries would function, he'd get periods again, and if he gained weight, he'd gain it like a girl. The voice, though, that would stay low forever. But J wasn't really worried about the physical changes. It was deeper than that. Despite what his mother or father wished, despite what his friends thought of him, despite being barely old enough to vote or buy cigarettes, despite his own brain convulsing at times with confusion, here he was: making a change dictated entirely by his suffering. It felt like a matter of life or death. But if this suffering turned on him later, well, the change would have already set in his soul. Psychically speaking, he couldn't just knock down the building, find the hole, and fill himself back up with dirt. There would always be a scar.

Describe an event that changed your life, he thought, remembering the essay question from the stack of college applications that sat on Melissa's kitchen table. He resolved to write his essay before Thursday after next— before the scheduled injection.

There were some other things, too, that J wanted to clean up before he took his first T. Like that day in the pet store with Blue. Testosterone, in his mind, was becoming like a spiritual rite. He wanted to be pure for it, and his experience with Blue was anything but pure.

He had lied to Blue—that much was clear. He had lied about the poem and where he came from. Even the necklace wasn't a present he'd picked out, the way he'd led her to believe. J wasn't sure if he loved Blue or if he loved the way she saw him—as a male named Jason (it was Jason, wasn't it?), a heterosexual, normal guy, whatever that was.

The guys in the transgender group called it "disclosing," and they all had lots of opinions about it. Some felt as Chanelle did—with straight girls, they thought, the less you said, the better. Others, like Zak, thought you should "disclose your status" right away, to avoid more pain later. J didn't know where he stood.

The phone rang three times before Blue picked up.

"'Sup?" J tried to sound equal parts friendly and disinterested.

"Nothing. I'm just painting. Wassup with you?"

It was lunchtime on a school day. J had expected Blue's voice mail. "You skipping school?"

Blue said it was her sister's birthday, so she was outside Saint Patrick's Cathedral on Fifth Avenue, painting her a card.

"Aren't you cold?"

"Freezing."

"Wait for me. I'll be there in a few."

Blue was crouched on the steps in front of the church, squinting up at the Gothic towers, when J padded up behind her. She clutched a postcard-size canvas in her left hand and had a paintbrush in her teeth. *Cute*, J thought. *Always so damn cute.*

J handed her a cappuccino. "Looks good," he said.

Blue jumped, startled. When she'd given him a (brief, stiff) hug and regained her composure, she took a long, grateful drink of the cappuccino and held her painting out at arm's length. There was one tower, all in watery blues, reaching toward a strip of sky. The topmost point was sharp, but the lower spires and the triangular windows were twisted—tangling, almost—in their effort to reach the apex.

"I know it's not realistic," Blue said, cocking her head, "but I think Jadzia will recognize it."

"No monsters in this one?" J lit a cigarette, and Blue took it from him, pulling a long, thoughtful inhale.

"Not for Jadzia. She doesn't have any demons."

J wondered how deep the foundation was for this cathedral; it had to be more than thirty stories high. "How old is this church?"

"Dunno." Blue nodded at the bunch of tourists knotted at the entrance. "Want to go in?"

J shook his head. It had been years since he'd been in a church. First Communion had been his mother's idea, and something Manny tolerated. After that, J went occasionally with Carolina, but by the time he was ten, both he and his mother had pretty much given up. As far as he knew, his father hadn't been in a church since his own wedding day; and he never went to temple. Apparently, he'd even begged out of J's christening and just showed up for the party.

J didn't want to go inside because of the guilt that was already percolating pretty strongly beneath his rib cage; big, vaulted sanctuaries tended to exacerbate that feeling. He'd deceived Blue, made her think that he was angry with her, when he was really just tumbling around inside his own pain. He'd ignored her and then begged her back, hoping to win a double date with her for Chanelle. And here she was, sweetly painting a watercolor for her sister. The last time he saw her paint, all he could think about was getting busy with her. And his hormones. Those ever-present hormones. Had he ever really looked at Blue before? Had he ever looked at anyone?

"Blue, I haven't been totally straight with you." Blue was shaking her paper cup in slow circles to blend the foam into the coffee. She gazed at the cup as though it required her entire attention. "That necklace—I didn't buy it for you. I mean, it was mine. It came from my tía Yola."

"You stole the necklace from your aunt?"

"I didn't steal it! She gave it to me. For my First Communion."

"Whoa," Blue said. "Understanding aunt. That necklace was pretty girly."

J narrowed his eyes in confusion, but Blue continued. "I haven't been totally honest with you, either."

J reached into his pocket for a smoke, but the pack was empty. He gestured for her to continue.

"I followed you to your school one day. I know where you go."

J sat down hard on the cement step. This he wasn't expecting. But then he remembered having seen flashes of blue one day when he walked to school; he hadn't been imagining things. "So, you know about me."

Blue nodded her assent, but J couldn't see her. He was staring at his hands. When he spoke again, his voice came out lower, darker than usual. "Why'd you do that?"

Blue sat down next to him. "Because, J, I didn't know what to do. Every day it was like you were a different person. One day warm, the next day cold, the next day missing," she said. "Then I understood. You had a secret."

"It's not a secret!" J kicked over Blue's now-empty cup. Calling it a secret made it seem bad, dirty, something to hide. When here he was—he'd risked everything—his parents, his home, his best friend, his school—to live the life that was coursing through his blood. "You're the one who kept a secret! Following me around like a spy. Damn."

"You're right, J. I'm sorry." Blue quickly tried to

touch J's knee but then pulled her hand back just as fast. "But how is it not a secret if you never told me you were gay? When you were kissing me and everything?"

J looked at her, astonished. "What?" Now he was really pissed. "Gay is different from trans!"

"What are you talking about, *trans*? Trans what?" Blue's tone, for once, seemed to be ratcheting up as quickly as J's.

J knew that people scrambled gay and transgender all the time; they thought that every lesbian wanted to be a man and that every gay boy wore dresses. But Blue was too smart for that. J didn't like being thought of as gay; it reminded him of the time everyone thought he was a lesbian. He was a boy, and if he was a boy, he was straight. Well, queer. But queer-straight. Or whatever.

J got up to throw Blue's coffee cup into the trash can. This talk was supposed to clear the air between them; he didn't want to be angry at her. But he didn't want to educate her, either; he'd already done plenty of that with his mother and Melissa. And he was sure there would be others down the line. When he turned back, Blue was scowling.

"What do you mean, *trans*?" she asked again.

"Transgender." *Is she playing me?* J thought.

"You mean you're really a girl?"

"Born that way."

Blue's jaw dropped. J closed it for her with one gloved finger, but she didn't look at him, just stared off at some indistinct spot in the horizon. "Like that god," she said softly.

"Who?"

"From the Greek myths. There was a god who had both male and female parts—I forgot his name," she said. "It's weird. When I used to paint nudes, I would sometimes paint them with both male and female parts."

"I don't have both sets of parts."

Blue looked at him. "Oh."

They sat together awhile, watching the tourists stream in and out of the cathedral. Tourists made J nervous. The light shifted, signaling afternoon's descent.

"I'm glad you were my first boyfriend," Blue said.

"So, I'm not anymore?" J wasn't sure he wanted a girlfriend right now, with testosterone coming up, and college, and finishing high school, and Blue was so—so difficult. He didn't have another word. Still, his pride was hurt.

"I don't know," Blue said, still staring into space. "I mean, I think we've both lied to each other too much. It'd be weird."

"I didn't lie to you about being male. I mean, I am that. I'm trying to be better at that."

Blue looked at J and held his gaze. Her eyes welled. "We're all trying to be better at something."

Blue stood up to go. "I've got to get back. We're celebrating Jadzia's birthday after school, which is where I was supposed to be right now."

J raised an eyebrow. "So you lie to them." *Like you lied to me.*

Blue considered this. "I let them think what they want to think about me, and I keep what I know about myself to myself. That way we all agree."

Like me, J thought. Blue was deep, no doubt about that. He felt a sharp stab of regret for breaking up like this—under the shadow of a church, no less—but the feeling ebbed when she hugged him. This hug was real and long, and Blue laid her head against J's collarbone. It was half-sexual and half-sisterly, this hug: Blue didn't press her body against his as hard as she had in the past, but he could feel her lips brush against his neck. He didn't need this confusion right now, these mixed messages; why were girls so weird? If he gave in, he knew, Blue would either accuse him of violating the breakup they'd just settled or else be mad that he didn't call her enough in a few days' time. Blue was deep, but she was also a teenager, and J was about to become a man. Eighteen and testosterone equaled man in practically any nature documentary. He wriggled himself free and squeezed Blue gently on the shoulders. She got on her tiptoes and kissed him on the nose.

"I'm keeping the necklace," she said. "I still like it."

"Good," J said. He helped her gather her paints that were scattered about the ground. "It doesn't fit me."

J watched Blue walk away, her old-man overcoat open to the wind and flapping behind her. J waved, but Blue didn't see.

Describe an event that changed your life. J stared at the computer screen, chewing on a pen. He was sitting in the computer room at school, a tattered poster of Sylvia Rivera looking down on him. He'd learned about the Stonewall riots in class, and about how, back in the fifties and sixties, it was illegal to be a person like him. Anyone who was caught even wearing clothes of the opposite sex could be arrested. But one night, Sylvia Rivera fought back. She was in a bar, the Stonewall Inn, in 1969, when the cops raided the place. They wanted to arrest all the gay and transgender people who hung out there. Sylvia, who was "assigned" male at birth, threw the first bottle, and, as his teacher explained, the modern gay rights movement was born. The fight lasted three days. *That* was an event to write a college essay about.

The fights J had endured mostly ended in humiliation, and they certainly didn't lead to anybody's liberation. But he hoped he could do some damage with his camera. The pictures he'd been taking were getting better; they were telling stories, he knew—but he wanted them to do more. The photos he snapped of Zak and Chanelle had inspired him; he imagined a series of portraits of the people his father would have called freaks, making their way into magazines and books and, hell, maybe even galleries. Not that he went to galleries, but Melissa did. Forget shooting musicians; that dream was tired, it had been done; J wanted his pictures, his people, to fight back. He didn't want Melissa to dance his story; he wanted to photograph it.

J didn't even know what he meant; these were the kind of loose, disjointed thoughts he had when he woke up from a dream. Or tried to write an essay. How could he be accepted for a photography major if he couldn't even articulate a sound idea for a project? *Describe an event.* J looked around the empty room. The collected Shakespeare works was still sitting on the table where Chanelle had left it; she obviously wasn't worried about someone pocketing that. J started typing.

On the second day starting my new school, J wrote.

He knew the grammar sounded wrong, but he kept going. *I met a girl named Chanelle. This event changed my life. Chanelle is like me in some ways—we both are easily misunderstood.* J worried this sounded simple, or vague, or both. Couldn't you just buy essays online? *Before Chanelle, I was often hateful, but Chanelle wasn't afraid. She wasn't afraid to go back to high school, even though she is already twenty years old. She isn't afraid to write poems or read them to strangers. She isn't afraid to tell people she's transgender.* Might as well come out, J thought. They'll know it from the transcripts. And if Zak can be a doctor of gender, then hell. *The first day I met Chanelle, she asked if I was an artist. With Chanelle, I knew I could be transgender and an artist. She was my first transgender friend. Meeting her was an event that changed my life. Next Friday, I'm showing my photographs in public for the first time. I'm sending you some photographs, and I hope very much to get into your college and your photography program.*

"Needs more of an arc," Chanelle said when she phoned J to tell him she read his essay. "But it's so sweet."

"I didn't write it to be sweet," J said. He felt embarrassed. "Do you think I'll get in?"

"With this essay? No." J could practically hear her playing with her bangs over the phone. "But writing about me is a good idea. It's a subject I happen to know a lot about. I'll help you with it."

"Thanks."

"Hey, J?" Chanelle's voice was gentle. "When are you getting your shot, again?"

"Next Thursday."

"I'll be there."

CHAPTER TWELVE

J was glad he'd worn his baggiest jeans. Not that any pair wouldn't have done the trick, but he wasn't accustomed to dropping his drawers for strangers. Sitting on the paper that draped the doctor's exam table, he wished he hadn't forbidden Chanelle from coming with him; medical clinics were so sterile, they almost seemed hostile. *Couldn't they play some music in here?* At least Chanelle would have distracted him. Blown up the latex gloves into balloons or something.

A nurse had asked J to roll his jeans high enough to expose the top of his right thigh; he stopped his feet from dangling and stiffened up. *Take it like a man*, he thought. Very slowly he pulled out the piece of paper he'd copied from the Internet the night before. The *she-hecheyanu*. It was a prayer his dad had taught him during his "let's all be Jewish" phase, when they'd eaten Shabbos dinners together for those brief months when he was ten. Of course, he didn't remember how to say the *shehecheyanu*, but he remembered what it meant. His dad had said it with him on his first day of school; you recited the prayer whenever something new or important happened. After the prayer, he had left for fourth grade feeling protected somehow, as if he had an invisible shield around him, delivered by a superhero.

The paper was crumpled, and the words were a little smudged from J's sweat. He hadn't been aware that he'd fiddled with the things in his pocket on his walk to the clinic, but he must have. Still, the prayer was readable. Under his breath, he sounded out the words slowly and carefully. *"Baruch ata adonai elohenu melech ha olam, shehecheyanu, v'kiyimanu, v'higiyanu laz'man hazeh."*

The same doctor who'd drawn his blood a few weeks back knocked once, then walked in. "How you doing?" he asked, glancing at a clipboard.

"Fine," J said, forcing himself to make eye contact. *I'm not sick.* He stuffed the prayer back in his pocket.

"You ready?"

J nodded, a quick jut of the chin.

"Okay, then." The doctor swabbed J's thigh with some wet gauze and unwrapped a syringe. A small amber bottle materialized from the countertop (*had that been sitting there the whole time?*), and he poked the needle through the top and drew back the plunger. "We can teach you to do this yourself at some point in the future," he said, staring carefully at the syringe. "People often find that's easier than coming in."

The doctor gave J's thigh a gentle squeeze, told him to relax. And then—*ping*—it was in. J glanced at his leg and noticed there was no blood, and then the doctor was pulling out the needle and pressing down a small square of gauze.

That was it? J thought. Where was the rush, the high he'd expected, been promised from reading stories online? Some guys thought they could feel their bodies changing right away, swore they could sense the liquid seeping and soaking its way through their muscles, but J didn't feel anything at all. He hopped off the table and rolled down the leg of his pants. He blinked twice, patted his thigh. *There's no going back*, he told himself, hoping for a bump in emotion. He thanked the doctor, and his voice came out steady, sounding the same as always. For a brief moment, he wondered if this all was even real.

*   *   *

But then in the waiting room he saw Chanelle. She had come, after all; he couldn't be dreaming. She was talking to somebody, a man. When they both turned to look at J, he saw that it was Zak.

"J, you did it!" Chanelle said, running up to hug him.

J hugged her back, but stiffly; there were other transguys in the waiting room, and they were watching.

"You know each other?" J said, motioning to Zak, who was throwing his arm around him and grinning like a fool.

"Yeah, we met years ago at a trans youth thing," Chanelle said. "Back when we were babies."

"*You* were the baby," Zak said, quickly running his eyes over Chanelle's body. "*I* was an organizer, remember?"

"And *I* have a boyfriend," Chanelle said, smiling flirtily at Zak but turning back to J. "You okay?"

"Yeah," J said, feeling dazed. "Didn't hurt." He looked at Zak and gave a quick nod of his head. "I don't feel any pain where they put in the shot. Maybe you had a bad doctor."

There was a flurry of movement and color and chaos at the door as a coat was flung off, bags were tossed to the floor, and a swirl of curls popped out of a bright red hat. Melissa rushed over to J, squeezing past Zak and Chanelle.

"Is it already over? God, I got here as fast as I could!" Melissa gushed, breathless, grabbing J in a quick hug. "We were setting up the space for tomorrow. There's still so much to get done! I can't believe it's tomorrow. My God, J, did you get the shot already?"

J nodded. "Melissa, this is Chanelle. Oh, and Zak."

Melissa blinked and then quickly composed her face into a flat smile, as though guests she hadn't expected had suddenly dropped in on her at home. "I'm sorry," she said, extending a hand. "Hi. I'm Melissa."

Chanelle and Zak nodded their hellos, and then suddenly J felt it: here were his friends, all in one place, gathered together for *him*. It was like a family, a holiday, a graduation, a birthday, a plane taking off, a circuit overload. He felt a slight throb in his thigh where the syringe had gone in. Testosterone!

"Can we go outside?" J asked.

The group bundled up, and as soon as J hit the door, he ran to the corner at full sprint. The light was red, so he jumped—tagging the bus-stop sign, making a loud *thwack*. Testosterone! T! He'd done it, and in two weeks he'd do it again. Everything, everything had led to this moment, and J wanted to hug the street—take it all in his arms and pull it inside. He could hold it now. He turned around. There were his friends, halfway down the block, watching him, laughing. And what did he feel? Love. J felt love for each of them—so much, it could almost kill him. For Zak, who'd been doing T for years and made it through; for Chanelle, his first trans friend, who made him feel smarter than he was; and for Melissa—complicated, beautiful Melissa, who loved him despite it all.

He ran back. "Aaaaaaaaaaaaahhhhhhhh!" he shouted, his breath making a huge cloud of steam. "I feel so damn good!"

"That's what hormones do," Zak said, smiling. Chanelle just nodded.

"God, maybe I should try some," Melissa said. "I feel kind of jealous."

"We should celebrate," Chanelle offered.

They went to a diner around the corner and ordered waffles. For once, Melissa didn't mention calories when J ordered extra ice cream and scooped some on her plate. Zak ordered a side of bacon, which everyone thought was disgusting, but it actually tasted delicious mixed in with all the sweetness.

"Can you eat bacon, J?" Chanelle asked, between bites. "Aren't you part Jewish?"

"His dad's, like, the least observant Jew in New York," Melissa answered for him.

My dad, J thought. *If Manny could see me now. Sitting with two transpeople and a girl I once kissed. Just after I took a hormone shot.* He felt proud. "I don't care what my dad thinks," he said.

"Right," Zak said, but he was smiling. It seemed he hadn't stopped smiling since he met J at the clinic.

"Here's to overcoming our parents' dreams for us," Chanelle said, raising her water glass. They all toasted.

"Here's to J," Melissa added.

J raised his glass and took a long, delicious swallow.

J arrived at the performance space three hours before the show, lugging one of Melissa's suitcases. He'd wrapped each of his framed photographs in a few T-shirts or a sweatshirt, but he'd taken a cab and carried the bag in his arms just to be safe. He had a hammer, nails, a level, and a roll of measuring tape in his backpack.

Dancers were running around everywhere. A cage with two doves sat unattended in a corner, and the birds hopped around nervously. A big guy with dreadlocks was unloading a drum set, and a girl on roller skates was zipping around, barking orders.

"Can you scoot the drums farther back?" the skater asked, her ponytails bobbing. "We need a lot of room for the water feature."

Melissa was nowhere to be seen, but J found his "hallway" easily enough. It was a ten-by-twenty-foot wall made of thin plywood, which formed a backdrop for the chairs in the audience. It was the first thing people would see when they walked in the door.

J started unwrapping pictures. The first one was the jackhammer cutting through his shadow. He laid it on the floor. Next came the print of his hand punching the phone booth, smashing the "man." He'd printed up his photos at the shop where Melissa had bought the frames, and they'd done a good job; the colors were even, the lines sharp. Luckily, they had two more frames identical to the others, and now he had a series, of sorts.

The next photo was the shot of Chanelle's eyes. He'd blown up the image and cropped out the rest of her face, so only her eyes, looking both determined and lonely, stared back, with the raised eyebrow, like his own. Then came Zak's muscle shot. This was J's favorite. He hadn't noticed when he pushed the button, but when the picture was developed, you could see Zak's stack of books behind his bulging bicep and the blurred profile of his face. A muscled scholar; J liked it. And the final photo was the one J had shot at the pier the day he ran away—the single gray bird against an even grayer sky. A shadow, then a punch, a stare, then muscles, then flight: the story of J's life thus far.

"Do you have an artist's statement?"

J jumped. It was Melissa, standing behind him,

looking down at the photographs he'd arranged on the floor.

"A what?"

"You know, a little bio or something that explains who you are and why you did this work," she said. She'd piled all her hair into a cone on the top of her head and wrapped yellow DO NOT CROSS police tape around it. She looked crazy.

"No," J answered. He hadn't thought of it. "Do I have to?"

Melissa stamped her foot. "J! Do I have to think of everything?"

J hung the pictures by himself, carefully measuring fourteen inches of space between each frame. The girl on roller skates wheeled by, screeching to a dead stop in front of Chanelle's eyes.

"Whoa, those eyes are amazing," she said. "Is that a man or a woman?"

J shrugged. "Does it matter?"

The girl gave him a funny look. "You're really good," she said, and skated off. J smiled at the floor.

J still had enough time before the show to make it back to Melissa's and type something up. On the train, he decided he'd write PHOTOS BY J SILVER and skip the bio.

The more he thought about it, the better it sounded; *photos* was casual and not too pretentious, and he'd always liked his name. Just a plain letter, not short for anything, able to stand on its own. And the pictures weren't bad; maybe if people liked them, it would be okay if they knew he took them. Then again, maybe people wouldn't notice the sign; maybe they wouldn't even notice the pictures—they were coming for the dance, anyway. Except for Zak and Chanelle, who were now showing up for this stupid thing, thanks to Melissa, who'd invited them.

"Oof, you stink. You've gotta quit that habit," Karyn said to him when J pushed through the door, reeking of cigarettes. J turned on the computer, but Karyn kept talking. "Do you know anything about this dance tonight? Melissa wouldn't tell me a thing."

J shook his head. Ever since she promised that she wouldn't dance about anything transgender, Melissa had kept mum about the whole endeavor.

"I guess it'll be a surprise, then."

J was grateful he could catch a ride with Karyn and hide behind her as they entered the warehouse; people were actually *looking* at his photographs. An old man with a mustache was peering at the shot of Zak's muscles, and two girls J thought he recognized from his old high school were staring at the jackhammer. J felt like he might be sick.

"It's kind of creepy," one girl said to the other.

"What is it?"

The first girl, who was about sixteen, squinted her eyes. "It's like a jackhammer going into a dead body or something. But the light's making a halo—see around the head? Maybe it's an angel."

J almost burst out laughing. *People will see whatever they want to see. Parallax.* He surreptitiously stuck his name to the wall and went in, taking a seat next to Karyn.

The first few dances were kind of boring—just bendy, sweeping things with girls in serious faces falling to the ground and getting up again. Thankfully, they didn't release the doves—they just danced around them at one point and dragged out a human-size cage to lock themselves into. A metaphor, he supposed. The word *Threshold* was printed on a banner above the audience, which was crowded with bodies and thick winter coats. It was so warm, J had to chew on his cheek to stay awake.

Finally, it was Melissa's turn. She started the piece on her toes; she was wearing pointe shoes and a thick wool blanket in a mummy wrap, so tight she could barely move her feet. Her eyes were closed, and the drummer hit the bass in a steady heartbeat rhythm. Melissa pointe-tipped her way across the stage, gently swaying her head, toward a hook that was bolted to the wall. She caught the edge of the blanket on the hook and struggled, pulling and yanking, until finally she tumbled out of the blanket and landed in a heap on the floor, yelling like a baby. The inside of the blanket was shiny and red. A birth, J supposed. Why were these dancers so into metaphors?

After she'd untied her pointe shoes, Melissa danced her way through childhood—first crawling, then walking, then swirling and leaping, hunching into a small toadstool shape and jumping up to a star, then around and around, dervish-style, arms flailing in a falling spin. The drums were wild and ecstatic until, suddenly, they stopped. But Melissa kept dancing as though she hadn't noticed, as though she had an internal meter and rhythm of her own.

But then Melissa stopped, too. She cocked her head, listening. The audience watched her heaving chest. Her eyes grew wide and angry. She marched back to the drummer, who sat with a placid expression, his drumsticks loose in his hands. Melissa, her back to the audience, raised her hands, stomped her feet, mimed drumming, but the drummer didn't even look her way. Melissa jumped up and down, trying to get his attention, throwing a silent fit. Finally, she just hung her head and walked away.

She went back to the blanket, crumpled on the floor by the hook. She sat on it, cross-legged, and lifted the edge of it to her mouth. She tasted it, smelled it, rubbed it against the caution tape in her hair. Then she started searching the red shiny lining, feeling the countours of it lovingly. The room was silent. She found a pocket and pulled something out. Something small and square. A razor.

J didn't breathe. Melissa held the razor up to the light and slowly, carefully, drew it up the inside of her forearm. A thin line of blood beaded up. Not enough to gush—she hadn't hit a major vein—but enough to catch the light and shine against her skin. Someone gasped. Melissa raised her hand to do it again.

"Stop!" someone shouted from the audience. But Melissa appeared to be in a trance. This time, she flipped her arm over and made three quick nicks in the top of her forearm. The drum started again—the heartbeat, slow and steady. Melissa smiled, and the stage went dark.

"Oh, my God," Karyn breathed beside J. "My fucking God." Then, as the audience slowly started to applaud, Karyn stood up and shoved past him and the rest of the people sitting nearby, making her way backstage.

It was intermission. J didn't know where Karyn and Melissa were. People were hovering around the entrance and going outside to smoke. He spotted Zak and Chanelle.

"That was intense!" Chanelle said, squeezing around some teenagers blocking the way. "Melissa's bold."

"Yeah, but look at us," Zak said, nodding at the photographs on the wall. "We're famous!"

J tried to smile, but he was distracted, worried about what was going down between Karyn and Melissa. Still, for the second time in two days, he accepted congratulations from his friends. Chanelle told him she thought he'd definitely get into a photography program, with talent like this. Zak didn't even know J had applied, but he agreed with Chanelle.

"Thanks," J said. "Listen, are you guys staying 'til the end? Will you tell Melissa I said she did a great job?"

It was eight-thirty on a cold winter night. The third Friday in February. J realized he had somewhere else he needed to be.

The last time J had been to Martino's, it was summer, and the back patio was open. His grandma had been visiting from Puerto Rico, and they'd gone there to celebrate her birthday. It was probably three years ago. J remembered that his dad had been particuarly sullen over the clams in wine sauce—too salty, he said—and he went inside to watch the game at the bar.

He didn't know whether his grandmother would be there tonight, as she wasn't the biggest fan of Manny, and his mother hadn't mentioned anything about a trip. Still, a twenty-year anniversary party was a big deal, so who knew. Mercie would definitely be there, and probably some of his dad's friends from the union, maybe that couple they used to go to movies with—J couldn't remember their names. For sure, Carolina's boss and some of the other nurses, and J's old babysitter, Alfie, whom they still talked to. Alfie was a lonely old guy who lived on 205th Street; he needed a party.

J remembered there was an alcove near the coat check at Martino's, just before you got to the back room. He could hide out there for a while and watch. Maybe he could slip a waiter some cash to bring him a drink, so he could arrive at the podium with a glass in his hand. He was sure there'd be some kind of podium or microphone setup for people to give toasts, like at a wedding.

"To the best parents in the world," he would say, raising his glass high. His mother would be shocked, but she'd force a smile, look nervously around at her friends. "Here's to twenty years!"

But after everyone cheered and clanked glasses, J would go on. "Thank you for raising me," he'd say. "And for staying married."

He'd wait for a laugh—the old, shy J gone for the moment, the new, testosterone-filled J confident and charming. He'd smile into the microphone, gathering attention. "To Manny and Carolina. A beautiful couple. A couple that always puts themselves first."

Here the room would start to shift uncomfortably, but J would continue. "To Carolina, who protects Manny at all costs, including the cost of their only child—me. And to Manny, who was once my hero but is now too much of a coward to even talk to me. My parents may have been too ashamed to invite me tonight, but I am not ashamed of who I am. I came to this party to toast who they are. Who they *really* are."

This is the speech J would give, and when the doors opened at his old station, he was just determined enough, and angry enough, to do it.

Martino's looked less fancy and festive than he'd remembered it—just a plain old brick restaurant with an Italian flag on the door. *Be a man*, he told himself as he gripped the handle, but his hand was shaking.

"The kitchen's closed," a waiter told him when J walked in. The waiter's top button was undone, and he looked tired.

"I'm here for the party in the back," J said.

"Oh, the Silver party? I think most everyone's gone. But go on back."

J took off his hat and smoothed what there was of his short hair. The razor stripes had entirely grown out. He briefly considered hiding in a bathroom stall for a while, but he didn't want to bump into anyone he knew, and there was always the question of which restroom to choose. He walked slowly toward the back room, careful to hold his chin high.

Five people sat around a table cluttered with bottles. He recognized his father's backside, broad and doughy, stuffed into his best checkered shirt. His mother was next to him, laughing at something a woman was saying. J didn't recognize her. Two other men in sweaters and slacks nodded along.

"J!" his mother yelped when she saw him.

"You got back early!" his father said, standing up. Manny walked up to J and pulled him into an awkward hug. "Everybody, this is my daughter, J. She just got back from a trip to D.C."

The other three people at the table stood, smiling, and shook J's hand. "Have a seat, have a seat," one of the men offered, pulling up a chair from one of the other tables, also covered with discarded plates and glasses.

"When'd you get back, J?" his father asked. His

words were slurred, but J couldn't decide whether alcohol was confusing him or he was supplying some kind of secret code for J to follow in front of these strangers.

"Um, I just came to give you guys a toast," J said.

Carolina cut her eyes into slits. "You missed the party."

"That's okay—you're here now," the unknown woman said. Her dark hair was piled into a swirly updo on her head, and her earrings were shaped like bees. She patted J on the knee.

One of the sweater men told the updo they had to get going; the babysitter was going to cost them a bundle. Carolina begged them not to go.

"How was D.C.?" Manny asked, turning to J.

"What are you talking about?" J asked. This was not the vision he'd had on the train.

"You can tell him about your trip later," Carolina said, pouring some bourbon into her watered-down Coke. Her voice was shrill, her expression tight. "Right now we've got guests."

"What do you mean, D.C.?"

"Honey, we've got to go." Sweater Man was tugging at Updo's dress.

"What do you mean, what do I mean?" Manny said. J couldn't tell whether it was anger or alcohol rising in his cheeks. "You've been living there for months."

J looked at Carolina, but she was standing up, helping her friends put on their coats.

"No, I haven't. I've been at Melissa's."

"Cari!" Manny practically shouted, followed by J's "Mom?"

Carolina was ushering her three friends toward the front of the restaurant. They looked more eager to leave now, with Carolina shoving at their backs, and they barely mumbled a "happy anniversary" in Manny's direction.

"I'll be back in a minute," Carolina said. "I need to show our friends to the door."

J and Manny stared at each other. "What's going on?" Manny finally said.

"You tell me," J answered. He felt sullen, defiant, and entirely confused.

"No, J, you tell me." Manny slammed his hand on the table. "You've been staying at *Melissa's*? Don't you have a *crush* on that girl?" He shuddered in disgust.

"Not anymore." Good old Manny. Always months behind.

"So, what's this about a college prep course in D.C.? Staying on the Georgetown campus? Studying computers?"

"I have no idea. First I've heard of it."

His father shook his head in amazement. "So, you're saying Mami's lying."

"I don't know," J answered. He looked at the tablecloth. It was stained with red sauce. "What did Mami tell you about me?"

"What did she tell me? Nothing. Just that you got into this program in D.C."

"And you didn't think of asking her anything about it? You never wanted to call me?" All this time he had thought his father hated him. And now maybe he still would. J wanted desperately to reach for one of the half-empty bottles of beer.

"So, now I'm the bad guy? J, I never call you on the phone. Why would I start?"

"Why would Mami lie to you?" J asked. And where was she? It was taking a long time to get back from the front door.

"I don't know," Manny answered. He stared down into his glass and shook his head. "It wouldn't be the first time she lied."

J looked at the tablecloth stains again, unsure of where to direct his rage. At his mother—who had deceived him, making him think it was his father who wouldn't let him come home? Or at his father, who was so detached and indifferent that he couldn't be bothered to inquire about J's life?

"Let me tell you something about your mother, J,"

Manny started. His voice was still slurred, but his eyes were clear. "You're eighteen now. You should know the truth."

J wasn't sure he wanted to know the truth, if there was even a truth in all this strangeness going on. But his dad continued.

"This whole anniversary party bullshit—it was all for her. She always wants to make everything look good on the outside, when the inside can be going to hell," Manny said. "She wants to have the perfect job, the perfect husband, the perfect kid. She's a very driven woman."

J remembered his conversation with Carolina that day by the river. *I wasn't in love with your father*, she'd said. And, *I was a very determined kid.*

"And when things aren't perfect on the outside, J, Mami wants to make them just disappear until they're perfect again. Why do you think I've been gone so much? I haven't been perfect to Mami in a long time."

She wanted to make me disappear, too, J thought. "I'm not perfect, either," he said.

"How are you not perfect, J?" Manny asked. "This is between Mami and me."

J swallowed. "I'm transgender, Pops."

"What does that mean?"

"It means," he paused, "that I'm really male. I was

supposed to be born male, except I wasn't, so I'm doing things to change it."

Manny's jaw dropped for a second, then he closed his mouth. "Jesus, J. That's disgusting." He rubbed his eyes, and when he looked back up, his sockets were bulging, almost pleading, but his mouth was twisted into a snarl of contempt. He gripped a beer bottle as though he might break it. "You're sick. You need help."

"No, I'm not." J was shaking, but he held his father's stare.

Manny sat for several long minutes, glaring at his bottle and picking at the label. "Man, what a night," he finally said, sighing. "You find out that your wife's been lying to you and then that your kid's got major problems in the head. Happy anniversary to me."

J looked at his father. Manny was balding, and sweat beaded up around the receding hairline. What used to be muscle had drooped into fat, and his eyes looked dim and unfocused. This was the man J used to worship?

"Yes, Pops, happy anniversary to you. And happy birthday to me. Which you forgot."

Manny stared at him, uncomprehending. "Wasn't that months ago?" He looked toward the door, searching for Carolina. "And you were supposed to be in D.C."

"You could have called my cell phone; you have

the number." His father was always full of excuses; if Manny had actually tuned' in for once instead of relying on Carolina for everything, this whole mess could have been sorted out much sooner. J felt a surge of strength, standing up to his father this way, and Manny even seemed to shrink back in his chair just a bit.

"Is your birthday really the point, J? What are we even talking about here?" Manny looked genuinely confused and, more than that, despairing. He was holding on to the tablecloth as if it would save his life. And, yes, J decided, his birthday *was* the point. From here on out, he'd have a new birthday. February 16: the day of his first testosterone shot.

"We're talking about respect," J said, though by this time he, too, was a little confused about where the conversation was going. Still, while his courage was running high, he wanted to make a point. "Respect for your only son."

"My *what*?" Manny sputtered.

"Your son," J said, standing up. "Call me when you can say the word."

J pushed open the door to Martino's, and the winter air was harsh and dry. On the corner, he saw his mother, stooped against the cold and leaning on a lamppost. She was crying. He marched straight up to her.

"Mami!" he shouted. "What the hell?"

They were alone on the block. A siren sounded from far away, and a few dogs howled in response. Carolina looked up at him, her face tear-streaked and miserable. She shook her head.

"Answer me!" J said. "What did you tell Pops?"

"I couldn't," she breathed. "I couldn't." And her face crumpled into more sobbing.

"Couldn't what, Mami?" He balled his right hand into a fist and stuffed it deep into his pocket. Her tears disgusted him. "Couldn't what?"

Carolina's eyes widened. "I needed more time, J."

"Time for *what*?" J kicked the lamppost, and his mother jumped. "I'm not going to kick you, Mami. Jesus."

Carolina just mutely shook her head, the tears still streaming.

"But you told me he was the one who couldn't deal with me, that he was the one who wasn't ready. You let me think he hated me." J felt bile rising in his throat, and his eyes burned in their sockets. "You were the one who was ashamed of me."

"He would have, J! I was protecting you," Carolina said. "And how can you say I was ashamed? I wrote you that letter!"

The letter. Testosterone. His mother had written the letter, had met with him; his father hadn't even called for his birthday. *A kid who's got major problems in the head.* Who was better? He was begging for scraps. "You were too late with that letter, Mami. I got the hormones myself. I'm an adult now."

Carolina leaned her head back against the pole and slid down so she was sitting on the sidewalk, her legs stretched out in front of her. "You don't know about your father, J. He thinks I've spoiled you."

Oh, God, not again, J thought, his head swimming. *What am I, some kind of marriage counselor? Try talking to each other about your problems.* "You married him," he said bitterly.

"Yes, I did, " Carolina answered from the ground. "And all my life, I've been trying to make things right."

Carolina was silent then, staring at her gloves. J felt weird, standing above her, but he didn't want to sit on the cold sidewalk. He remembered his father's words. "Did you think that if I went away, I would just stop being transgender?"

"I thought..." Carolina started. "I thought...I just thought if you went away for a while, I could have more time. To think. I just needed more time. It wasn't going to be forever."

"You used me!" J felt his voice straining, and he lowered his tone to a growl. "You let me think he hated me."

"He would have, J, I promise you. What did he say to you in there?"

He said I was disgusting. But he might not have thrown me out. J was silent.

His mother started crying again. "J, at Melissa's you could be yourself—you could grow the way you needed to grow. And that's what happened, right?"

J considered this, but he didn't want to give his mother the benefit of a nod.

"At home I couldn't have provided that for you." Carolina was speaking so softly, J could barely make out the words. "Sometimes we can't do everything we want to for our children."

"So sometimes you lie to them?"

Carolina wiped her nose on her glove and stood up. J hadn't realized how much shorter she was; could he have grown in just a few months? "I thought if I had more time, you'd have a better family to come home to."

So all this time it wasn't even about me, J thought, backing away a few inches. *It was about you and your fears of what he'd think—of* you *and how you've raised me.* J hadn't considered his parents' marriage too deeply before, the way his father was gone so much, the way Carolina backed away from arguments like a wounded animal but then instigated them, too, with little pecks and insults, tossed from a room away. He knew that his dad thought Carolina coddled J; was she afraid Manny would blame her for J's being trans? Was it his fault that his parents were too afraid to face their own problems to take on his? *Am I braver than you both?*

"J, what are you thinking?" Carolina asked, stepping in to bridge the gap he'd created between them. "I was going to tell him; I really was. But then, well, a lot of time passed. And—we just do the best we can."

J was thinking about getting home to Melissa, about how Karyn had probably consulted all her psychology textbooks on cutting or called her shrink friends to get the name of a good doctor. Melissa would need him now.

"I'm sorry, m'i—" Carolina paused. "M'ijo. I love you."

J could tell she wanted to hug him, but he didn't move. The strands of the conversation were starting to fray: His mother loved him and lied; his father hadn't hated him but wasn't accepting, either. Everybody had their problems. All he really knew was that his life was no longer a secret and no longer anyone else's to control.

He reached for his mother's hand and gave it a single squeeze. "Go back inside," he said quietly. "Pops has probably fallen asleep in there." And he turned to walk toward the train.

CHAPTER THIRTEEN

It was spring, no doubt about it. Crocuses were up in the park, and the pretzel stands had started selling ice creams. J could only justify triple-shirting for a few weeks more; pretty soon he'd be down to a tank and a tee. But Zak's hand-me-down chest binder had stopped chafing so much, and J's arms were already looking bigger, so maybe this summer wouldn't be so bad.

He turned his key in Melissa's door.

"You got something in the mail!" Melissa yelled from the kitchen. She was cooking again—part of the "ten-point plan to health" that her new therapist had instituted. This meant J and Karyn were eating a lot of experimental recipes involving flaxseeds or Kombucha. Unfortunately, Melissa was still a terrible cook.

"Smells delicious," J grunted, thinking that if he took up his parents' offer to move back home, at least he'd be able to eat some real food. But he'd talked it over with Philip and Chanelle, and he realized he liked living with Melissa and visiting his parents on weekends. He could walk to school and to his meetings and not have to worry about daily encounters with kids from his old neighborhood as he went through his transition. And his parents were on good behavior when he visited. Carolina still felt guilty about the lie, so she babied him, and Manny avoided the topic of anything trans but still came home for dinner. Just last weekend, they'd talked about college.

"You hear from any schools yet?" his father had asked. He'd brought home some Junior's cheesecake and was slicing up healthy portions for each of them.

J shook his head slowly, careful not to trip the thin wire his family was walking on.

"He will," Carolina asserted. She was becoming more comfortable with the *he* pronoun, though Manny desperately avoided any third-person reference to J. Carolina traced the raspberry icing on the cheesecake and delicately licked her spoon.

"We've saved a lot of money for you, kid," Manny

continued. "And just because you've got this, this *thing* happening…doesn't mean you shouldn't get an education. You can't stay at your girlfriend's house forever."

J protested that he'd applied; he was just waiting to hear. Carolina backed him up. "These things take time. And Melissa's not his girlfriend."

Like the old days, J hated it when his parents started in on the slow simmer of a fight, but he felt newly supported by his dad, somehow. At least he was taking an interest.

"Don't worry, Pops, I'll get in," J had said. And he believed it. Karyn had pulled the star card from her tarot deck, which she said was the card of hope. Charlie, his English teacher from school, had written him a recommendation that made him sound like the king of a small nation. And Melissa had been having one of her "good feelings," which were almost never wrong. Melissa had always been intuitive, but ever since she'd stopped cutting, she said she felt downright psychic. And she claimed she owed it all to J. When Karyn made her go to a residency program for traumatized teenagers, Melissa was resentful at first, even angry at J for encouraging her to dance about her cutting. But now, she said, she felt access to a range of emotions she never knew she had. Which, unfortunately for J, she could never shut up about. She felt free now; she felt that the cutting was some abstract way to get even with her father; she felt that her body was her temple and she would honor it forever—on and on went their late-night talks until J's head would drop in exhaustion. Melissa was postponing college for a year so she could volunteer at the residency program and keep up with her therapy; she said she would live vicariously through J. She was positive he'd go away to school.

"I'm not saying you won't," Manny had answered, scraping the last bits of cheesecake off his plate and reaching to finish J's. "I guess I'm just a little anxious about this whole thing." Manny paused. He licked his fork. "Or excited. Maybe I'm excited about you getting to go to college."

And that was it. J had gone from feeling like the most alone person in the world to someone people believed in and were even a little bit excited for. He remembered Marcia from the hotel; she had told him to be patient with his family, and that's what he was being—Manny still had a long way to go, and J still hadn't fully forgiven Carolina. But he was like a camera before things went digital; the film in its roll could imprint any picture at all. People could project images into his line of sight all they wanted, but he was the one who pushed the shutter.

Back in the kitchen, Melissa ignored J's comment about the stench emanating from her cooking. "Envelope's on the table," she yelled, and dropped a pot into the sink.

At first he thought there had been a mistake. Next to Karyn's books and a few flyers for someone running for the city council was a manila envelope. It was addressed to "Mr. Silver." *Why is my dad getting mail here?* he thought, but quickly corrected himself. It was from the college.

J sat down and peeled back the seal. *Dear Mr. Silver,* he read.

We're delighted to accept you for our incoming fall term and our prestigious photography program in upstate New York. Enclosed you will find material about housing, financial aid, and registering for classes. We welcome you with our warmest congratulations.

J let out a whoop, startling the cat.

"I did it!" he shouted to Melissa. "Get ready to miss me, 'cause I'm getting my own room now!" His new, deep voice didn't crack.

AUTHOR'S NOTE

Dear Readers,

I was inspired to write *I Am J* more than ten years ago, when I was researching my first book, *Transparent*, about transgender teenagers in Los Angeles. At that time, there were almost no books, movies, or television specials about trans kids; they had few ways to see themselves reflected and, at the initial stages of my research, I wanted to help give voice to all the dozens of brave, creative, and resilient kids I came across. As the book took form, however, I focused on fewer and fewer specific characters, to give the book more narrative depth. As transgender boys and girls (especially at that time) tended to run in very separate circles, the boys were largely excised from the work. At that point, I wanted my nonfiction to portray the history, culture, and challenges in the young, urban trans community—but I dreamed of one day returning to my notes and to the transgender boys. I imagined writing a book that would speak directly *to* them as adolescents—rather than *about* them in a book for adults. I wanted to write fiction, with all the flexibility that fiction affords, and thereby tell a different kind of truth—an emotional truth—that can cut right through to readers.

In one way, the character J is an amalgam of some aspects of several transboys I know, and yet he's evolved as very much his own person. Some of these young people are first- or second-generation immigrants, who struggle both with what it means to be trans as well as with what these changes will mean to their families and their ethnic identities. What all of these real people share with J, and what they have taught me, are the ways that anger and pain implode when one's internal reality collides with an often unforgiving outside world.

And yet this outside world is changing—especially in the urban areas of this country—amazingly fast, and it's becoming a somewhat more forgiving, and definitely more dynamic, place. There are more out and visible young transgender men than ever before, and their growing ranks are bolstering the courage of the generation behind them (and in queer terms, a generation can be just a few years long) at an exponential rate. Definitions of masculinity and femininity are expanding every day, and adolescent transboys are finding more creative ways to discover, and be, themselves. As their ranks grow, I imagine, they'll look for even more reflections of who they are and are becoming. And their teenage friends, who know them or wonder about them, need and often crave a way to understand their experience. That is why I'm so excited and hopeful about *I Am J* and about the many books that others are writing about themselves and their friends right now. There are still so many kinds of transgender stories to be told and cherished—and so much room on the shelves.

Of course, it's scary to take an imaginative leap and write a character who is not you. I have known and loved several people who are *like* J, but J is not me. I'm not of trans experience, and I know what tricky territory this is, partly because there are still not enough published works by transgender authors, proclaiming their lived experience. I can only know a kind of truth by proxy. I'm blessed that my foster daughter, Christina, is transgender, and my partner is gender variant—so my immediate family and my deepest ties are trans in nature (or nurture!). Aside from the benefit

of having any of my residual gender assumptions chal-
lenged daily, my family keeps me open to the rich, brilliant, and often spicy dialogue that's so vibrant in our
growing trans communities. J is, at best, only one character, one voice, in an enormous ongoing conversation.
I welcome your letters and your thoughts.

Warmly,
Cris

RESOURCES

The following resources are recommended by the
author and are current as of the date of publication.

For Youth

Websites
YouthResource
By and for lesbian, gay, bisexual, transgender, and
    questioning youth
www.amplifyyourvoice.org/youthresource

Youth Guardian Services
Safe space online for LGBTQ youth
www.youth-guard.org

National Youth Advocacy Coalition
NYAC advocates for and with young people who are
lesbian, gay, bisexual, transgender, or questioning.
www.nyacyouth.org

24-hour Suicide Prevention Hotline for GLBTQ Youth
1-866-4-U-TREVOR (1-866-488-7386)

Female-to-Male Transition Websites
FTMInternational Website
www.ftmi.org

Hudson's FTM Resource Guide
www.ftmguide.org

The Transitional Male
www.thetransitionalmale.com

Books
Beam, Cris. *Transparent: Love, Family, and Living
the T with Transgender Teenagers.* New York:
Harcourt, 2007. ISBN 978-0-15-101196-4 (hc) /
978-0-15-603377-0 (pb)

Peters, Julie Anne. *Luna*. New York: Little, Brown and
    Company, 2004. ISBN 978-0-316-73369-4 (hc) /
    978-0-316-01127-3 (pb)

Wittlinger, Ellen. *Parrotfish*. New York: Simon &
    Schuster, 2007. ISBN 978-1-4169-1622-2 (hc) /
    978-1-4424-0621-6 (pb)

For Parents, Teachers, and Other Supporters

Websites
*Children's National Medical Center Outreach
    Program for Children with Gender-Variant
    Behaviors and Their Families*
A basic primer on gender variance in children
www.childrensnational.org/dcchildrens/about/pdf/
    GenVar.pdf

PFLAG (Parents and Friends of Lesbians and Gays)
PFLAG has a transgender chapter, too.
www.pflag.org

*Gay, Lesbian and Straight Education Network
    (GLSEN)*
www.glsen.org

TransFamily
A support site for families and transpeople
www.transfamily.org

LAMBDA GLBT Community Services
www.lambda.org

Books

Brill, Stephanie A., and Rachel Pepper. *The Transgender Child: A Handbook for Families and Professionals.* San Francisco: Cleis Press, 2008. ISBN 978-1-57344-318-0

Ewert, Marcus, and Rex Ray. *10,000 Dresses.* New York: Seven Stories Press, 2008. ISBN 978-1-58322-850-0
A great picture book for young children

Lev, Arlene Istar. *Transgender Emergence: Therapeutic Guidelines for Working With Gender-Variant People and Their Families.* Binghamton, NY: The Haworth Clinical Practice Press, 2004. ISBN 978-0-7890-0708-7 (hc) / 978-0-7890-2117-5 (pb)

ACKNOWLEDGMENTS

Many people helped bring J to life and helped me understand the interior world of a young transperson a little better. I'd like to thank my students at EAGLES Academy in Los Angeles for sharing their stories over so many years, and all the young people I profiled in my first book, *Transparent*. My primary acknowledgment goes to my daughter, Christina, with her courageous heart, who taught me about the street and about fighting for your life and then for your family, in that order. Foxxjazell provided early lessons about gender and heartbreak and the redemptive power of art. Chris

Haiss shared writing and stories about his transition, as did Max, Eli, Jose, and several other friends: thank you for your trust.

Alex Thornton read a very early draft, and Shawn Luby read a late one, and their critical insights kept me honest. Joy Ladin is a marvelous poet, and she helped me locate a more nuanced voice and point of view. Pascale and Louis Hurst fed me delicious meals during a key writing surge in Switzerland, Krystyna Srutek helped me understand the Polish immigrant community in New York, and Juan Miranda double-checked my Spanish. Merrill Feitell and Elyssa East provided vital theories on plot and structure, and Sharon Krum, who did it first, always cheered me on. Carol Paik, Kelly McMasters, and Jennie Yabroff read multiple drafts of multiple chapters and somehow managed to keep me laughing; thank you for your diligence, your patience, and your fiery pens. To Claire Hertz, thank you for listening.

Teresa Dinaburg Dias became a mama just as J was born; you are my sister and my light. Batyah Shtrum, my champion, was beside me throughout the entire process, and I am forever grateful. Diamond Patty O'Toole has kindly steered my career at more crossroads than I care to count; thank you will never ever be enough. Thank you also to Robin, Trista, Lacy, Karen, Lisa, and Gemma, my oldest friends, and my family.

My agent, Amy Williams, is steadfast and true; thank you for believing in me and in this project and for finding J his rightful home. Thank you to T. S. Ferguson for your early edits and enthusiasm, and to Alvina Ling, for your fresh and insightful read. My editor, Julie Scheina, is a shining and thorough editor; thank you for your broad vision and your critical eye.

My deepest gratitude goes to my beloved Lo, who shows me every day that gender can be fluid and curious, excruciating and intoxicating. And that when we're lost in the madness, kindness is wisdom. This book is for you.